"WHY DID MAZURI

"My friend, you are spiracy theorists. I ha on who killed Council President Mazurıch than you'd ever care to write."

"Mr. Maxwell—"

"You want to know what I have? Police reports, forensic reports, digital images of the scene. The man killed himself. If there was anything to any of these conspiracy—"

"*Mr. Maxwell*—"

"I'd be the first to report it—"

"*Mr. Maxwell!*"

I stopped talking for a moment.

"Mr. Maxwell, I am not delusional. I offer you nothing that cannot be substantiated. I am aware that he killed himself."

"What then?"

"*Why* did he kill himself?"

I remained quiet.

"Mr. Maxwell?"

"Okay," I said, "why did he?"

"Not over the phone. My life is in danger. I've talked too long already. Meet me in the Old Arcade at 6:30."

"How will I know you?"

"I will know you . . ."

DAW Novels from S. ANDREW SWANN

Fantasy:

THE DWARVES OF WHISKEY ISLAND
THE DRAGONS OF THE CUYAHOGA

BROKEN CRESCENT

GOD'S DICE

Fiction:

ZIMMERMAN'S ALGORITHM

Science Fiction:

HOSTILE TAKEOVER
omnibus:
Profiteer \ Partisan \ Revolutionary

THE MOREAU NOVELS

MOREAU OMNIBUS:
*Forests of the Night \ Emperors of the Twilight \ Specters
of the Dawn*

FEARFUL SYMMETRIES

THE DWARVES OF WHISKEY ISLAND

S. ANDREW SWANN

DAW BOOKS, INC.
DONALD A. WOLLHEIM, FOUNDER
375 Hudson Street, New York, NY 10014
ELIZABETH R. WOLLHEIM
SHEILA E. GILBERT
PUBLISHERS
www.dawbooks.com

First Printing, October 2005
1 2 3 4 5 6 7 8 9

Dedicated to the citizens of
Cleveland, Ohio

PROLOGUE

W HAT I KNOW—what anyone knows—of Dominic Lloyd Mazurich's last few hours, is pieced
together from police and forensic reports, a few wit-
nesses, and public records. It goes something like
this . . .

Mazurich holds his last press conference at Cleveland City Hall at about 6:30 in the afternoon. It is in a
small meeting room off of Council Chambers that is
packed with reporters. The scene of the press conference, as was the City Council session that preceded it,
is more hectic than usual. The Supreme Court has just
issued a ruling against the city about jurisdiction over
the Portal, which happens to be the city's prime—
pretty much only—natural resource. The expectation,
of course, is that Mazurich will issue some sort of statement about impending federal annexation of northeast
Ohio's golden goose.

That is not what is on Mazurich's mind.

Mazurich is a large man in every conceivable dimension. Tall and wide, with an expansive personality. He started as a union organizer, and he retains that blue-collar air. He can stand at the head of a roomful of a thousand people and make everyone feel as if he is one of them. He can give anyone the impression that he is on their side, if he wants to.

He walked out of a shutdown West Side steel plant two decades ago, and walked into City Council with a promise that he would pull his ward out of the economic depression the steel collapse had left it in. In his first three years, he pulled off a minor miracle, halving an unemployment rate that had started at nearly forty percent. By the time the Portal opened, the decommissioned steel plant had been replaced by a high-tech office park—built largely by the local labor force.

When the chaos from the Portal hit, he hooked his star to Mayor Rayburn, and managed to get the companies in his ward a major slice of the city contracts rebuilding the information infrastructure in Cleveland. When the dust settled, two years later, the unemployment rate in his ward was below the city average for the first time in a quarter century.

When Rayburn won reelection, Mazurich was elected as council president. He's been council president for eight years, and the current consensus is that the only thing that might keep him from serving eight more would be a successful run for the mayor's office.

Mazurich walks in frowning, an uncharacteristic expression. He steps in front of the lectern, facing the room of reporters. For a few moments, the assumption is that his displeasure is due to the Supreme Court ruling. No one in city government is happy about it. The federalization of the Portal represents a loss of jobs, money, and power for the city of Cleveland.

Mazurich clears his throat and pulls a dirty, wrinkled piece of paper out of his pocket. He glances down at it and says, "I only have a short statement, and I'm afraid I will not be taking any questions."

He takes a deep breath and deflates a little. His tie is somewhat askew, a detail picked up by many political cartoonists. Suit and tie have never worn well on Mazurich's large frame.

"Effective 7:30 PM today I have resigned my position on City Council."

There is, perhaps, a second or two of shocked silence. Something rare in the journalistic profession, complete, sincere, and universal surprise. There have been no rumors, no leaks, no hint of anything like this on Lakeside Avenue or off.

"Brenda Carlson will be acting councilwoman in my absence, and I have directed my staff to work with the next council president to effect a smooth transition. I have served my ward for twenty years, and it is my deep regret that I cannot serve them any longer."

Then, of course, the questions. Everyone shouts at once in the vain hope that Mazurich—who'd been, up to his announcement, the second most powerful man in Cleveland—might break and answer a question out of frustration, if nothing else. People ask him if he plans to run for mayor, if he consulted with Mayor Rayburn—or anyone—about his decision, and, of course, everyone wants to know—

Why?

Mazurich stares at them. His expression is odd. He's a career politician, but he looks shocked and slightly afraid, as if the attack of journalists is a surprise to him. He stands at the lectern as if dumbfounded, a state so incongruous that the questions slack off a bit.

To the consternation of his audience, Mazurich doesn't utter a single word more. He turns and exits the room without any further acknowledgment. As the door closes behind him, the sound of shouted questions is replaced by electronic clicks and beeps as the reporters rush to make cell phone calls and e-mails to catch the next edition, and in a few cases, the next broadcast.

Mazurich dismisses all his staff around 6:45 PM. They are all loyal, and have been working for him for over a decade in some cases. The feelings range from betrayal to despair. No one understands what he is doing, and the impact leaves the half dozen city employees shell-shocked and mute. Most of them end up in a bar down the street from City Hall and remain there for the next four hours.

Mazurich's secretary, Pam Lebowitz—who's worked for him the longest, close to eighteen years—doesn't join the others at the bar. At 7:00 pm, she walks into Mazurich's office to see him sitting at his computer. Mazurich looks up at her and closes the briefcase on his desk.

"Why are you doing this?" she asks.

His answer is abrupt and uncharacteristically cold, "I've said all I'm going to say on the subject."

"You owe me, all of us, an explanation."

"Owe you?" Mazurich shakes his head. "*Owe* you? I've given my life to this city. I lost a marriage and two kids. I gave and gave until this thankless job is all I have left. Now I've given *that*. How dare you. Owe? *Owe?*" He slams a large fist down on the desk, and stands up, toppling the precariously balanced brief-case. It tumbles to the floor spilling papers and CDs. *"This city owes me!"*

His dumbfounded secretary looks down at the spilled briefcase and bends over. "I'll get that, sir."

He steps in front of it and says, "You'll get out. I don't want you in here."

"But."

Mazurich's expression softens. "Please, Pam. I can't tell you what you want to hear. It's over. Leave it at that."

"But—"

"Let an old man go home."

Pam knows him well. She senses the pain, which only adds to her own confusion. She's run this man's life for nearly two decades, set up his meetings, his travel plans, rallies large and small. She's been a part of every decision he's made in his public life—except this one.

"Please, Pam. You can't help me anymore."

Something in his voice causes her to back away, a

decision she will regret the rest of her life. "Dominic, please, if you need to talk . . ."

He just nods.

"I'm your friend. We all are."

"I know. I just need to be alone now, please."

Pam leaves him as he picks the papers up off of the floor. Behind him, the screen of his workstation is flashing block letters on an otherwise blank screen, "Format Complete."

At some point before 8:30, he drives though his hometown neighborhood, and pulls into the driveway of his two-story frame house. The house belonged to his father, and his grandfather, both steelworkers and union to the core. Twenty years ago, you could have seen the stacks of the steel plant from the front porch.

No lights greet him as he pulls in the driveway. His two children are grown and his wife is separated from him—has been for three years now. The only thing preventing their divorce is the fact that both of them still hold Catholic beliefs.

He sits in the driveway of the empty house for some time. According to a later statement to investigators, a neighbor walks his dog past Mazurich's house and sees him sitting in the darkened vehicle at 8:30, then at 8:45.

A little before 9:00, Mazurich walks into his house. He doesn't turn on any lights, and he doesn't lock the side door behind him. At this point, he knows what he's doing. He walks upstairs, feeling his way in the dark. In the bedroom he sits down on the edge of the bed, by the nightstand. He takes off his shoes and sets them neatly on the floor by the nightstand. He loosens his tie and slips it off over his head, hanging it on the corner of the headboard. He takes his wedding ring off and sets it on the nightstand. He places his wallet next to it.

Then, he opens the drawer to the nightstand and pulls out a thirty-two caliber automatic. He takes out the magazine and removes every bullet except one, setting the ammunition neatly back in the drawer. With one bullet, he replaces the magazine and chambers the round. He places the barrel in his mouth.

Sometime before 10:00 PM, he pulls the trigger.

CHAPTER ONE

"WE MUST NEVER FORGET that Cleveland is a *city*."

Gregory Washington stood at a podium at the head of the Lakeside Baptist Church. The rally was deep in his home territory on the East Side—"Energizing the base," as political wonks like myself would say. I sat in a front pew reserved for local press, keying shorthand notes into my PDA with a stylus.

The man oozed charisma, and had the presence of a young James Earl Jones. There was a fair bit of lay preaching in his background and it came out in his speaking voice without devolving into parody.

"Let me say again. Cleveland is a *city*. Homes. Businesses. People. Too long our leaders have bowed down before this 'Portal' which has appeared on our shores. The city's budget has tripled in ten years. Have you seen that money?"

A chorus of "Noes."

"Have your schools seen that money?"

"*No.*"

"Is it in the roads? Is it in the fire department?"

"*No.*"

"You know why? Because almost all that money has been fed into the Portal. We've paid lawyers millions of dollars to help us to keep this thing that's costing us tens of millions. Last year, half our city budget—*I said half*—went to expenses related to the Portal. Let the federal government have it."

I made a silent promise to myself that I would be the one political reporter this election who would refrain from using the phrase "paradigm shift" in an article. The rhetoric that Washington was using would have been politically inconceivable two years ago. The Portal, a mystical phenomenon about twelve years old now, had been the raison d'être of city government for a decade. The Portal had granted Cleveland, Ohio, an association with the supernatural so pervasive and widely acknowledged that my hometown's relationship to elves, dragons, and sorcerers was as fundamental as gaming was to Las Vegas, technology was to Silicon Valley, and politics was to Washington D.C.

However, some politically disastrous moves by the administration of the outgoing Mayor Rayburn, followed by a series of new Supreme Court rulings, had cast the relationship of the Portal to city government in a whole new light. The fact was, the Feds now had physical control of the Portal and passage through it, and the world had not ended. The streets of Northeastern Ohio were still awash with mana, mages still brokered their potions, and dragons still flew in the nighttime sky.

Of course, when federalization happened, people started asking the obvious questions; what was the big deal? Why did we waste all that money on lawyers? Even Gabriel Clifton, Mayor Rayburn's spiritual successor and Washington's only real opposition in the race for the Democratic spot in the next mayoral election, did not go to the mat defending the city's stand against federalization.

Even Rayburn himself didn't much talk about it anymore.

The fact was, what marked Cleveland's economic boom wasn't the Portal. It was the supernatural radiation flowing out of it. Immigration had been important, at least at the beginning, but while the novelty of passage to another universe initially commanded prices usually reserved for tickets into suborbital flight, the income from that had been surpassed by income from tourism within two years. It was always the case that more people wanted to visit the circus than there were who wanted to run away and join it.

So even with federal regulation of passage, customs, and a drop in ticket prices that made the cost closer to a one-way flight to Europe than a seat on the space shuttle, the hit to the northeast Ohio economy was practically nil.

Even if the Feds ever shut the door completely, a dozen years of near-unlimited passage from the universe next door had given Northeast Ohio enough local color to last into the next century.

So, despite the protests from the folks who ran the city, in pure economic terms it was pretty much irrelevant who had physical control of the Portal. One councilman had put it this way, "If we gave the Feds immigration control over the Sun, it wouldn't make our streets any darker."

People linked to the current administration were having a lot of trouble explaining how they had been on the wrong side of that argument.

Washington's rival for the Democratic nomination, Gabriel Clifton, might have the establishment's blessing, and the support of the man who was, at one point, the city's most powerful and popular mayor, but people had been talking about "Rayburn Fatigue" for six months before the current mayor made the announcement that he wasn't going to run for reelection. And there wasn't enough daylight between Gabe Clifton and Dave Rayburn to grow a mushroom.

And, given the state of the Republican Party in Cuyahoga County, that meant that there was a pretty good chance that I was watching the next mayor of the city. Unlike Clifton, Washington had both street cred and the currently enviable position of being a complete outsider. That gave Washington, a relative unknown, a better-than-even chance to win the nomination, and—barring a massive screwup—the election.

"Do we want a city government that gives away millions in tax 'incentives' to corporate cronies? Two billion dollars—I said *billion*—two billion dollars in new construction downtown. Office buildings, hotels, malls. Do you know how much of that pays back the city any property taxes? *Any?* Fifteen million."

There was a chorus of hoots.

"Ninety-nine percent of new construction since the

Portal opened has been built under an 'emergency tax-abatement incentive' begun under the previous administration. Don't you think the emergency is over?"

"*Yes.*"

I shook my head. His figures were a little dubious. A hell of a lot of that two billion figure represented construction by the city itself for city facilities, including the containment structure around the old Browns Stadium and the Portal inside. That probably accounted for a quarter of that figure.

Still, he did have a point. A lot of the executive bureaucracy of the city was a patchwork of ad hoc measures and emergency provisions that, when examined as a whole, made little sense. The blanket tax abatement was a case in point. The Portal opening had been an economic disaster in the short term. No one had been thinking about what things would look like a decade hence; the worry was about the social and economic collapse of the city.

But, while the emergency was long since over, it's a fact of politics that it is a lot easier to get a tax abatement passed than it is to get one repealed.

About the time Washington began delving into a comparison between the growth rates between the city budget as a whole, versus the budget for the city schools—along with the same figures for various outlying suburbs that *still* outperformed the city in proficiency achievements and graduation rates—my cell phone started vibrating at me.

I spent a moment assessing the likelihood that Washington might deviate from the speech he distributed to the press, and whether any extemporaneous comments might be newsworthy, before I slid out of the pew and headed toward the back of the church.

When I was back and off to the side, I pulled the phone out, flipped it open, and said, "Kline Maxwell, *Cleveland Press*. Make it quick."

"Mr. Maxwell, I wish to meet with you."

It wasn't a voice I recognized. I glanced up toward Washington. "I'm on assignment at the moment. You can call the main desk at the *Press* and leave me a message."

"Please. I expended much effort to contact you. You, specifically."

The voice had an accent. I couldn't identify it, because my caller was disguising his voice. All I got was the occasional too-hard consonant. Middle Eastern, dwarven, or German, I couldn't tell.

"I'm flattered," I said. "Tell me who you are and what you want to discuss, and we'll see if I can accommodate you."

"I cannot over the phone. My life is in danger."

Not German . . .

"You have to tell me something if you want me to take you seriously. Why should I be interested?"

The crowd in the church broke into a standing ovation. I had to turn to the wall and cover my other ear to hear what my caller was saying.

"What?"

"—Mazurich."

Mazurich?

"What about him?"

"Why did he die, Mr. Maxwell?"

I grunted. "My friend, you are the latest in a long line of conspiracy theorists. I have more letters on who killed Mazurich than you'd ever care to write. I could write a dissertation of the cover-up using theories more creative than you could think up—"

"Mr. Maxwell—"

"You also want to know what I have? Police reports, forensic reports, digital images of the scene. The man killed himself. If there was anything to any of these conspiracy—"

"Mr. Maxwell—"

"I'd be the first to report it—"

"*Mr. Maxwell!*"

I stopped talking for a moment.

"Mr. Maxwell, I am not delusional. I offer you nothing that cannot be substantiated. I am aware that he killed himself."

"What then?"

"*Why* did he kill himself?"

I remained quiet.

"Mr. Maxwell?"

"Okay," I said, "Why did he?"

"Not over the phone. I've talked too long already. Meet me in the Old Arcade, mezzanine level, at 6:30."

"How will I know you?"

"I will know you." The phone clicked. I switched it off, turning around. As I watched Washington basking in the glow of potential constituents, I told myself that the call was a wild-goose chase.

I also knew where I was going to be at 6:30 tonight.

*   *   *

When I left the rally and returned to my Volkswagen, someone had brushed the snow away enough to slip a neon-green flyer under my windshield wiper. I had parked only a block away from the church, so I wasn't particularly surprised when I pulled it free. On the cover was a stylized whirlpool graphic around which swirled the phrase "God's Plan or The Devil's Handiwork?"

The question was rhetorical for anyone who had seen one of these pamphlets before. The whole trifold was a warning how the Portal was a threat to my immortal soul and a gateway to hell itself. The inside showed a crude graphic of Satan lording over it the Cleveland skyline, surrounded by half a dozen quotes from "Leviticus" and "Deuteronomy."

"Give no regard to mediums and familiar spirits; do not seek after them, to be defiled by them: I am the Lord your God."

I looked around at the other cars parked down the street. All had Day-Glo flyers tucked under the wipers. I wondered if the author was independently motivated, or was part of Washington's base. Attitudes might be shifting, but I was pretty sure that the voters in this city were still a few steps away from condemning the Cleveland Growth Association to "the lake that burns with fire and brimstone."

I pocketed the evangelical pamphlet and got into my car.

The drive back to the *Press* offices was a little rougher than usual. In addition to a short flurry of lake-effect snow that unloaded during the rally, an accident on the Shoreway tied up pre-rush hour traffic downtown in both directions. A semi had jackknifed on Dead Man's

Curve trying to avoid a griffin. The guy on the traffic report speculated that the griffin had been a brand-new arrival out of the Portal, which was pretty close by, and it
didn't know about interstates, and that a semi wasn't a
good choice of prey.

While it was true that the griffins that had been here
any length of time knew enough to hang out in the
Metroparks and thin out the deer population, the idea
that the victim of the accident had just popped from the
recently federalized Portal implied that the Feds didn't
have as tight a lid on things as the Port Authority had
had, which was kind of scary.

I passed by the mess, where the cops had traffic downtown narrowed to one lane. Not pretty. The griffin car-
cass had been removed, but the signs remained. Blood
and feathers covered the eastbound lanes like a voodoo
ceremony gone horribly awry. Police wreckers were still
trying to remove the semi, the front of which was caved
in as if it had run into the business end of God's own
place kicker.

The driver had probably taken the curve going fifty,
and from the looks of things, the ill-fated heraldic beast
had been diving in the other direction, from the lake, just
on the wrong side of an overpass for the driver to see him
in time.

As I inched by the scene, the radio informed me that
the driver had lived, and had been life-flighted to Metro
Health Medical Center.

Well, I knew what the lead Metro story was probably
going to be. The driver's miraculous survival cinched it.
The Portal might have killed local television and TV jour-

nalism, but the ascendance of blogs and print hadn't changed the dynamics of local news coverage all that much—and the only thing better than a gory accident, was a gory accident with survivors. Gave you someone to interview.

Back at the office, I wrote my piece on Washington's political destiny. I even managed to work in a bit of evangelical politics, a nod to the serendipitous pamphlet. I would probably be the only reporter to give even a passing mention to the born-again vote, given the fact that Cuyahoga County was one of the most aggressively liberal pieces of real estate between Boston and San Francisco, but there's always something to be said for the organization and passion of a vocal minority in the political process.

As I typed, I heard with half an ear people talking about griffins. Someone walked up to my desk and said, "Say, Maxwell, who's the prof at Case, the guy you used on the dragon story?"

I kept typing. "Shafran, Dr. Newman Shafran."

"Thanks."

I muttered something polite, keeping my annoyance in check. I was a political reporter, but one story about a dragon's murder and I was the expert on any supernatural critter that met an untimely end. I had been dealing with this for the past two years.

Even if it had been, arguably, the biggest story to break out of the Portal after the Portal opening itself, I didn't want to be the dragon expert, or the elf expert, or the talking frog expert.

We supposedly had a reporter on the "fuzzy gnome" beat. It was unfortunate for me that the position had a high turnover and the people Columbia Jennings, my boss, tended to pick for the job tended to creep out the other reporters.

"Mr. Maxwell?"

Speak of the devil.

I looked up to see Nina Johannessen standing next to my desk. The current *Cleveland Press* journalist on the supernatural beat. She was a Nordic blonde suitable for a Wagner opera, or a lite beer commercial during the Superbowl. The only disconcerting note were eyes that were nowhere near shallow enough to make the average male comfortable talking to a woman that attractive.

"Please tell me that you don't want to talk about griffins . . ."

She gave me a puzzled look and shook her head. "Why would I?"

"I wouldn't know . . ."

She reached over and picked up the neon-green pamphlet off of my desk. I felt slightly embarrassed when she opened it. Considering the kind of sources she used for her stories, it was sort of like having one of my Jewish coworkers pick up a neo-Nazi tract from my desk.

She stared at the devil picture for a long time and I mentally prepared a long explanation about Washington's candidacy and changing attitudes toward the Portal.

She set the pamphlet devil faceup on my desk. "Has anything strange happened to you lately?"

"No, what?" I was left conversationally disoriented by

a question I wasn't expecting. She looked at me deeply enough that I had the uncomfortable sense that she was seeing much more than I was saying. "What do you mean?"

"Unexpected changes or influences? Anything new or threatening?"

I was suddenly looking for sinister influences in every part of my life over the past few days. It took a bit of an effort to rein myself in. As a reporter I was naturally paranoid, but that impulse did quite well enough without outside help.

"Nina, the only thing I can think that might match that description is that question."

"I'm sorry, I didn't mean to disturb you."

"The only thing disturbing me is wondering why you're asking in the first place."

"A vision." She tapped the pamphlet. "It wasn't completely clear, and I thought it might involve you."

"Might? You don't know?"

"Sometimes the Oracle is unclear."

"And how would you know?"

She shrugged. "Have you seen Death or the Devil recently?"

I had the feeling she wasn't kidding.

CHAPTER TWO

I SHOULD HAVE known better.

Hell, I *did* know better. At quarter to seven I was staring up at the vast glass canopy that roofed the Old Arcade and telling myself that I never really expected anything to come from my anonymous caller. I sat back in one of the chairs lining the railing of the first mezzanine level and looked at my little neon-green pamphlet.

The author had certainly gotten his money's worth out of me. Something about it had me thinking about the backlash coming against the Portal. What exactly would happen when the author's point of view became a majority position, or even a plurality?

Federalization might be the least of our worries.

A shadow glimpsed out of the corner of my eye brought me back to the here and now. A very *tall* shadow. I looked up and saw an elf standing by my table. Not just any elf either.

"Maelgwyn Caledvwlch," I said, still butchering the name after two years.

"*Commander* Maelgwyn Caledvwlch," he responded with none of the irritation that a human would lend to the correction. His voice was cultured and much too light for someone eight-and-a-half feet tall. His accent carried a hint of the West Indies, though the magical influence of the Portal would keep him from ever traveling any farther south than the edge of Columbus before the life drained out of him.

When I first met him, under less pleasant circumstances, he was a senior detective in the Special Paranormal Unit. He had since graduated to running the whole SPU, which made him probably the highest ranking nonhuman in the city government.

But his suits were still cheap, and they still didn't fit right.

"What can I do for you?" I asked. I reached over and picked up my coffee, trying to remain casual in front of Caledvwlch. It took an effort. Not just because he was physically intimidating; he ran tall even for an elf, and his eyes were featureless metallic reflections that hid any slight emotion that might pass over his impassive face. What really made me ill at ease was the fact he was a cop, the SPU commander, and in two years he had never once said one word to me that was not part of some official communication.

For one brief moment I thought that he might have been my anonymous caller. But that wasn't Caledvwlch's style, and he certainly would not have any issues contacting me whenever he wanted.

"I wish to ask you some questions in connection with a police investigation." He drew the seat away from the other side of my small table. He folded into the seat without asking my permission. Even seated, I had to look up to see his face.

Reading his expression was hopeless. I took a sip from my coffee and asked, "Am I a suspect, a witness, or a victim?" I told myself not to be too worried. For the past two years my brushes with the law had been largely benign, limited to two speeding tickets, contempt of court for not revealing a source, and one bogus trespassing charge brought by a councilman who felt I shouldn't be spending time watching city employees unload kegs of Miller Lite behind a bar owned by the councilman's brother.

"Witness, Mr. Maxwell. I need to know what you know about a gentleman named Ossian Parthalán."

"The name doesn't ring any bells."

"Perhaps, then, you may recognize his face."

Caledvwlch reached into his breast pocket and pulled out a picture. His long fingers covered it as he slid it facedown across the table.

I looked down at the white glossy back of the picture as his hand withdrew. Fresh inkjet print on cheap paper, still curling a little, as if it had just come out of the printer.

I set down the coffee feeling a little trepidation as I lifted the picture, half expecting what I saw.

Cops, even elven ones, are nothing if not predictable. If Ossian Parthalán had meant anything to me, looking at a picture of his mutilated corpse probably would have provoked some incriminating reaction.

I was very aware of Caledvwlch watching me stare at the gruesome crime scene picture.

Someone really did not like Mr. Parthalán. They had cut out his eyes, sliced his mouth open, and chopped off his hands, among other things. The blood was so bad that it took a moment for me to realize that Parthalán wasn't human.

I lowered the picture to the table and said, "Dwarven?"

"Yes."

"I don't know him."

"Look again, please. Mr. Parthalán knows you."

I lifted the picture reluctantly. "Dwarves," in this case, referred to the humanoid race that came over from the other side of the Portal. Dwarves weren't squat humans. Their skin was different, wrinkled, thick, the color and texture of weathered leather. Their skulls were flatter and wider, a thick jaw usually hidden behind a thick beard. There were a whole litany of subtle differences in internal organs and skeletal structure . . .

"Who'd do this to someone?" I whispered.

The body was sprawled on a hardwood floor. Blood had spattered everywhere. The camera looked straight down, framing the body. There were few other details visible. I looked up at Caledvwlch and asked, though I already suspected the answer, "How does he know me?"

"The last time we know Mr. Parthalán contacted anyone while he was alive was one phone call he made at 12:45 PM today."

"And you know who he called?"

"You, Mr. Maxwell. He called your cell phone."

I looked back down at the body. This was the person I had come here to meet. The person who knew why Council President Dominic Lloyd Mazurich put a gun in his mouth and pulled the trigger.

What did you know? What were you going to tell me?

"I got a call," I said.

"What did Mr. Parthalán talk to you about?"

"He wanted to meet with me. He didn't give his name."

"Why did he want to meet with you?"

I looked up at Caledvwlch and felt a little uneasy. I had been dismissive about conspiracies involving Mazurich's suicide, but the dwarf's death lent substantial weight to whatever suspicions he did have.

However, while Caledvwlch was one of the few cops in the city I could say for certain wasn't crooked, that didn't mean I trusted him.

"How did you find him?" I asked. "What happened?"

"The investigation is ongoing."

I slid the photo back across the table. "You know us humans, we tend to have faulty memories."

Caledvwlch shook his head. "I know humans, Mr. Maxwell. I know you. What did Mr. Parthalán discuss with you?"

I sipped my coffee. I have two personality traits that, in most professions, would be self-destructive. The first was a cultivated paranoia that, in my more self-aware moments, I told myself was a natural journalist's instinct not to take people's motivations at face value.

The second was, whenever anyone attempted to pressure me to do anything, I tended to behave in the exact contrary manner.

"You know me," I said. "And I'm under no obligation to continue this conversation with you."

"I cannot detail our investigation—"

"No, but you can give me enough facts about the case to satisfy my curiosity."

Caledvwlch retrieved his photograph and replaced it in his pocket. "There are very few facts. Mr. Parthalán died two hours ago. He was killed in rooms above a tourist bar, the *Nazgûl*, on the West Side of the Flats. Authorities there for an unrelated matter became aware of a disturbance and broke into the room Mr. Parthalán had locked himself inside. He was dead when they found him. In the room was the phone he had used to call you."

"Locked from inside?"

"Yes."

"Was any sort of ritual involved?"

"Dwarves do not use magic," Caledvwlch said. "They cannot manipulate mana, and are largely immune to its effects."

"That's not quite an answer to my question."

Caledvwlch stared at me. "You have not answered mine. Do you wish to, or shall I leave you now?"

Despite my contrary streak, I saw no good reason to obstruct a police investigation. "He said that his life was in danger, and he wanted to talk to me about Mazurich."

Very, very slightly, an eyebrow arched on the elf's face. Given their almost pathological reserve, I counted that as the equivalent to a human expression of stunned disbelief. Nothing altered in the timbre of his voice, so I might have imagined it. "Council President Mazurich?"

I nodded. "One of the hundreds of conspiracy theorists out there. He said he knew something about his death but couldn't talk about it on the phone. That's pretty much it."

Caledvwlch nodded and stood. "Thank you, Mr. Maxwell. I will contact you if we need to discuss this further."

He turned to go, and I asked again, "*Was* there a ritual involved?"

"Perhaps we will talk later," Caledvwlch walked away without looking back at me.

I sipped my coffee.

One of the hundreds of conspiracy theorists . . .

True.

But the only one I knew of who had been murdered.

I drove home thinking of the late Councilman Mazurich, and about dwarves.

Mazurich was union to the core, the kind of traditional working-class Democrat that didn't even have to ask the locals for support. It just sort of happened. So it made sense that dwarves had an interest in him.

Dwarves were labor personified. One of the dwarf

clans in Cleveland was responsible for most of the construction that Gregory Washington had been complaining about. The dwarves at the local Ford plant were, to my understanding, the most productive workers on the North American continent. During the exodus of skilled labor in the chaotic years following the Portal's opening, dwarves had slid into dozens of niches in the economy, from plumbing to civil engineering.

And, while a lot of dwarven individuals were part of the Teamsters, or the UAW, and so on, the dwarven clan system was more powerful than any union. You cross a dwarf, you'll not only lose your dwarven employees, but your clients will lose theirs. And their dwarven customers. Down to dwarven contractors abandoning construction sites if the owner was too cozy with someone on their shit list.

I was certain that dwarves would have a political affinity with Mazurich. A lot more so than with the opposite pole of Cleveland politics, Mayor Rayburn.

Rayburn was, according to his critics, autocratic, authoritarian, elitist. . . . A top-down type of politician whose view of the world was more in sync with elves and dragons.

Mazurich, to the same people, was populist, egalitarian, a small "d" democrat . . . a man whose grassroots politics would certainly be more in tune with the dwarven clans.

I sighed to myself. I was a political reporter, but the politics I reported on were almost universally human. It was inevitable, I suppose, a white journalist in the Deep South during the days of Jim Crow wasn't going to be very good at discerning the internal politics of the civil rights movement. I was in the same position, trying to understand a culture—a series of cultures—I wasn't a part of.

However, when I parked behind my condo, I had enough professional sense to realize that all my speculation up to that point was just that. Speculation. Non-human politics happened behind closed doors, out of view of the media.

I stepped out of my Volkswagen, raised my collar against the snow, and walked around my building to the front entrance.

Willie Czestzyk—the doorman for my building who looked at least as old as it was—let me in to my condo.

"Long day, Mr. Maxwell?"

"Longer than some, shorter than others."

"What's the news?" he asked, like always.

"Old politicians never die, they just become the focus of conspiracy theories." I shook my head and walked into the lobby. I didn't like that I was still thinking about the dead dwarf. Ever since my divorce I had made an effort to leave my job at the office—as if I was still trying to fix my marriage.

The sad thing was that I did a pretty good job at it once my marriage wasn't on the line.

So, trying to think happy thoughts about my daughter's coming visit this weekend, I gathered my mail and took the elevator up to my condo. I noticed a new set of charms riveted to the doors as they slid open. Building management must be upgrading security again.

My condo lived on the third floor of a line of buildings built in the nineteen-thirties. Originally intended as apartments for professionals commuting via the brand new light-rail line downtown, it sat just on the suburban side of Shaker Square. My place was one of the lesser residences, some of the suites here ran larger than some good-sized houses, with an inflated mortgage to match.

I had one of the more reasonable condos, four rooms if you counted the bathroom, five if you designated the living/dining room space as two separate areas.

I let myself in and collapsed on the couch that dominated half of the living room area, and scattered my mail on the coffee table. Bills mostly.

I checked my watch and saw that it was still before five on the West Coast. My daughter usually didn't call until after she ate dinner, so I picked up the remote, intent on watching something brainless on my new fifty-inch Panasonic LCD flat-screen. I powered it on and waited while the electronics between it and the satellite dish established a reliable digital connection and filtered enough of an incoming signal through the Portal interference.

While I waited, I saw that one of the envelopes I had brought up wasn't a bill.

I set down the remote and picked up the envelope. It was an odd size, and a little lumpy. My address was written across the front in an elaborate cursive hand. The postmark was local, a post office downtown, dated yesterday. Two fifty-cent Ronald Reagan stamps. No return address.

The television was flashing a "signal error" message at me. I shut it off.

Okay, are we paranoid yet?

Holding the corners of the envelope, I walked to the kitchen with it. I set it down in the basin of the sink and pondered what to do with it.

Unfortunately, I work in a profession that is a lot more likely to receive dangerous things in the mail than most.

I went into the bedroom, grabbed a table lamp, stripped off the shade, and carried it into the kitchen. I plugged it in and turned the thing on.

Then, feeling like an idiot, I grabbed a pair of tongs and picked the letter up by the corner and held it up between me and the incandescent bulb. I stared at it, lit from behind.

The good news: no wires, no electronics. It contained a folded piece of paper with some writing on it in the same hand as the envelope. The lumpy bit was something else, rectangular, about the size of the two stamps on the envelope. There seemed to be some transparency to it. When I tilted the letter, it stayed in the same place, as if it was taped there.

There didn't seem to be signs of anything loose inside the envelope.

I set it down on the counter.

"So?" I asked it. "Are you safe or not?"

The fact was my self-destructive curiosity was getting the better of me. I figured I was safe from most hostile magic, I certainly paid enough for the wards in this building, a nasty enchantment shouldn't have made it through the front doors. Mundanely, there didn't seem to be any surprises inside this letter.

Even so, I got a pair of latex gloves out from under the sink and dug out the sharpest paring knife I could find. With the envelope flat on the table, I very carefully slit open one side of the letter. Then I backed up and spread the opening with the end of my tongs.

Just a folded letter with something taped to it.

Figuring I was safe, I drew the letter out of the envelope. Still wearing the gloves, I opened it and laid it flat on the table.

What the hell?

The letter was a single line long:

"This is why he killed himself."

Somehow, I had a pretty good idea who "he" was.

The object taped to the letter was a small ziplock bag that contained a few grams of some granular white substance. I looked at it and shook my head.

"What were you into, Mazurich?"

CHAPTER THREE

THE LETTER STAYED on the counter, slipped
back into its envelope, and the envelope, in turn,
isolated in the biggest ziplock bag I could find. I figured that there was a good chance it was evidence of
something, and I didn't want too much contamina-
tion from myself or from my apartment on the thing.

Not that I was about to turn it over to the cops.

Not yet, anyway.

What I did do was grab a beer from the fridge and
settle down in front of my TV. I turned it on and it
was still having signal difficulties.

"Damn it."

One would think that with a dozen years working
on the signal problems in this city, they could come
up with a reliable television. I had paid almost double the national standard to get a TV and satellite
hookup that had the custom electronics to work
within the Portal's influence—and the damn thing
couldn't lock on a signal.

I leaned back and sighed.

I couldn't bitch too much. The Portal's influence on data transmission was why I had a job in the first place. The interference, the inability to transmit or receive video without special equipment, was why there were no local broadcast or cable TV stations around the Portal. That meant no local TV news. That meant the revival of print journalism to the tune of five local dailies in the Greater Cleveland area along with hundreds of regional weeklies.

TV in northeast Ohio was an elitist luxury.

It was still annoying.

I shut it off again and walked over to the windows. I looked out at the purple sky where a swollen yellow moon competed with the streetlight glare off of Shaker Square. Signal blackouts usually happened because of weather conditions, storms, thick cloud cover . . .

The sky was perfectly clear.

The phone rang.

I walked over and picked up the phone, "Maxwell."

"Dad?"

"Hey there," I said, staring up into the cloudless night sky. I effortlessly forgot Mazurich, dwarves, and political conspiracies as I slid into Father mode. Something I've gotten a lot better at in the years since me and Margaret split. "All ready for this weekend?"

"More than ready." I could pick up the exasperation in her voice all the way from California.

"What's the matter?"

"Nothing."

"What particular nothing is it this time?"

"Oh, you know, Mom."

She wasn't a little girl any more, but I could hear the childlike frustration in her voice—probably half calculated to catch my sympathy. A long veteran of long-distance parenting, I asked, "So, why are you upset with your mother?"

"She can't stop it with telling me what to do. I'm seventeen, Dad. I'm not a kid who needs to be told how to cross the street."

"She just worries about you."

"She's acting like I'm going into a war zone. Like goblins are going to eat me or something."

I hoped my sigh wasn't audible. When the Portal opened up, the whole area was thrown into chaos for a good eighteen months. Everything from power outages and the failure of most of the electronic infrastructure of the city, to a federal blockade and a small invasion by magical critters of every description. It was the story of my career, and I didn't have the good sense to listen to my wife's concerns about living in the epicenter of all this. I've never been able to blame her for that, which is one of the reasons that up until now every family visit I've had involved me buying the ticket.

This time around, though, Sarah had insisted on visiting *me*. She wanted to see the town where she had been born.

This, of course, drove her mother nuts.

"Sarah, your mother has very bad memories of this place. Try to understand where she's coming from."

"She's being irrational. She wants me to lock myself in your condo until I take my return flight."

"I'm sure you're exaggerating."

"You think so? I said I wanted to see the Portal, and she went nuts. She almost tore up my boarding pass . . ."

"Sarah, there's no reason to bait your mother like that."

"I have a right to see you, Dad—"

"Correction. *I* have a right to see *you*. You have a right to do whatever your parents tell you."

"Dad."

"Don't 'Dad' me. Just because your mother has buttons doesn't mean you have to push them. Just be happy she's letting you come here for once."

"Okay, but you don't have to live with her."

At this point, that was probably a good thing.

"Anyway, I got a surprise for you, Dad."

"Oh, what?"

"Hey, that would be telling."

The paternal instinct kicked in. "Is this a surprise I'm going to like?"

"Uh-huh . . ."

"Why do you sound uncertain about that?"

"It's just . . . I haven't told Mom yet."

Okay, now I was really worried. "Tell me."

"I wanted to tell you in person—"

"Honey, unless you want me to have nightmares

about you eloping with a biker with a ring through his nose, tell me what it is."

"Ick. Okay, if you promise not to tell Mom."

"Sarah, you know I—"

"I'm going to tell her, I just need to let her calm down first."

"What is it?"

"I got an acceptance letter from one of my college applications."

"Hey, that is good news. Congratulations!" As I said it I began to realize that there was more going on here.

"What aren't you telling me?"

She sucked in a breath and said, "It was my application to Kent State."

"You applied to Kent?"

"And Oberlin."

"Uh-huh?"

"And Antioch, and Case Western . . ." She rattled off a list of a half dozen other schools.

"Is there a university in Northeast Ohio you didn't apply to?"

"Cleveland State."

I placed my hand on my forehead. "Did Margaret let you send out those applications?"

"Uh, no."

"Did she know you applied to these places?"

Silence.

"Honey, you aren't eighteen, wasn't a parent supposed to sign your applications?"

"She did . . . sort of."

"You didn't forge your mother's signature, did you?"

"Not really."

"Sarah!"

"I filled out a stack of twenty or thirty, Dad. I just slipped a few more in when she was signing them for me. Can I help it if she wasn't reading closely?"

I tried to stifle a laugh.

"Dad?"

I gritted my teeth and said, "You have until this weekend to come clean with your mother."

"You're angry with me?"

"I will be if you continue this feud with your mom. Think of who's going to be paying for half of this education. She has a right to be part of that decision."

"You know how she feels—"

"And you're making assumptions. If you don't want me talking to your mom, do it yourself. She might surprise you."

"I doubt it."

"Perhaps, but you're a year away from having the right to make those decisions unilaterally." I walked away from the window, holding the phone.

"Okay, I will."

"Promise?"

"Yeah, I—"

"Honey?"

"—ble hearing you, Dad." Her voice was small and weak. I could hear the distance in it now.

"I think we're losing the connection."

"—is weekend—ve you, Dad."

"I love you, too."

A rattle, a hiss, and a shaking dial tone. I turned off the wireless and tossed it on the couch.

"Kent State?" I muttered to myself, smiling. I was going to catch hell from Margaret about this one. She would think I put our daughter up to it. And, knowing my daughter, I doubted that there was anything Margaret would be able to do to keep her from moving up here.

There were God knows how many parents of God knows how many teenagers living perfectly normal lives here. More all the time.

However, despite all the times I had told my ex that things were okay up here, now that the possibility was staring me in the face, I wasn't sure how I felt about it.

CHAPTER FOUR

A S SOON AS I HIT the office, I spread the competition across my desk. The *Herald*, the *Leader*, and the *Plain Dealer*, all had at least some ink devoted to the late Mr. Ossian Parthalán. The *Plain Dealer* had little more than a police blotter, but the other two pretty much confirmed what Commander Maelgwyn Caledvwlch had told me.

At Club *Nazgûl*, at about six-thirty yesterday, they found the corpse of our dwarf. The one detail I picked up from the stories that Caledvwlch hadn't volunteered was the fact that the "authorities" who broke in on our decedent were FBI agents, not local cops.

Of course, the glaring omission in every story was what Federal agents were doing there in the first place. After plumbing the record, such as it was, I decided to check the *Press'* own resource.

Reggie Sommers had been a veteran of the crime beat longer than I'd been paying attention to politics, much less covering it. He'd been a rookie back in the

Danny Greene era and probably had the numbers of more mob guys in his head than were in the Youngstown phone book.

He looked like the guys he covered; squat, beefy, snow-white hair, with a cigar—always unlit in the non-smoking building—clamped in his mouth.

He looked up as I stopped in front of his desk. "Hey, Maxwell, what brings you to my side of the tracks? Another kickback story?"

"No." I pulled up a chair. "Murder, actually."

Reggie arched an eyebrow and took the unlit cigar out of his mouth. "A little off your beat, isn't it? They didn't find another dragon, did they?"

They're probably going to carve that story on my tombstone.

I shook my head.

"Thank God for that."

"No," I said, "this was a source. Well, he might have been a source. . . . Someone killed him before we met."

"That sucks."

"I want to know if you heard anything. I got a feeling that the FBI might have had my guy under surveillance."

"This guy wouldn't have just turned up dead in a Goth nightclub, would he?"

"Ossian Parthalán."

"Holy crap. I knew I had a bad feeling about that one."

"What do you mean?"

"The guys I usually talk to, they might hire mages here and there, but they have a good Catholic fear of the kind of voodoo that flies out of the Portal. The nasty stuff, they don't want to touch."

"A ritual killing, you think?"

Reggie laughed, "You see any crime scene pictures? Kind of thing that can make a forensic mage lose his lunch. This was a dwarf thing, and the dwarves in this town are up to their little skulls in the nasty stuff."

"I thought dwarves weren't involved in magic."

"Well, I can't count the stories of guys who crossed the wrong dwarf and ended up like your friend Parthalán. Guys a century removed from the old country will give you the evil eye if you mention dwarven business."

"So no one's talking about Parthalán?"

"I didn't say that."

"So what have you heard?"

Reggie leaned forward and lowered his voice. "Now, I didn't hear this from who I heard it from, and you didn't hear it from anyone. The wise-guy gossip is that your dwarf had left the reservation. He was selling out someone, and this was payback."

"Who?"

Reggie shrugged. "Someone involved with the clans, and big in the dark side of things."

"Things a good Catholic mobster doesn't mess with?"

"You got it." Reggie looked at me with a little concern. "And, frankly, if he was talking to you, I'd watch your back."

I grunted a "Thanks," and changed the subject. "So you have any idea what the FBI was doing there?"

"I haven't got a clear answer from anyone, but there are rumors about some sort of dwarven smuggling operation." I thought of the little plastic bag of white crystals. "My guess is they were tailing the dwarf, and considering how he was cut up, probably a good chance that he was about to become an informant, if he hadn't already."

I nodded.

"So want to tell me what he was a source on?"

After a long conversation with Reggie, I slipped out to have lunch with one of the few good, reliable contacts I had on the investigative side of law enforcement.

Like any good reporter, I cultivated cops for sources. But I'm a political reporter, and that skews the people I cultivate. All the cops I dealt with were either in the city administration or in the union hierarchy. Basically old guys with a lot socked away for their pension and within spitting distance of retirement. Folks whose secure position made them reluctant to openly criticize anything, but, ironically, made them more likely to be my unnamed source. The guys I usually talked to weren't going to be the first ones—or the last ones—at a crime scene.

However, there was one guy I knew who was still actively involved in criminal investigation more than politics. The guy wasn't even a cop. His name was Dr. Russell Kawata, and he was a forensic pathologist. I'd met him over a liquor store shooting a few years ago. It wasn't something I normally get involved with, but it was a high profile case with some racial overtones—

which meant that someone decided to make political hay out of what happened. Speeches, public trial, all very ugly. Kawata had been offended at the way some public figures were misstating the facts of the case, and fed me details on what *really* happened.

It wasn't often that a political reporter needed the help of a forensic pathologist, and it had been over a year since I talked to him about a story, but, thankfully, he was free for lunch at a small deli downtown. He was waiting for me when I walked in.

"Maxwell, how're you doing?"

"Good. Thanks for meeting on such short notice."

He held out a beefy hand and I shook it.

Kawata was dark and round, with black hair and Asiatic features. He spoke with an accent unfamiliar to most Midwesterners. He told me once that about half the people he met thought he was Indian or Pakistani, the other half thought he was some weird Puerto Rican half-breed. He actually was a full-blooded native Hawaiian. I never asked why he came to Cleveland, but I suspect it had something to do with the Portal.

"No problem, Maxwell. I was thinking of you the other day. I saw the story about the bar."

I nodded. "I was hoping that you could do me a favor."

"What?"

I pulled out my letter, contained in its Ziplock bag. I placed it on the table. "You do drug tests when you do an autopsy, right?"

"Yes?"

"So if I asked you to, you could identify what's in this envelope?"

"If there's enough for a spectral analysis." He picked up the bag. "We just got a new toy. They finally bought us a mass spectrometer that gives accurate readings."

"There was a problem with the old one?"

"I never told you? Same problem every TV had. Analog signal. Up to now we had to ship tests to an out-of-state lab, or take about twenty-five readings on one sample and average out the noise. Got a brand-new machine now, though, does all that for us."

"Glad to hear it."

"Only took a decade . . ." Kawata held up the bag and looked at it. "Addressed to you?"

"Someone sent me a present."

Kawata nodded. "You know, all I'm competent to do is a chemical analysis. If you want anything more thorough—handwriting, fingerprinting . . ."

"I have a good idea who sent it."

"Okay."

"But you should probably treat it like crime scene evidence, just in case."

He lowered the envelope. "Is it?"

"I don't know yet."

When I got back to the office, I tried to research what I could about Ossian Parthalán. Mazurich aside, Ossian Parthalán's life and death already counted as a minor news story even if he was just a dwarven conspiracy buff blowing smoke out his ass.

I sat at my desk, running searches through my com-

puter through periodical databases at the *Press*, at the
local library, and at two subscription services, as well
as the basic Internet search engines.

The pickings were slim. In two hours of searching, I
only had three solid hits, and only one of them directly
concerned the dwarf in question.

The direct hit was a minor story from about three
years ago about a legal battle between my Mr.
Parthalán and State Farm insurance. It seems that Ossian Parthalán made a trade out of auto bodywork. He
worked out of a small garage on the near West Side
called *Thor's Hammer*. State Farm wasn't compensating
my dwarf for work he did because, apparently, he did
too good a job. State Farm thought the claims were
fraudulent. Their adjusters were convinced that, based
on the damage done to the cars involved, they
wouldn't be salvageable.

Mr. Parthalán won that case.

The first indirect hit was from almost ten years ago.
It was someone's attempt to do a story about dwarven
politics. My caveat about reporters on the outside looking in applied here in spades. The article was mostly a
description of some sort of dwarven council meeting
that was held in the Tower City Hilton, the mechanics
of which the reporter obviously wasn't privy to. The
whole story amounted to little more than saying: "the
dwarves here have a clan-based system that has something to do with blood relation, and after a lot of rau-
cous infighting, one of these clans is dominant."

The picture accompanying the story showed a half
dozen dwarves yelling and pointing at each other

around a circular meeting table. By the caption, third from the left was my guy, Ossian Parthalán.

So my guy was active in dwarven politics at one point. I wondered at what point that interest carried over into Cleveland City Council.

The second indirect hit was from one of my Internet searches, and at first look the Web page seemed to have nothing to do with my dwarf at all:

The Dwarven Armorer:

Highest quality arms and armor. Serving the Midrealm for ten years. If your marshal doesn't pass it, we'll take it back!

Specializing in:

- Full Plate
- Chain Mail
- Functional Historic Reproductions

Gauntlets to Gorgets and everything in between. Reasonable prices, financing, Master Card and Visa accepted. Prop. Sir Thorndyke of Dover (mundanely Teaghue Parthalán)

It was located at another West Side address. I would have passed it off as simply a coincidence of names, but the address was only a block or two from the *Thor's Hammer* body shop, and—when you think about it— there is some similarity between making plate mail and doing auto bodywork.

At least there seems to be, to a reporter looking for leads and who knows nothing about either.

*   *   *

There is some truth to the argument that once you cross the Cuyahoga River you are entering a different city. When Kipling wrote, "West is West and East is East," he could have very well been talking about my hometown. A lot of people simplify the thing by pointing out the racial fault lines. It's easy to do, since Cleveland is—even post-Portal—one of the most segregated communities north of the Mason-Dixon line. But the differences go a lot deeper than that.

The histories of the two halves of Cleveland over the past hundred years have been radically different. The East Side had the race riots in the '60s, while the West Side had its working class communities plowed under and split in half by interstate construction. Almost every museum was built east of the river, every factory built on the west. The East Side has Case Western and University Circle. The West Side has the airport. Hispanic people drift west. Middle Eastern people drift east. Rayburn was a solidly West Side mayor, and Gregory Washington was firmly East Side.

On the East Side we've got elves.

The West Side got the dwarves.

I was thinking of the Portal's contribution to the yin-yang nature of this city as I left the Shoreway and started looking for *The Dwarven Armorer*.

It was hard to miss.

If the heraldic banners flapping in front of the doorway didn't give it away, the suit of plate mail standing in front of the shop was a dead giveaway. I found a parking spot across the street and looked at the building. It wasn't a regular storefront. The building was a

low red-brick structure with large garage doors set in
the side. A small lot on one end was surrounded by
chain-link. The snow-covered lot was piled high with
scrap metal of every description—old plumbing, wheel
rims, twisted rebar still dangling fragments of concrete,
and the occasional engine block.

We were obviously zoned for light industrial here,
and I wondered what the building used to produce. I
suspected that it was a machine shop of one sort or another, which probably closed up when this town's last
steel mill shut down for good, about twenty years ago.

I got out and walked to the door and its metallic
guardsman.

I was impressed. I've seen the medieval armor dis-
played at the art museum here, the best collection in
this half of the world, and you could place this guy's
work right up there with it. All it lacked was the patina
of age.

Teaghue Parthalán also did something a bit unusual.
Every suit of armor I'd ever seen had been in a static
upright display. This one was mounted on some sort of
articulated skeleton that allowed it to be posed in the
midst of delivering a blow to an unseen attacker. It
helped show off the mail underneath and the way the
joints moved.

Apparently, you had a much wider range of motion
in one of those things than you'd expect.

I slipped under the broadsword and pushed
through the door into the shop.

If the showroom was any indication, business was
pretty good. There were glass-fronted display cabinets

on every wall, and a couple taking up floor space in the center of the showroom. While there were a couple of full suits on display, most of the space was devoted to individual pieces. Helmets, gauntlets, shields, swords, breastplates, and innumerable other metal parts whose names escaped me.

I was busy studying an intricately engraved broadsword with an eight hundred dollar price tag when Mr. Parthalán emerged from one of the rooms in back. He announced himself in a gruff voice, "Is your interest display or function, good sir?"

I tapped on the glass in front of the broadsword. "What would you consider this?"

"Display, my lord." He chuckled. "That pretty little number is meant for a wall, or for fancy dress."

"I see."

He seemed to measure me up. "What is it you're looking for?"

"A story." I turned around and held out my hand. "My name's Kline Maxwell, *Cleveland Press*."

He cocked an eyebrow and took my hand. It felt as if I were shaking hands with a cinder block. "Ahh, you didn't look like any Cleftlander I know."

"Cleftlander?"

"Barony of the Cleftlands, the local chapter of the Society for Creative Anachronism. Are you familiar with it?"

"Somewhat. I had a friend in college who would go out every Wednesday with a bunch of people who'd beat each other with sticks. I didn't think it was this so-phisticated, though."

"Well, it's a little more than that. The S.C.A. re-creates all aspects of the Middle Ages: arts, sciences, as well as combat. It happens to be that armory is my own particular specialty."

"If I recall, my friend's armor was mostly blue plastic and duct tape."

The dwarf laughed. "I doubt any marshal would pass that nowadays, even before the Portal opened. There are strict safety rules."

I shook my head. "So how did someone from the other side of the Portal become involved in the S.C.A.?"

Teaghue shrugged. "Many of us had to change specialties, I preferred to find out what market existed for what I had always done."

"You seem to have done well."

"Why would anyone engage in labor to do poorly?"

"Your workmanship is incredible, but I was referring to your business."

"As was I, good sir."

I looked down at him and saw him smiling. He obviously enjoyed talking about what he did, a trait that will endear you to any journalist. I tried to see any familial resemblance to the late Ossian, but I wasn't familiar enough with dwarven appearance in general. The kinky brown hair and beard, flat nose, and brown face were similar, but were also similar to just about every dwarf I had ever seen.

"A story, you say?" he asked. "On the S.C.A., my lord?"

"No. I am looking for background on a person named Ossian Parthalán."

I paused for a moment. I had no idea if Teaghue was a close relation to the dead Ossian or not.

"Go on." No overt reaction to Ossian's name, but I had the feeling that he knew Ossian. The way his humor seemed to fade, I suspected that he knew Ossian's fate.

"I cover city politics," I told him. "And I am looking for connections between him and the late Councilman Mazurich."

"Sad end, that," Teaghue said. He could have been referring to Ossian or Mazurich. "The councilman was a friend to me and mine. There was a feast when he died." He looked up at me. "You don't do poetry, do you?"

"No."

"Pity, a soul like Mazurich should have an epic written to him."

"Ossian thought highly of him, then?"

"Ossian Parthalán is not of any clan of mine and I shall not speak for him."

"But the councilman is well thought of in the dwarven community?"

"It was his work that found us homes, and labor worth pursuing. Without him, those of us that came from the Portal would be as rootless as the elves." Teaghue glanced away as if he was seeing something else. "Without him there would be no halls under Erie."

The "halls" he spoke of were the remnants of another industry collapse caused by the Portal's opening. The salt mines under Lake Erie, particularly those

around the spit of land called Whiskey Island closest to
the Portal, suffered some severe issues with "mana"
that resulted in about a dozen deaths before the operation was shut down.

The dwarves ended up resident in those mines, apparently immune to the magical influence that tended
to drive anyone else mad. I'd personally never paid
much attention to the details of how that happened. At
the time there was a federal blockade of the city, an economic meltdown, and a thousand other crises.

"He participated in the dwarven settlement in the
mines?"

"He initiated it." Teaghue looked up at me with a
suspicious expression. "You ask about dwarves and
you do not know this?"

"Just trying to get your perspective," I lied. The fact
was, I tried to avoid inhuman interest stuff that simply
existed to announce, "See, it's magic here! See? We're
special." It's a strange bias to have in this city, I admit,
but I've always been more interested in the political
ramifications of the Portal than its material manifesta-
tions. Usually, considering my seniority at the *Press*,
and my particular beat, it wasn't an issue.

Usually.

Still it does tend to be a bit of a blind spot.

"I see," Teaghue said. I could feel the guy closing up.

"Can you tell me anything about Ossian's relationship with the councilman?"

"Ossian is nothing to me or mine. For the Councilman, he was a good man, ill-used."

"How so?"

"That is my perspective, Mr. Maxwell. Should you ever be interested in the purchase of quality arms or armor, feel free to return. Right now I have work to attend to."

Teaghue ended my interview by walking into the back of the shop, leaving me alone in the showroom.

A good man, ill-used.

I couldn't help but think, *Used by whom?*

CHAPTER FIVE

OF COURSE, SINCE *The Dwarven Armorer* was only two blocks away from Ossian's body shop, I swung my Volkswagen around to take a look at the place where the late Ossian Parthalán made his living.

Thor's Hammer wasn't much to look at. A brick garage with a rolling metal door, an asphalt lot with half a dozen cars in varying states of destruction, a high chain-link fence topped with razor wire. Only one of the cars gave a hint at what Ossian was capable of, a '68 Mustang that, from the back, was a mint cherry-red muscle car, and from the front was a rusted-out hulk. It was obviously a restoration job, not a wreck. The front of the car was jacked on its rims, the hood was gone, and the engine compartment was empty. The contrast between front and back made me wonder if dwarves actually were capable of magic.

I got out of my car and looked around, and I wasn't surprised to see the yellow police stickers sealing the garage door. It was the standard warning about a sealed investigation scene, along with a complex glyph that you did not want to break, unless you were into pain and felony convictions.

I had sort of been hoping to find a cop or two on the scene that I could talk to. No such luck.

I walked over to the side door opposite the chain-link and the lot, and stopped.

Someone *was* here.

Not cops.

The seal on the door had been torn open, along with most of the doorframe. The warning tag still smoldered with the aftereffects of the torn rune. The discharge should have dropped anyone opening the door.

However, judging from the splintered state of the door, whoever had smashed it was probably well past being affected by such nuisance enchantments.

I heard movement inside the building, and I flattened myself against the wall. Not being the action-hero type myself, I pulled out my cell phone and dialed 911.

"911. What is the nature of your emergency?"

"I'm at *Thor's Hammer* an autobody shop by West 50th and Detroit," I whispered into the phone. "There's been a break-in."

"Sir? I have tro . . . king you out."

I spoke a little louder, "Detroit and West 50th, break-in at *Thor's Hammer*."

". . . t and Wes . . . at right?"

Christ, of all the times to get funky reception.

"Detroit and West 50th!"

". . ."

Nothing.

But the motion inside the body shop had stopped.

I decided that was not a good sign. I turned and ran back toward my car. Halfway there, a large panel of frosted glass windows exploded beside me. It happened suddenly, and about all I could do was throw my arms up to cover my face from the flying glass.

So I didn't see what yanked me inside.

I sailed in through the window, and slammed face-down into the hood of a Lincoln Town Car parked inside the garage. I felt the impact in every joint, as if every bone in my body had snapped in half. Even my teeth hurt. I rolled over and groaned, sliding down the slope of the hood. I couldn't even manage to get my arms up in front of me to defend myself.

Lucky me, I didn't need to. While I lay there, stunned, my assailant retreated out the window. I didn't get a good look at it, backlit by sun outside. However, what I did see made me think I didn't really want to get a good look.

Despite what the Cleveland Growth Association has to say about it, the born-again authors of my green evangelical pamphlet had a point. A lot of *nasty* things came out of the Portal. It's not all fairies and elves and unicorns. The thing that cleaned my clock would not make it into any convention brochures.

The face was a human skull covered by red glistening flesh, held in place by metal wires. It wore a trench coat that covered most of its body, and the fabric was spotted with stains from fluid that oozed from its exposed flesh.

When its hand gripped the edge of the window frame, I could see the tendons move, and the glint of metal.

Then the thing was gone.

I lay there until the sirens came.

Commander Maelgwyn Caledvwlch was, predictably, not pleased with me.

He walked up to me as a paramedic was giving me the once-over. Caledvwlch stood by the ambulance, watching as the medic waved some charms around my head and neck. The medic shook his head and said, "You'll be fine."

I rubbed my neck. "You're sure?" I still hurt all over.

"If you want me to, I can take you the Emergency Room."

I stood up and shook my head. "No, if you think I'm fine."

"Take some Advil."

"Mr. Maxwell," Caledvwlch announced himself as I stepped away from the ambulance.

"Commander Caledvwlch."

"How is it we find you assaulted in the late Ossian Parthalán's place of business?"

"I'm working on a story." I brushed some of the dirt off my clothes. "You should know, you showed me the picture."

"What did you expect to find here?"

"To be honest? Some cops who would be more forthcoming about Mr. Parthalán's death than you are." I looked into *Thor's Hammer*. It was easy now the window was gone, the view only obstructed by some yellow rune-stamped police tape draping the entrance.

My friend the zombie had been busy. He'd gutted the place. Filing cabinets had been torn open, the contents scattered everywhere. Tools, fragments of computer hardware, and broken office furniture littered the garage floor. A safe lay on its back next to the Lincoln, the door missing.

That made me rub my neck.

The Lincoln itself had been torn apart by this thing. The seats had been pulled out and shredded, the doors and fenders ripped off, bumpers on the ground.

Amidst the chaos, two things struck me:

First, the car had out-of-state plates, *California* plates. Not terribly common, even in the tourist-trap areas downtown.

Second was the number of people going over the crime scene. Three carloads of forensic investigators was overkill for a B&E, even one by something like zombie-boy.

They seemed to pay particular attention to the fenders on the Lincoln.

"What was zombie-boy looking for?"

"I would make a suggestion, Mr. Maxwell."

"What?"

"That you leave this particular investigation to those with the expertise to undergo it."

I backed up a bit as Caledvwlch made a pass with his hand and folded his tall angular frame under the police tape. I called after him, not really expecting an answer, "Can you tell me why this investigation rates the personal attention of the SPU commander?"

Caledvwlch ignored me.

They had my statement, so there was nothing to keep me here. I did, however, slip out my phone and take a few discreet shots of the inside of *Thor's Hammer*.

Camera phones are a wonderful invention.

I revised my opinion of my phone when I'd driven to the Flats and had parked long enough to look at what I shot.

My phone was an expensive Cleveland model. That meant that it had some very hefty software that—in theory—could filter and do error correction to limit interference from the Portal's magical influence. Using a film camera anywhere around here would give you a picture, but the picture would be something out of Timothy Leary's id. Same thing with most pre-Portal electronics. Signals into any device—cameras, tape recorders, television, Xerox machines, cell phones, computers—tended to pick up hitchhikers generated by the mana around the Portal.

Of course, after over a decade of dealing with it, most of the problems have been worked out. If you duplicate a signal enough times, you can filter out a real image. It's just a matter of storage, bandwidth, and money.

And I had paid a lot for this phone.

For all the good it did.

The pictures were garbage. Demonic faces drooling at the camera, snakes coiling around twisted machinery, murky landscapes that looked as if David Lynch did underwater filming of the Cinderella castle at Disneyland. In one or two shots, I could make out parts of the Lincoln. That was it.

"Fuck it."

Just to check, I took a shot out the windshield.

Perfect. Murphy's law, I guess.

I was parked in a lot near the Club *Nazgûl*, trying to get a feel for the place before I stepped inside. Caledvwlch had called it a tourist club, but there are tourists, and there are *tourists*.

The building had been a warehouse in a prior life. Now it had been painted completely black. The only detail in the exterior came from subtle patterns done in glossy black, over the matte-black exterior. They looked like wards of some sort, which I suspect they were, since the city inspectors wouldn't let you inscribe anything really dangerous in a public place.

But looking at the outside gave me a good idea of the clientele they were trying to attract. My guess was the tourists who frequented this place probably came to this city alone looking to find some patron of the "dark arts." This place, I suspected, helped connect those wayward souls with mages who were more than happy to fulfill someone's faux-satanic heavy-metal fantasies.

Also gave the evangelicals a reason to reread "Leviticus."

The mages that cruised clubs like this weren't really black sorcerers, at least as far as city ordinances on necromancy, curses, and dangerous incantations went.

Usually they were only a step up the food chain from the teenagers they conned. They didn't want to buy your soul. Just your body for a few nights—and if you had any drugs or cash, that would be nice, too. I reached the door, embossed in screaming black skulls, and thought of my daughter.

Maybe her mother is right . . .

I had the brief Dad argument with myself, one side saying how I really should give Sarah a lot more credit, the other thinking about all the kids that were given too much credit by their folks.

Is it different than anywhere else? There're predators everywhere. She'll be in more danger during spring break in Florida—

Maybe I should just lock her up when she gets here.

I grabbed a skull, pulled the door open, and walked inside.

The decor wasn't particularly innovative. Call it early Inquisition, though they one-upped Torquemada by putting in a dance floor. While my eyes adjusted to the gloom, someone in the back yelled at me, "Hey, we're closed today."

I blinked until I could identify the speaker. It took a moment because, until he moved, I thought he was a prop. The guy had a shaved head, a sleeveless black T-shirt, and a combination of tattoos and obnoxious piercings that would severely limit his career options.

"Hello, Kline Maxwell, *Cleveland Press*."

The guy walked toward me, carrying a mop. "You a reporter?"

Add "not particularly bright" to my list of first impressions. "I understand you had some problems here last night."

"Fucking-A."

I'll take that as a yes. "Would you mind talking about it?"

"You going to put me in the paper?"

"You'll only be a named source if you want to be."

"That's cool." He set down the mop and held out his hand. "I'm Christian."

This kid got first place in line when they were handing out irony. I shook his hand. "Pleased to meet you."

"You're here about the dwarf, aren't you?"

"What's the story there?"

"Wish I knew. It's all fucked up." He pointed back toward a row of caskets on the other side of the dance floor. "I was working the bar. We'd just opened up at four. And this dwarf dude comes in and pays for one of the private party rooms upstairs." Christian pointed up into the vast loft space at a line of windows overlooking the dance floor. If the lighting were in full party mode, the rooms up there wouldn't be visible.

"Did you know him?"

"The dwarf? No, never talked to him and he wasn't a regular."

"You get a lot of dwarves?"

"A few, the little motherfuckers can get tanked . . ." Christian shook his head. "Anyway, this guy gets his room—"

"Alone?"

"Yeah, that's the weird bit. Those rooms are to party, you know? Hard to party alone."

But they'd be a good place to meet someone. Private, but in a public place. I wondered why the dwarf in question didn't ask me to meet him here.

Considering his fate, it was probably a good thing he didn't.

"What happened?"

"Place was just filling up at six, 6:30, then we start hearing the dude screaming. I mean nasty. Worst thing I ever heard." Christian leaned toward me. "The fucking Feds were already here."

"Undercover?"

He nodded. "Five guys pull guns and yell, 'FBI,' and run upstairs and find this guy chopped to pieces."

"How long between the scream and when they found him?"

"What, a minute. Less."

That was a lot to do to someone in a short time.

"Anything else, man? I got to clean up around here."

"Yeah, can you let me take a look at where they found him?"

The room Christian showed me was still sealed off by the cops. However, since they'd destroyed the door getting in here, the only barrier was some strategically placed yellow tape. That gave me enough of an opening to look inside and see the final resting place of Ossian Parthalán.

The room itself was designed for some ugly scenes. Chains dangled from walls and ceiling, waiting someone's bondage scenario. The table in the room also seemed to be a functional rack, right out of the Tower of London. One corner had a five-by-five metal cage, in case someone wanted to play Vietnamese POW.

All of it seemed a little tacky in the face of the real blood, and the outline marking the middle of the floor.

A white circle had been drawn on the floor, the outline of Ossian's body crossing a broken edge. Dwarves might not deal in magic, but this one had been trying to cast some protective spell. Apparently it didn't work.

I tried to take a picture, but my camera phone was having glitches again.

"I suppose it's too much to expect any security cameras up here?"

Christian laughed. "No, man, only in the parking lot, and the Feds got all of that."

I nodded. Not only was that kind of security expensive to maintain around magic-heavy sites, I suspect that it would kill a good part of the *Nazgûl's* business. The kind of party they were set up for wasn't meant to be recorded—except by the parties involved.

I carefully pushed the yellow ward-tape back so I could lean in a bit and get a better look.

"Careful there, man."

"I know what I'm doing." In theory, as long as I didn't actually break the line formed by the seal, I was okay.

I don't know exactly what I was looking for. I don't pretend I'm a crime scene investigator, and anything beyond the patently obvious was going to escape me. I needed a look at the actual case file, but since the Feds were involved, the chance of me getting someone to leak it were slim to none.

I looked at the doorframe, and one of the patently obvious deductions I was able to make was the fact that the Feds did, in fact, bust down a locked door. I could still see a size-twelve footprint next to the doorknob where the door had been kicked in. Kicked in hard enough to splinter the doorframe.

"No other way in or out?"

Christian shook his head. The upper floor was so quiet I heard his piercings rattle.

"This bothers me." I looked around the party room, at all the S&M gear. It took a second for me to pick up on exactly what it was. "You said everyone heard the dwarf scream, right?"

"Damn straight."

I stepped back from the opening and let the barrier swing back to a natural rest position. "Considering the kind of partying that goes on in these rooms, aren't they soundproofed pretty well?"

Christian's eyes widened as if I had just performed some mage sleight of hand. "Hey, that's right . . ."

"And the dance floor gets kind of loud, doesn't it?"

"Shit, then what the fuck was that noise?"

"Don't know, but I suspect that our dwarf was dead a while before you heard it."

CHAPTER SIX

"CALEDVWLCH, YOU BASTARD," I cursed as I drove back to the office. The elf cop never really lied to me, but he had a habit of leaving out critical information. Information, such as federal involvement in whatever was going on.

While it might be coincidence that the FBI was staked out at the *Nazgûl*, I had a strong suspicion that the "unrelated matter" the Feds were investigating was unrelated only in so far as they weren't on a murder investigation.

Caledvwlch can be very literal when he wants to be.

And, if I needed anything more to convince me that the elf wasn't completely forthcoming—which I didn't—there was a matter of timing.

If Christian was right about his time line, then the Feds were busting down the door at the *Nazgûl*, about the time I was sitting down at the Old Arcade.

Caledvwlch was on my case with a crime scene picture within the hour. Even with a forensic mage and the authority of the Feds, no one could have identified the corpse, traced the phone log, and found me at my table in the Arcade in that space of time, unless the dwarf was under surveillance and his phone was already tapped.

So Ossian Parthalán was involved in something that the Feds were interested in. And to me it looked as if he was meeting someone in the bowels of the *Nazgûl*. Someone who scared him enough to attempt some sort of protective circle, however ineffective. The meeting goes badly, and if I trusted Caledvwlch's offhand estimate of the time of death—two hours ago when he caught up with me at seven—then Mr. Parthalán is eviscerated sometime shortly after five.

It's not until an hour later that someone—or something—screams, and the FBI breaks in and finds the dwarf's body.

You can do a lot in an hour, especially if you're adept at any black arts and have a sacrifice to work with. At the very least I suspected some highly illegal necromancy, especially when I thought of zombie-boy wading through the *Thor's Hammer* garage.

None of which explained the Feds' involvement.

And let's not forget zombie-boy . . .

When I got back to the office, Nina Johannessen was there, and I wasn't sure whether I was thankful or not. Her desk was off in one corner of the pressroom.

"Nina? You asked if anything strange happened to me lately?"

She looked up at me as I walked up to her desk. She set down a pen with which she was making some incomprehensible chicken-scratches on a notepad. I'd say it was all Greek to me, but there were clear traces of Latin and Hebrew around some of the symbols she was jotting down.

"Yes, I'm sorry about bothering you yesterday." She looked up and smiled. "Sometimes I feel a sense of urgency, and—"

"I don't know if it counts as Death or the Devil, but I've certainly scored one for 'new and threatening' since I talked to you."

"Oh." The smile left and her already pale skin lost whatever color it had to begin with. The sudden concern in her expression gave me the same sense of unease as hearing the word "Oops" in an operating theater. "What happened?"

"Well, I have a dwarf as the victim of a ritualistic homicide, and I had the bad fortune of running into an extra from the set of *Night of the Living Dead* when I checked out his place of business."

Nina leaned forward. "You ran into what?"

I shrugged. "I don't follow paranormal crap that closely. I wouldn't know what to call this thing."

"Describe it."

"A skeleton held together with raw meat and piano wire."

Nina frowned. "It did concern you, what I saw."

"What did you see?"

"Three trumps from the tarot."

Nina opened a drawer and pulled out an oversized deck of cards and after searching through it, placed three cards on the desk in front of her. One looked like a lighthouse snapping in half and tumbling a victim to rocks below, the next was a goat-legged demon framed by a pentacle and squatting on a rock where a pair of damned souls were chained, and the last was a skeletal figure in black armor, mounted on a horse.

The cards were labeled "The Tower," "The Devil," and "Death."

"The vision I had, was these cards—or embodiments of these three cards—"

I picked up the death card.

"That one, Death, isn't as bad as it looks, really." She sounded as if she was trying to convince herself. "It mostly represents change. The Tower is a much worse omen—"

"You use these to tell fortunes, right? If you were reading this," I tapped the desk with the card and put Death back with the doomsayer's triumvirate. "What would you tell me?"

"Death traditionally means change, the end of something and the start of something else. The Devil is pretty much a symbol of material desire, money and power. The Tower . . . ruin, destruction. A three-card spread tends to be past, present, and future." She looked down at the cards. "If I were reading this for someone, I couldn't leave out the net effect of the more mundane negative connotations. They're not good to see together like this."

"In a nutshell?"

"Someone with this spread has undergone a life change, one that set him or her on a path to pursue money, power, or lust, and that path is going to lead to destruction . . ."

The interpretation Nina just gave me could fit Mazurich. Possibly the late dwarf. I didn't like the thought that it might apply to me.

She was shaking her head as she stared at the cards.

"What is it?" I asked.

"Visions are never entirely what they first appear to be. That's the nature of the Oracle."

"What do you mean?"

"Reading it like a normal spread, it doesn't seem right to me." She shuddered slightly. "The skeletal apparition you described, it makes me afraid that what I saw was something more . . . *literal*."

I laughed, "I don't think I'm going to run into the Devil."

"But you've already seen Death in at least two forms, haven't you?"

I looked at Death in his suit of armor, and thought of the zombie that had cleaned my clock, and of my friend, the dwarven armorer. A skeleton wrapped in metal . . .

Touché.

She gathered up the cards and replaced them in the drawer in her desk. "Tell me what's going on with you. I think you may need help."

"If you tell me something."

"What?"

"Why did you think the vision was about me?"

Nina looked up and hesitated a moment. "I just had a sense it was tied to you."

Now I'm not one to dismiss gut feelings, especially those of someone who made her living tied into the psychic network that wrapped this city. However, I am pretty good at telling when someone was flat-out lying. Most people just aren't that good at it.

"Come on, Nina, I know bullshit when I hear it."

"Part of the vision. In the Tower. I saw you."

"And that isn't good."

She shook her head. "No, it isn't."

I got the sense that she wasn't telling me the whole truth. However, whatever she had seen had obviously been disturbing. I could see the stress in her eyes, and to be honest I suspected she was avoiding something just because she found it too painful to go over. I made a decision not to press her on it, since she seemed more than willing to help me in the here and now.

That would turn out to be one of the worst mistakes of my entire life.

"Okay," I said, "see if you can help me make sense of what I'm dealing with here." I gave her the Cliff Notes version of the last thirty-six hours. She took her pad and made quite a few notes as I talked.

"So," I finished, "does any of this ring any bells? Have you come across anything that might connect with this?"

"I think you're right." She looked at her notes and frowned. "What you describe indicates someone trying to cast a protective circle. The circle was either unsuccessful or subsequently broken."

"You sound unsure about that."

"Dwarves do not cast magic—"

"That's what I thought. But there's a first time for everything, right?"

"It's not that simple. It isn't that dwarves don't. They

can't." She shook her head. "Their nature makes them a suppressive force, diminishing the power of everything cast in their presence. For a dwarf to cast something, even the simplest protective spell, it would require energies beyond the ability of most mages."

"Well, apparently it didn't work."

"The point is, he thought it would, or why bother casting it?"

"Can't some rituals focus energy—"

Nina laughed. "Our dwarf would have to build up ritual potential for a week or two to cast anything—" She stopped laughing.

"What?"

"Well, if someone else cast a ritual, and embodied the power in some charm or fetish. That could give enough potential for him to make an attempt."

"I hear a 'but.'"

"Well, not only would such an object be inherently dangerous, it would require weeks of work by some mage simply to amass undirected power. A legal mage isn't going to do that, and I can't even imagine what the cost of that would be on the black market."

I wondered if something like that would be enough to interest the FBI. Maybe, but it didn't seem likely. While there was a thriving industry of black market mages around town, the nature of the crime made it inherently local. The nature of the radiation through the Portal meant that those mages' influence stopped outside the boundaries of northeast Ohio. The Feds tended to be more interested in things that might leave the state.

She shook her head. "No, it makes more sense if someone else cast the circle—maybe he met with someone besides his killer?"

"That's as plausible as anything else I have . . ."

"Now you sound unsure."

"If there was someone besides his killer around, why aren't there two bodies?" I shook my head. "Not enough information. Can you tell me anything about zombie-boy?"

"That name seems an accurate description, flesh animated by some necromancer—but there are some oddities about it."

"Only some?"

"The more decayed a body is, the more energy is required simply to have it move. Your zombie not only moves quickly, but shows more strength than I'd expect in even a freshly animated corpse. What you describe is certainly not fresh. And the wires and metal you describe are completely new to me."

"Any idea what the wires might be for?"

"A framework? A matrix to focus additional power? Armor, perhaps."

I wondered if she was intentionally referencing the Death trump.

She kept looking at her notes. "I can do some research on both of those. Find out if there are some magically plausible explanations I haven't thought of."

"Thanks."

She reached out and touched my hand. "Please, be careful."

"I always am," I lied.

*   *   *

I hadn't gotten out of the office before my extension rang. My mind was still churning with images of Death, the Devil, and the Tower when I answered.

A familiar voice told me, "My office, Maxwell. Now."

My boss, Columbia Jennings, wasn't the Devil, but she could give the witches from *Macbeth* a run for their money. She lorded it over the Metro editor's desk from an office filled with a chain-smoking haze, and if anyone ever had the balls to tell her this was a nonsmoking building, I hadn't heard of it.

When I walked into her office she looked at me and shook her head. "First off, don't shut off your cell phone while you're working. It makes me feel like you're avoiding me."

"What?" I pulled out my phone. "I didn't—" I looked at it and the screen was dark. Apparently I had. "Damn it. This thing's been acting up all day."

"Fix it."

I nodded.

"That's not what I wanted to talk to you about."

"I had that feeling."

"Shut the door."

When I did, she asked me, "Now, do you mind telling me how a story on the Washington mayoral campaign became involved with the SPU, a ritual murder, and the trashing of a crime scene?"

I shrugged. "Things got a little sidetracked."

"I gather."

"The dwarf was trying to pass me some information before he was killed. I'm just trying to follow up on it."

"Information about the Washington campaign?"

"Ah, no."

"What, then?"

I hesitated a bit before I said, quietly, "Mazurich."

"I didn't quite hear that."

"Mazurich, damn it. The dwarf claimed he knew the motive behind his suicide."

Columbia rolled her eyes at me. "I didn't figure you for chasing conspiracy theories."

"The dwarf was killed. That's a story in itself."

"And you became a crime reporter . . . when?"

"Look, I just want—"

"Maxwell, don't tell me what you want. You're one of the best paid reporters on the staff, you have a hell of a lot of latitude, but you don't get to make ad hoc decisions like that while you're on the payroll. This isn't some random op-ed piece. If the city public safety director starts calling me and asking what my reporter is doing, *I* should know why, at least."

"You're ordering me off this?"

"Please, lay off the journalistic martyrdom. You know you have to run this by me." She waved at a chair. "Now sit down, and convince me you should be doing this story."

She was right, of course. And she kept me there for ninety minutes, more, I think, to punish me than because she needed any convincing.

I left smelling like an ashtray, but with full editorial sanction.

CHAPTER SEVEN

THE NEXT DAY was almost painfully clear and cold, the sky a near cloudless, razor-sharp blue. All of which made the atmospheric display over the Portal that much more spectacular. I was passing by on the way to City Hall, and when I parked my car it was hard not to look up and stare like a tourist.

The Portal is pretty much what it sounds like, a hole between this universe and the next about fifty feet in diameter. And while it was hidden from Lakeside Avenue by the retrofitted fortress that used to be Browns Stadium, its effect on the environment was visible for miles.

More poured out of the thing than magic and dwarves—it also contributed a permanent standing weather front thanks to differentials in temperature, pressure, and humidity between here and there. Today it was particularly active, building roiling black clouds stacked up for miles, swirling with hail, sleet, and lighting, all lit by piercing winter sun. Ice crystals fractured rainbows in the sky while the occasional bolt of lighting traced across the clouds.

When you told newcomers that the whole display actually had nothing to do with magic, they tended not to believe you.

As influential as the damn thing is, comparatively few people had ever seen it outside of those who actually passed through the thing. No photographs or video of it existed; the interference inside the stadium was too great for any software engineers to filter out. Even regular electrical appliances, floodlights, power tools, and forklifts began acting weird when they got within a few dozen feet of the Portal.

Other than those who had a close encounter with the object itself, the best image anyone had was artistic representations of the thing. None of which did it justice. Even the best drawings I'd seen made the thing look like a giant chromed Christmas ornament, a sphere reflecting the image of another universe.

Nothing I'd seen caught the sense of depth the actual phenomenon had, the feeling of looking deep into a direction that didn't actually exist.

I turned away from the storm and bought a copy of *USA Today* from one of the vending machines on the corner. Having been one of the people in the stands when the Portal was created, opening on the Pittsburgh thirty-five yard line, you'd think I'd be used to the damn thing by now.

I carried my paper and walked toward City Hall, serendipitously close to the epicenter of the last dozen years of city politics.

I took a station in the hall outside Council Chambers and opened the paper. The Supreme Court's discussion on the Portal jurisdiction had long slipped off the front page of the national consciousness. The news was dominated by Congressional debates on Medicare and illegal immigration. The President was on a trip to North Africa. And the cover picture showed about three hundred protesters circling an offshore oil platform in the Gulf of Mexico with yellow rubber dinghies.

I tended to get so focused on local events that it was nice to remind myself there was a world outside of Cuyahoga County. It helped me gain some perspective.

I read the paper for about fifteen minutes. Then the Council meeting recessed, and the members began filing out of the chamber. I folded my paper and waited for the current council president, Brenda Carlson.

"Thanks for meeting me on such short notice." I held out my hand when she came out to meet me. She smiled and shook it.

Carlson was just coming out of a marathon Council session, but she had the skill of not looking as drained as she must have felt. She had an easy smile, a red suit that appeared freshly pressed, and her hair was perfectly in place for any cameras that might be around.

By contrast, her late predecessor, Mazurich, used to come out of Council Chambers looking as if he had just been in a bar fight.

"Should I buy you a coffee?" she asked. "Or would that be a blatant attempt to influence the media?"

We left City Hall and found a booth in a coffee shop around the corner. I made a point of getting our coffee, despite her offer. I'm a purist and prefer my coffee unadulterated by sugar, cream, mocha, or whatever is Starbucks' flavor of the day. When I came back with our caffeine, she said, "I read your profile on Greg Washington."

"What did you think?"

"He's going to beat Clifton."

I chuckled. "Is that on the record?"

"It's common knowledge. Besides, no one on Council gets a warm fuzzy feeling when they think of Gabe Clifton."

"How about you?"

"Oh, I'll work with whoever the people of this city decide to elect." She smiled. "So is this what you wanted to talk about?"

"I'm afraid not. I'm here about Councilman Mazurich." I sipped my coffee and looked at her, trying to gauge her reaction.

"Dom? What about?" I could hear the suspicion in her voice. It didn't surprise me. I was the political attack dog on the *Press*, and I was pretty well known for unearthing ugly secrets.

"A couple of things. Primarily, why would a dwarf concern himself with why Mazurich killed himself."

"A dwarf?"

"A dwarf."

"Who?"

"The name I have is Ossian Parthalán."

"That sounds slightly familiar . . ."

I leaned back and set down my cup. "I was hoping you might help me with Mazurich's history. You worked with him the first five years after the Portal opened. You must have seen a lot that was going on."

"He was a good man." She was quiet a long time, staring into her coffee. "You remember, back when the Portal opened. . . . The power failures, the blackouts, the federal blockade—"

Of course, anyone who lived through it would never forget. The first year no TV at all, radio so intermittent as to be almost useless. Computers and other electronics would eventually fail as digital garbage filled their memories. It would be two years before the engineers started producing consumer electronics that would work properly.

I was lucky enough to be one of the few to have benefited, at least professionally, during the chaos. But even if the collapse of local TV and radio caused the proliferation of news dailies that gave me my job, I was still rational enough not to be the least bit nostalgic about it.

"Yes?"

"You remember that most of the city government locked itself behind a National Guard barricade?"

That was when Mayor Rayburn made his famous stand against the federal government coming in and taking control of the Portal, the U.S. Army blockaded the city against the Ohio National Guard, and—if it weren't for the intervention of Congress—the President might have ordered the first military assault on a U.S. city since the Civil War.

While it had been in the guise of protecting a natural resource, over the years it had come to light that Rayburn had been, in fact, negotiating unilateral trade arrangements on the other side of the Portal—and with the help of the governor and the Ohio National Guard, had helped orchestrate a regime change in the kingdom of Ragnan, the government on the other side.

The only thing that prevented a constitutional crisis at the time was badly written legislation on the part of Congress that effectively annexed the Portal and gave jurisdiction of all of its "contents" to the local government of the area the Portal sat in.

Only now, with a rewritten law and a new Supreme Court ruling had the Feds managed to finally gain control of the Portal, and the commerce through it.

"Yeah," I remembered City Hall, Browns Stadium, all of Lakeside, packed with kids in fatigues carrying machine guns, all trying not to look at the storm swirling the sky above the stadium. The image was something out of the Iraqi insurgency. "I tried to get into City Hall a couple of times, not much luck."

"Well, Dom actually went out into the city, he saw people, did what he could."

She told me stories of what he did do. He not only saw the people in his ward, he visited the camps where refugees from the Portal were being held.

That's where he first met the dwarves.

Without a common language, he couldn't speak to them, but he managed to notice something that had been missed by most of the other humans commanding the influx from the Portal.

Mazurich saw that, even in the midst of escaping a genocidal war and finding themselves in the midst of a (super)natural disaster, the dwarves still worked. With little more than the possessions they carried through the Portal and the material lying about the refugee camp, they were able to craft amazing things—textiles, jewelry, statuary. Even with no common language, the dwarves had started their own economy, trading with other refugees and even with their human guards.

Seeing what the dwarves did, and seeing the major problem of the day as the breakdown of infrastructure in the city combined with the panicked departure of much of the available skilled labor, Mazurich became Rayburn's ally in getting the nonhuman population legal recognition. Rayburn had high-level geopolitical motivations, mostly concerned with preventing a federal takeover of the city. Mazurich was much more practical. He saw the potential to integrate these new people into the city and get things working again. The dwarves were quick studies and picked up English—and shovels and jackhammers—all within a few short weeks.

Mazurich talked with the leaders of all the clans, always in an effort to try and meld the existing dwarven society into our own. It wasn't an easy task. Dwarves weren't solitary, and the clans tended to act as a unit—including in the acquisition of living space. Finding facilities to house several thousand dwarves in one place wasn't easy, especially for a race that preferred living underground.

Mazurich managed to pull it off, though. He managed to get the Port Authority and the county to buy up all of the remaining private property on a spit of land called Whiskey Island and designate it a relocation area for the dwarven population.

He managed to get his hands on the prime lakefront property and longtime political football by the simple expedient of political blackmail. There was still a federal blockade, and while the Feds were letting people out, no one was getting back in. In the space of a few months, Mazurich's dwarven contractors were pretty much the only game in town. Sewer, water, power, roads, name it and Mazurich's dwarven allies were maintaining it.

Keeping the dwarves happy became high on everyone's priority list.

And whatever the history, and whoever's ox was getting gored, Whiskey Island was a perfect solution for the dwarves. Not only was it spitting distance down the coast from the Portal, it was home to acres and acres of subterranean salt mines under the lake. Pretty much a perfect environment for the dwarves.

"I seem to remember some nasty stories coming out of the salt mines, before the dwarves moved in."

She frowned at me. "Are you trying to imply something?"

Actually, I wasn't. "I just remember some news stories from back then."

"Alarmist bullshit. It was the same stuff that was happening everywhere at the time—a salt mine just happens to be a dangerous place to panic."

"Uh-huh." I sipped my coffee, wondering exactly what she wasn't telling me. "What about recently? How were things with him and the dwarves?"

She smiled. "They loved him, he was practically one of their clan."

Mazurich managed to be human advocate and power

broker to his new nonhuman constituency. His dwarves managed to form a bloc that was a political counterweight to Rayburn. They weren't particularly glamorous, but they ran the city, and because of them, Mazurich managed to keep the City Council tightly under his control. When you got down to the nitty-gritty, it *mattered* where your ward was on the priority list to get potholes fixed.

In return, Mazurich's own ward benefited greatly from dwarven labor. The technology park that lived over the remains of the old steel industry grew threefold, built by low-bidding dwarves. Dozens of new businesses set up shop, dwarven-owned and operated, ranging from one-dwarf operations like *Thor's Hammer*, to multimillion dollar R&D outfits like Magetech.

"Magetech? That's a dwarven operation?"

"Right in the heart of the Kucinich Technology Park. In fact, now I know why that name's familiar . . ."

"What name?" I was still absorbing the idea that Magetech had anything to do with dwarves. I had heard of it, of course. It was a magnet for venture capital. The next Internet boom and all that. The idea that it might be the first to viably apply magic to *any* modern technological process was like crack for investors. If anything, I would have expected a dragon or two to be involved.

But dwarves?

"Parthalán. That clan name. Their clan leader happens to hold the CEO position there, and a bunch of others sit on the board."

"No kidding . . ."

CHAPTER EIGHT

SURPRISINGLY, ONE PHONE CALL got me a meeting with the Chief Operations Officer of Magetech. It was unexpected enough that I had to reorder my whole day to fit in the sudden appointment. When I called to reschedule with members of Mazurich's staff, most of them sounded relieved.

Magetech was housed in a cluster of office buildings sheathed in mirrored glass. Even before I reached the parking lot, I could tell there was something unusual going on here. If you looked at the right angle, you could see something else in the mirror, something dark that traced glyphs and symbols that barely registered in the conscious mind.

The wards, if that's what they were, seemed only to register on my peripheral vision, and when I tried to look at them directly, my eyes hurt and I felt something between paranoia and dread.

I had to blink a couple of times to get the feeling to pass.

One of the annoying things about the world post-Portal was the fact you couldn't readily dismiss sensations like that. The sense that this was not a good place might actually have a concrete source outside my own subconscious.

Of course, dismissed or not, there was little I could do about the feeling anyway.

I pulled up and into the visitor parking area, feeling the uncharacteristic hope that this was a wild goose chase. As I stepped out of the car, I pulled my jacket close against the chill in the air. I walked up to the building, under a logo hovering in midair, and into a cavernous neo-industrial lobby: a few cubic acres of glass, exposed steel, and ductwork. Everything had been polished, so that even the rivets in the exposed girders gleamed.

Display cases lined the polished granite floor between the lobby doors and the reception desk. Floating in rune-carved Lexan cubes were artifacts of Magetech's R&D efforts. The objects were all pretty mundane and wouldn't have made much of an impression on someone who wasn't a Cleveland native; PDAs, cell phones, laptop computers, televisions, radios, digital cameras . . . so what?

The "so what" was the Portal. The mana flowing out from the world next door caused interference, severe interference, in every type of recording and communication media known to man. Magetech was jumpstarted by being the first to patent ways to correct for the problem. Because of that, Magetech got a piece of nearly every electronic device sold in Northeast Ohio.

I walked up to the reception desk. It was staffed by a woman who looked like a cross between a librarian and one of the nastier guards at a women's prison. She looked at me over the top of her glasses.

"Can I help you?"

"Kline Maxwell, *Cleveland Press*. I have an appointment with Simon Lucas."

"The *Cleveland Press*, I don't know—"

"It's okay, Nora," came a voice from behind me. "I approved it."

I turned and faced the Chief Operations Officer of Magetech. He was taller than I expected, and balder. There wasn't a lick of hair on his naked skull, and he was almost elven in his height and the way he moved. He held out a long-fingered hand and I shook it.

"Mr. Lucas?" I asked.

He nodded and looked toward the receptionist. "I apologize, Nora. Last minute addition."

Nora let out with an intimidating "Hrumph."

"Come with me, Mr. Maxwell."

Lucas led me past the reception desk, past a few corridors, and to a bank of elevators. "Nice setup you have here."

"These are just the corporate offices," Lucas said as he pressed the up button. "The heart of the operation is in Solon."

"Oh, I thought you had labs here?"

"Not for years," Lucas laughed.

The elevator slid open for us and we both stepped inside.

The interior of the elevator was all chrome and mirrors, and I again got the headache-inducing sense of seeing something out of the corner of my eye. As if something was written underneath the reflections, something old, arcane, and evil . . .

"Are you all right?" Lucas asked.

I realized I was rubbing my temple and I lowered my hand. "I'm fine. But I am correct? This is where operations started for you?"

"Oh, yes. On the location of an old blast furnace."

To my relief, the doors slid open. It was all I could do to avoid racing Lucas for the exit. Outside the elevator, there was a plush lobby where a glass wall opposite us looked out over the shorter buildings of Magetech corporate headquarters. Beyond that sat the rest of the Kucinich Technology Park, backed up by the Cleveland skyline.

The sky was clear enough that I could even see the cylindrical clouds marking the static weather front above the Portal itself.

"This way," Lucas said.

I followed him down a corridor dotted with portraits, most dwarven. I took out my notebook and jotted down names as I followed Lucas. No titles were provided, but I suspected I was looking at the founding members of Magetech.

Two of the portraits were of humans. The first, little surprise, was of Councilman Mazurich with tie uncharacteristically straight. The second was a man I wasn't familiar with at all. I suspected that meant that he wasn't a politician. The name on the engraved plaque was "Dr. Eric Pretorious."

I wondered what kind of doctor he was.

"Mr. Maxwell?"

Lucas stood by an open door, waiting for me. I stepped away from Dr. Pretorious and into Lucas' office. "So how did you come to be part of Magetech?"

Lucas closed the door after us. "I've always been a part of Magetech."

"Then why isn't your portrait on the founder's wall back there?"

"I do not work for that kind of recognition." He held out a hand toward a chair at a large oval conference table. "Have a seat."

The office was impressive, almost the size of the lobby downstairs. Two walls were glass, looking out at the Cleveland skyline, and everything was appointed in black-lacquered hardwood, chrome, and leather. It made me wonder what the CEO's office was like.

"You are here to talk about our history," Lucas said as he walked around me to fold himself into another chair across the table.

I held my notebook in front of me and nodded. "I'm doing a story about Councilman Mazurich's influence on the city."

"That was a tragedy," Lucas said. "He deserves a proper elegy."

At first, I thought Lucas misspoke. However, he didn't strike me as one to make a casual slip of the tongue. He was very controlled. It made me think of what Teaghue Parthalán said, "A soul like Mazurich should have an epic written to him."

I nodded, "I've talked to dwarves that have the same sentiment."

Lucas leaned forward. "They told you much of the late Councilman Mazurich?"

"They expressed gratitude for the efforts he conducted on their behalf."

Lucas leaned back. "Impressive efforts they were. He did much to create their world on this side of the Portal."

"Such as helping to found this company?"

"Yes, the councilman was instrumental. He brought all the initial people together, including myself. He was adept at recognizing a problem, and seeing who might have potential solutions."

"The interference from the Portal."

"Our first viable product was a police radio and a walkie-talkie for the National Guard. Those first government contracts were the seed money that allowed all of this to happen."

I rubbed my forehead. The phrase "government contract" clicked one of the journalistic circuit breakers in my brain. "Was Mazurich involved in getting Magetech that kind of business?"

It was the obvious question, but it was also a loaded one.

Politicians, especially at the city and county level, were always open to the charge of conflict of interest. It would be hard to find a local official who didn't have an incestuous relationship with local business. That was the nature of the beast. As long as the politician in question wasn't *directly* involved in the decision to award largesse, there wasn't anything criminal to it.

But there's something called, "the appearance of impropriety." And, of course, it's the job of every corporate hack and politician to keep that "appearance" minimal.

Therefore I wasn't prepared when Simon Lucas said, "Again, he was instrumental."

I looked up from my notes, "Are you saying that the councilman helped steer contracts toward Magetech?"

Lucas smiled. The grin was predatory, and disturbing. As if Hieronymus Bosch did a hairless portrait of Jack Nicholson. Though the surreal appearance of Mr. Lucas might have had more to do with the office I found myself in. I got the continual sense of something trying to pry itself into my skull.

"Mr. Maxwell, the councilman did everything in his power to help our enterprise . . . Are you feeling all right, Mr. Maxwell?"

It was the damn reflections again. With all the lacquer and chrome in the office, wherever I looked, evil gibberish tried to drill itself into my eye sockets. "I'm fine . . ." I closed my eyes and took a few deep breaths. "Did he benefit financially from those contracts?"

"Mr. Maxwell." Mr.Lucas steepled his too long fingers. "I assumed you realized he was part owner of this company."

He was still smiling. I couldn't read him at all. He had to know that he was dangling red meat for a political reporter like me. Mazurich was not just a corporate

kingmaker, bringing all the principals together, broker-
ing the deals that formed Magetech.

Lucas had just told me that he was a principal in-
vestor, and benefited personally from city contracts
with the new company.

"Mr. Lucas, are you saying . . . ?" I sucked in a breath
and looked down. I was getting a deep sense of vertigo.

"You do not look well. Let me get you a glass of
water."

I nodded as I heard Lucas get up. In a moment I
heard glass rattling.

"Are you saying that Mazurich helped award contracts that he benefited from?"

"Yes, he did." I heard water pouring over ice. "It was
a different time, and Magetech was the only company
available to do what needed to be done. As I said, he
recognized a problem, and found solutions."

My brain was swirling inside my head. *He's just told
me that our late council president was profiteering off the
chaos from the Portal.*

I felt his hand on my shoulder. "I think you need to
drink something . . ."

I nodded, weak and light-headed, the claws of a mi-
graine just beginning to bite into my forebrain. "How
much . . . ?" I couldn't actually complete the sentence. I
closed my eyes, knowing that this wasn't right, that
nothing about this was right.

Lucas asked for me, his voice low and breathy.
"How much is his portion of Magetech worth?"

I could just manage a nod.

Lucas told me a figure that would make a dragon blush.

I opened my eyes to take the glass. My hand shook.

I looked down into the icy water and saw a skull in the ice, laughing at me. The glass slid from my hand and, while I remember hearing a shattering noise, I don't think I ever saw it hit the ground.

CHAPTER NINE

I'M NOT OFTEN PRONE to nightmares. I usually don't remember my dreams at all. This one, however, was a bad one.

I chase someone. I run through back alleys and scrap yards piled with engine blocks and old suits of plate mail. I run through the ruins of old steel mills and find myself at the Magetech complex, a maze of mirrored glass.

I hear a muffled voice calling for me . . .

"Dad?"

"Sarah!" I scream at the mirrored glass, and pound at the doors.

In front of me, the building implodes. It shatters as if there's no substance to it other than the mirrored glass skin. Shards fall and swirl around me, like a lethal snowstorm, flying daggers all reflecting my daughter's face.

"Sarah!" I call again, feeling my flesh cut to ribbons.

The shards swirl into a glass vortex, a chromed tornado falling into a spherical void that becomes the twin of the Portal itself.

I take a step forward, naked, bleeding and sliding on my own blood.

I am thrown back as a quartet of horsemen erupts from the Portal. Upon the pale horse that tramples me, I see a skeleton wrapped with raw flesh stitched together with steel wires.

The figure of death leans toward me, opens its mouth, and makes an electronic beeping sound.

Waking up didn't make the beeping go away.

I kicked off the covers, completely disoriented as to time and place. Three things managed to sink in the first ten seconds. I was in my own bed, my phone was ringing, and I couldn't remember how I'd gotten here.

I grabbed the phone, hoping for some clue to how I got back here.

No such luck.

"How could you put her up to this?" I could tell it was bad. Margaret had already skipped two preliminary octaves in the conversation and was a just a few sentences away from dog-whistle pissed.

Despite my disorientation, something about talking to my ex made it very easy to slide right into the argument. "You know I didn't put our daughter up to anything."

"You didn't tell her *not* to apply to those places."

"In case you haven't noticed, you're living a few thousand miles away—"

"There's a reason for that."

"—and when the subject came up, I told her to tell you about it."

"And make me the bad guy? That isn't fair, and you know it!"

I sighed. I try hard to be a good long-distance father, and I've done my best to keep Sarah from playing us off against each other. But somehow, that never seemed good enough for Margaret.

"Damn it, Kline, what am I supposed to do?"

"You're supposed to be her goddamn *mother*." I must have really been stressed out, because I was harsh enough to actually leave Margaret speechless. "You're the parent, you set the boundaries. You *are* the bad guy, by definition."

"I just want some support."

"What the hell do you think I've given you? Do you have any idea how often she tries to get me to tell her that you're being stupid and unreasonable? How many times I've told her *you're* the boss, and I'm not going to second-guess you. I'm not there—"

"You should have told her that she shouldn't have applied—"

"I told her she shouldn't have lied to you."

"You should have never let her fly up there."

"*I shouldn't have let her?*" My hand was trembling and my teeth were clenched so tight that my voice could barely come out.

"Kline?"

"I gave you everything you asked for, the divorce, custody, the nodding assent of every stupid soft-headed hysterical parenting decision you ever made— But I am *not* going to tell my daughter that I don't want to see her."

"That's not what I'm asking—"

"What, then? What are you asking? I'll tell you right now that there's nothing I'm going to tell her that will keep her from resenting our breakup."

"That's not what this is about!"

"So you've talked to her?"

"I've told her—"

"I know exactly what you've told her. Did you ask her anything? Like why she feels she has no chance discussing this with you?"

"This isn't a negotiation! She knows how I feel about this, and she went ahead anyway."

"Went ahead and what, Margaret?"

"You know what she did. She went behind my back—"

"—and was accepted into Kent State University."

She was quiet for a moment.

"You know how most parents I know find out about their kids going behind their back? A call from the cops. I want to know if you'd be coming down nearly as hard on her if that had happened. She applied to a college— you want to know how many parents would give anything to see that kind of rebellion in their kids?"

"Stop it! You don't understand."

I took a few breaths and released my grip on the phone. It was the first time in a few years that I had really lost my temper and let loose on Margaret, and it made me feel like an asshole.

Not that I was completely pure in this relationship. In

my more self-aware moments I knew that a lot of my identity as a parent was tied up in being the reasonable one—an easy role when you're nowhere near the teenage epicenter.

"I'm sorry. I'm a little stressed out."

"A little?"

"She did wrong. I know it, and she knows it."

"What about her trip? She's coming to see you. She's been looking forward to this for a year."

My daughter's voice from my nightmare was ringing in my ears. "They're refundable tickets, aren't they?"

"I can't just cancel it."

"No, that would be a bit too much. But you can reschedule it, can't you?"

"You mean ground her for a month?"

"And send her over in January."

"You'd be willing to give up the holidays?"

I sighed. "I hate to say this, but it might actually work out better with my job."

"*Great.*" Somehow she was able to subliminally insert the entire history of our divorce in that one word.

"Let me know if you have any trouble changing the dates. I'll chip in any difference in the airfare."

"Thanks, but we have a good travel agent. I don't think it will be a problem."

"She's a good girl," I told her.

"I know."

"Tell her I love her."

"I will."

I hung up, feeling a mixture of relief and disappointment. I really had been looking forward to showing

Sarah around the local tourist traps. But the nightmare image of zombie-boy was fresh in my head, and for once, Margaret's fears about mana-infested Northeast Ohio seemed perfectly reasonable.

Not to mention, I was still trying to figure out what day and time it was. I stumbled out into my living room, still holding my phone.

I squinted at daylight streaming in my windows. The angle of the sun made it early evening. I glanced in the kitchen and the clock on my microwave read 4:30 PM.

I sat down, shaking my head. I never slept during the day and waking up twelve hours off my normal schedule threw my whole equilibrium out of balance. I had no idea if I'd been unconscious for four hours, or twenty-four. My last conscious memory before waking up was talking to the COO of Magetech, Simon Lucas.

I checked my phone messages.

First call at 12:45, shortly after my interview with Lucas. "Hello, Mr. Maxwell? This is Nora Abrams at Magetech. Mr. Lucas wanted me to call and make sure you made it home all right. You were suffering a bad reaction, and we just wanted to check up on you."

"A bad reaction?" I muttered. "To what?"

At 2:00, Sarah had called. "Dad, I told her. She went ballistic, just like I told you she would. I just know she's going to cancel my trip up there. Call me or I don't know what I'm going to do."

My cell phone rang.

I usually turn the cell off when I come home. I try to keep the cell for work, and the landline for my personal life. Not that it works particularly well.

Probably I wasn't in any state to remember to kill it when I came home, if I was having blackouts. *Christ, what happened to me?*

I hung up the landline and answered the cell phone, mostly because my argument with Margaret was still running through my head at that point and I was half-convinced that it was my ex or my daughter trying the other phone because I had the home line tied up.

I wasn't thinking very clearly. Otherwise I would have looked at the caller ID.

"Maxwell?"

"Hello?" Male voice, odd accent . . . I shifted mental gears when I realized who it was. "Dr. Kawata?"

"Yeah, I ran those tests like you wanted me to. You need to tell me what the hell's going on here."

"What do you mean?"

"Oh, you want a list? I put that sample in the county's brand-new spectrometer. The one that's supposed to filter out all that damn background noise, and the bastard doesn't work. Readings as crazy as anything on the old equipment. I ran it a dozen times to average it all out, and you know what I got?"

"What?"

"Run-of-the-mill sodium chloride."

"Salt?"

"Salt. Plain old salt, crushed fine with a few trace mineral impurities."

"Shit. Why would someone send me salt of all things?"

"That's not the question, Maxwell."

"There's more?"

"Yeah, there's more. I want to know why I just spent two hours being questioned by the FBI about your little package."

"What?"

"What did you get me into, Maxwell? I'm a civil servant, I got a pension, I don't need to be mixed up in this type of crap."

I shook my head. I hadn't expected the FBI to catch up with this so quickly. "I'm sorry. I think the feds were investigating the person who probably sent that to me. I didn't mean to get you involved with anything."

"Well, you find any other mystery powders, have someone else look at it. I like my job too much."

"What did the Feds want?"

"Why don't you ask them? I'm sure they'll be talking to you."

Dr. Kawata hung up.

"Salt?"

I got dressed, trying to remember my interview with Lucas. I couldn't remember anything past dropping the water glass. However, the sense of unease around the Magetech complex still clung to me like the stale smoke around Columbia Jennings' office. Every time I thought of Lucas, I felt something sour in the pit of my stomach.

There was something twisted about the guy—and my feelings about him made no objective logical sense whatsoever. Anyone looking at a transcript of my conversation with him wouldn't see anything but a very cooperative and open interview subject. I knew, because

I *had* that transcript. My notebook was covered with my handwriting. Notes I had no memory of jotting down

The guy had no problem answering every question I had, in detail.

"Maybe I was asking the wrong questions?"

The guy was way too open. He was telling me things about Mazurich's history with Magetech that no sane executive should be stating on the record to a political reporter.

I apparently had a more detailed conversation with Mr. Lucas than I remembered.

However, the highlights were clear from the prelude I could recall. I had conflict of interest in spades, and dollar amounts with enough zeros to give Gregory Washington's creative auditors an orgasm. The fact that Mazurich's assets were news to me meant that they were never publicly disclosed.

I flipped through my notes and saw a road map of Mazurich's secret finances, complete with quotes from Lucas that were marked as being on the record.

"What the hell?"

Lucas was giving me exactly what I should want.

For almost every line, I could think of at least two means of independent verification. With a few hours and a few phone calls, the right questions would have this story ironclad. I could easily reconfirm any quotes with Lucas before running the piece.

And I had a gut feeling that it was all completely accurate.

But that did nothing to dispel the sick sense of wrongness I felt about it all, and about Lucas in particular.

Stories aren't just handed out like that. And it was almost as if Lucas was intentionally sacrificing Mazurich, the founding father of his company. At the same time, he was allowing a PR catastrophe for Magetech. If I ran with this, people would call for hearings and investigations and . . .

It didn't make sense.

"This is why he killed himself."

Could it be a smoke screen? Throw something big at the reporter so he doesn't ask the really troublesome questions?

There was not a single thing in my notes about dwarves. Or zombies.

Or salt.

"Nina Johannessen, *Cleveland Press*."

I sat down on my couch, phone in one hand, cold beer in the other. I pressed the bottle to my forehead and said, "Nina—"

"Kline? Are you okay? You haven't been at the office."

"I've been working."

"Something's wrong."

I hesitated, I wasn't sure if I wanted to go into something like unexpected blackouts with her. Instead, I changed the subject. "You told me you would look into some things for me?"

"Yes." I heard rustling in the background. "I've actually tracked down rumors of dwarven magi. Nothing concrete, but from the sound of it there might actually be that unfocused charm or fetish we were speculating about."

"What about zombies?"

"Have you heard any stories about a company named Magetech?"

I sat up, almost spilling my beer. "What?"

"Magetech, they have the patents on most Portal-adapted consumer electronics—"

"I know who they are."

"Well, they've been trying to come up with fusions of magic and industrial technology for years."

"What? Are you saying my zombie—?"

"I can't find anything matching your description, but there're stories about Magetech hiring dark magi, necromancers, real left-hand path people for some type of black projects lab."

"The kind of people who might be reanimating corpses?"

"Your zombie was too decomposed and too active to be an efficient use of mana, unless the metallic components were some sort of superstructure. And the investment in time and energy to create that wouldn't make sense, unless—"

"Someone was mass-producing it?" I shook my head. "Christ, there're more of those out there?"

"It could be an R&D project, or I could be drawing the wrong conclusions."

I shook my head. "No, it makes sense. If this thing was unique, why risk it on a simple B&E?"

There was a long pause on the other end of the phone.

I got an uneasy feeling. "Nina, what aren't you telling me?"

"I don't know what . . ."

"Please, I smell bullshit for a living. What is it? Did you have another vision?"

Silence. I thought of my dream. The undead rider rising out of the shards of the Magetech complex.

"Is that how you thought to look into Magetech in the first place?"

"You know?"

I looked at the bottle, sweating in my hand. It was shaking. I felt a sick dread growing in my gut.

"What did you see?" I asked, "What did you hear?"

"The Oracle is sometimes unclear—"

"*I saw it, damn it!*" I slammed the bottle on the table in front of me. "I saw Death ride off your tarot card right out of the Magetech complex. I heard my *daughter*."

"I'm so sorry, Kline. I didn't want to upset—"

"My *daughter*, Nina. Did you see her in your visions?"

A long painful pause. "Yes."

"Don't make me pull this out of you."

Her voice was shaking. "It could all be symbolic—"

"Cut the crap and tell me."

"I saw the Devil," she said, near tears, "and your daughter was in his hand."

CHAPTER TEN

*N*INA IS PROBABLY *right, it is all symbolic.*

Even so, I did call Margaret back to make sure that we were on the same page and that Sarah wasn't coming anywhere near Cleveland for at least a month. I gave her some lame excuse, because I couldn't bring myself to say what really concerned me. I told myself that I didn't want to panic her, but it probably had more to do with the fact that I couldn't admit that she might be right about this city.

What really worried me was the idea that people who tried to cheat the Oracle tended to end up doing exactly what the ephemeral bitch wanted—from Oedipus to Macbeth.

The fact that both those examples were fictional didn't comfort me much. In my own life I had a brush with the Oracle that killed the soothsayer, and almost killed me.

All I could really think to do was keep my daughter as far out of the line of fire as possible, and do my job.

If someone was about to threaten my daughter, my best course was to try and expose him, her, or it as fast as I could—and something was definitely up with Magetech.

I left my apartment, my hands still unsteady from my blackout and my talk with Nina.

I had one major contact that was wired into the supernatural goings-on in the city. And, while that might all be Nina's job, I had pretty much reamed her over the phone and I needed a nonconfrontational conversation. Now. So I tried calling Dr. Newman Shafran three times as I drove toward Case.

Case Western Reserve University was only about ten minutes' drive from Shaker Square, and my condo, so I was parking my Volkswagen in the metallic shadow of the Peter B. Lewis Building by six. Dr. Shafran still wasn't answering.

I couldn't tell if my growing sense of urgency was some lingering dread from my lost time, or the aftereffects of grilling Nina. I sat behind the wheel and tried taking a few deep breaths.

I made my living with my head and my ability to think clearly. I didn't like the feeling that someone might be messing with that. Combine my lost time with a supernatural threat against my daughter, and I had lost any real sense of objectivity.

When I got out of the Volkswagen, my destination didn't help my state of mind.

In the entire history of Cleveland architecture, the Peter B. Lewis Building would be the structure voted most likely to induce migraines and epileptic fits. It

was hard to believe that someone managed to have a
psyche twisted enough to conceive the thing *before* the
Portal opened. My best attempt to describe it would be
if Salvador Dalí ate a Silver Surfer comic book, and
threw up.

After the Portal opened, it seemed to attract and
twist energies so that occasionally the curved metallic
shapes would throw out rainbow auras or plasmatic
arcs of energy.

It used to house the College of Business Administration, of all things. Nowadays it had been adapted to the
study of things more in tune with its surreal outlines.

When I closed the door of my Volkswagen, the metal
skin of the building draped me in a crimson blast of
static that shaded my vision for more than half a
minute. I saw spots in my eyes, one of which resembled
a massive dragon descending from the dusk-colored
sky.

I blinked a few times and it was gone.

Dr. Shafran wasn't in his office, and I had to walk the
non-Euclidean halls for about half an hour, asking random people where he might be. I was about to give up
when someone directed me to one of the subterranean
labs.

I walked down a shadowed hallway just in time to
hear a small explosion and shattering glass. Having no
idea what to expect, I ran down to an open doorway
where brownish-green smoke was just beginning to
roll across the ceiling.

"No. No. *No.*" I heard a familiar Eastern European
accent as I rounded the corner. In front of me were

ranks of lab tables with sinks and spigots for gas and oxygen. Two men flanked one of the tables in the middle of the lab; one easily seventy, the other in his early twenties.

On the surface of the table between them, a circle of runes was just fading from glowing yellow to a dull red. As the runes faded, a swirling mass of ugly, foul-smelling smoke rose upward from the table to spill against the ceiling. I heard exhaust fans working overtime to clear it.

In the middle of the fading circle was a pile of ash and broken glass.

"No." One last time, and Dr. Shafran threw up his hands. The younger man, a grad student I suspected, just looked at the ruins on the table. "This is not your mother's goulash recipe. Rituals are exact. The patterns must be maintained or the power you mass has no shape." He slapped the table, making the glass bounce a little. It was an impressive show of force for someone who looked like a German watchmaker and talked like Bela Lugosi.

The student shook his head. "It was a brand-new spell . . ."

"You cannot just throw words on a page or paint on a canvas and call it art!" Dr. Shafran took off his bifocals and pointed them at the student. "You must know the patterns you are changing, or this is all useless."

"But, sir,"

"Go, study what you just did here, and don't talk to me until you can explain what it is you did wrong."

Dr. Shafran stormed toward the door past me, then turned and said, "And clean this up."

The student looked at me as if he had just noticed I was there. I looked at him, then at Dr. Shafran walking down the hall. I faced him, shrugged, and told him, "Sorry," before I chased after Dr. Shafran.

"Doctor!" I called after him, running to catch up.

"What?" He sounded a little flustered. Then he turned and looked at me "I know you. Yes. Mr. Kline Maxwell."

"Yes."

"I got that grant request, thank you."

"Huh?"

"Our last conversation, dragons it was. Being quoted in a national story does wonders for the credibility of a scientist in an unpopular discipline." He waved me forward, toward the elevators. "Apologies for that display," he said as he gestured back toward the lab, where I could hear the student coughing.

"That's okay—"

"Somehow I cannot get through to the students that the presence of 'magic' does not invalidate the scientific method. Ten years of students, and how many have a solid science background? Three! A waiting list I have, and all astrologers, pagans, devotees of the Golden Dawn. From all over the country. And can I even get a basic physics prerequisite written into the course descriptions? Pheh." The elevator arrived and he turned toward me. "That is not what you want to discuss, is it, Mr. Maxwell?"

"No."

"Come, then. Share a cup of coffee and let us discuss the subjects of future news articles and research papers."

He took me to a refreshingly rectilinear cafeteria with a set of tables and vending machines. It was an odd hour, and we were the only ones there.

I made an effort to back myself up and act like a journalist. I sipped machine black coffee as I gave Dr. Shafran background on my dead dwarf, and where he had led me to date.

Dr. Shafran steepled his fingers and nodded in the right places and prodded me with the occasional monosyllable.

I paid particular attention to the oddities about my visit to Magetech, and the rumors Nina had passed on to me. The moment I mentioned Magetech, he seemed more interested.

"Really? I was offered a position there, a long time ago."

"You?"

"My expertise, you see. I was uncomfortable, however, with their—" I noticed a pause, as if he was deciding how much to tell me. "Their nondisclosure arrangements. It is hard enough to publish as it is, to conform to some corporate bylaw as well would be intolerable. At the university I study as I see fit and publish as I see fit." There was a pride in his voice that sounded almost familiar. "But I'm acquainted with the man you mentioned that they did employ."

"Dr. Pretorious?"

"Yes, a great mind. It's a blow to my own vanity to admit that he was the first to begin the scientific quantification of the phenomenon we call the Portal, at this university in fact. You might say I inherited his position. He joined that private enterprise at the beginning, and I understand the decision has been quite kind to him—in the material sense."

Knowing the figures I had jotted down for Mazurich, that had to be an understatement. And Pretorious had the added benefit of not having to keep things under wraps to protect a public position.

"So do you know anything about what he worked on for Magetech?"

Dr. Shafran shook his head. "Like me, he is—or he was—a scientist, a theoretician. The information the public sees coming out of Magetech is in the form of patents and end-user products. From that, you can see their engineering but not their research—and that is what would possess him. And anyone in my position will tell you that the time from pure research to practical applications is measured in decades."

"Could they be developing something like my zombie?"

"They could be developing anything, especially if they are employing black market mages. That begs the question, why would they?"

"Can you think of a reason?"

"There seems to be little chance of seeing a legal market for such an abomination, and I don't think the black market here is either wide enough or deep enough to support that sort of development."

"But someone did develop it."

"Which means that one of us is operating on a faulty assumption."

I looked into my coffee.

"Now," Dr. Shafran said, "your mention of dwarves is interesting."

"You think so?"

"Well, as you've been told, dwarves, in a sense, are antithetical to mana. Where mana pools into areas of ritual and pattern, both physical and cultural, the presence of dwarves tends to push it away. I've had no opportunity to study the effect closely. Dwarves seem too wary to volunteer for any experiments."

"I wonder why."

"My guess is that there's some inherent biological or mental antipattern that affects the collection of mana. It makes them unique as far as intelligent nonhumans go. They don't need mana to exist."

"You mean they can leave the influence of the Portal?"

Dr. Shafran nodded. "They like to remain close to their clan, but I have heard of dwarves traveling as far afield as California."

"Now why would a dwarf go to California?"

"Disneyland?" Dr. Shafran smiled.

"About Magetech—" I looked down into my coffee again. I was uncomfortable leaving the realm of journalism for the personal. I barely knew Dr. Shafran. I didn't know if that made it easier or harder to tell him about my blackout.

"I've never blacked out like that before. Could someone have cast something on me?" I asked him after describing my interview with Lucas.

"Certainly someone could have, but you describe unease before you even entered the building."

"What does that mean?"

Dr. Shafran leaned back. "The mechanisms by which human beings perceive mana are not fully understood. Just as a camera or a telephone without filtering software can pick up signals from the mana force itself, so does your brain. But while the brain of a living creature is an infinitely better filter than any microchip, signals can and do sneak through. I suspect that you passed close to an intense source of mana you're particularly sensitive to."

"Why would it make me black out?"

"That may be a medical or a psychological question. But I might suggest there is some slight evidence that such static is not wholly random, and is responsible for what some New Age victims refer to as the Oracle."

Please, tell me he didn't just say that . . .

I rubbed my forehead. As much as I wanted Dr. Shafran to be pulling my leg, he didn't look like it.

"You're saying that I had some prophetic vision?"

"I am saying that you might have seen something you were not physically or mentally capable of absorbing at the time. I won't say much more than that, since far more people claim to see the future than I can credit."

I tried to grasp a little rational reassurance. "I would think fortune-telling and soothsaying is outside your scientific purview. Mana or not."

"Such things are unproven and untested in the lab. We have, however, conducted very interesting experiments that demonstrate that these energies can violate our commonsense notions of causality, just as they mangle our not-so-commonsense notions of physics, matter, and energy."

Well, that isn't very reassuring.

I stood up, shaking my head. I wasn't absolutely sure I had learned much . . .

"Are you all right, son?"

"This whole thing is making me uneasy."

"Is there anything else you would like to ask?"

I paused, and realized there was.

"What about salt?"

"Salt?"

"Salt. The dwarf sent me a sample of salt. What could be the significance of that?"

Dr. Shafran reached over and grabbed a saltshaker and sprinkled the white crystals on the table. "When you speak of salt, you speak of possibly the most potent mineral symbol in human culture. Physically, it is crystalline, and it is a longtime symbol of purity taking part in rituals millennia before the Portal existed. Its crystal structure, and the cultural significance surrounding it, makes it a perfect matrix to absorb the mana flow out of the Portal."

"What would that make the salt mines under Lake Erie?"

"Possibly the most potent concentration of mana on either side of the Portal."

It started making sense. So much mana in one place,

no matter how dull someone was, the sheer force of all of that would leak through their mental filters. God help anyone who was sensitive or naturally adept. Of course, the mines became a disaster when the Portal opened.

"If dwarves are immune to the effects, they might be the only ones who *could* go down there."

Dr. Shafran nodded.

Christ, what happened when you refined the stuff?

CHAPTER ELEVEN

THAT DISTURBING SENSE of urgency kept me moving after I had talked to Dr. Shafran. My world felt out of joint, and I had the feeling that things were laughing at me from behind the reflection in my rearview mirror.

Be rational, damn it.

It was tied to the salt. The salt that I had given to Kawata, the salt that Ossian had given to me.

"This was why he killed himself."

Mazurich had led the dwarves into the salt mines. Mazurich and the dwarves had formed Magetech. The point of Magetech was to exploit the influence of the Portal, to apply twenty-first century science and engineering to it, or vice versa . . .

What kind of resource would that salt be?

I thought back to when I received the package. How my satellite and phone reception went, despite the filters for normal background mana. How Dr. Kawata complained about his brand-new spectrometer failing.

The camera on my phone failing at *Thor's Hammer*, and at the *Nazgûl*.

The white circle around Ossian's remains.

Potential.

Implication.

Nothing solid . . .

I wanted to talk to Dr. Pretorious.

The man I called was a private investigator of a rather specialized variety. His name was Quintin Valentino, and he didn't stake anyone out, didn't take incriminating pictures, didn't even own a gun. As far as I knew, the guy lived in his office. But you could give him a first name and where the person worked, and he could come back with a credit report, tax records, arrest record, and résumé.

"Quint?"

"Kline, darling. How long has it been . . . ?"

"Too long. Can you look someone up for me?"

"On your account? Anyone you want."

"Name's Pretorious. Dr. Eric Pretorious."

"Please tell me you can spell that."

I gave him the spelling from my notes.

"Any other identifiers?"

"Worked at, probably part owner of, a company called Magetech."

"Well, that won't be too hard. Tomorrow soon enough?"

"Yes, fine."

I hung up my cell phone as I drove up one of Solon's snaking industrial pathways. Solon was one of the outer suburban nets that caught a lot of the industry

shaken loose from the Cleveland metropolitan economy in the last quarter of the twentieth century. It was
the closest of a cluster of suburbs whose combination
of undeveloped acreage—read "farms"—and attractive real estate taxes attracted large box warehouses
and factories like a presidential campaign attracted unreasonable promises.

I drove by windowless boxes made of concrete and
corrugated steel, squatting in the midst of floodlit asphalt. Semi trucks backed into loading bays—industrial young sucking the teats of their mother. Every few
moments, a tractor trailer would drive past me, going
in the opposite direction. The side panels advertised
kitchen cabinets, soft drinks, or auto parts.

At the end of the road sat my destination.

The Magetech factory/warehouse complex
wrapped around the end of the street so completely
that it was able to build its massive logo into the island
in the center of the cul-de-sac.

I pulled into a small visitor's parking lot under the
watchful eye of a security camera. I sat in my car and
looked around, trying to get a sense of the place. The
scale was huge. Easily several hundred acres. A half
dozen separate buildings were immediately visible,
each marked with standardized runes which could be
wards, or could simply be some form of building mark-
ers. I could also see runes on the plowed surface of the
main parking lot.

The lot was down a long driveway from the five visitor spots, wrapped in chain-link, and protected by a
guard shack where a single uniformed dwarf sat, eye-

ing me suspiciously. The lot was mostly empty except for a quartet of charter buses, all bearing the Magetech logo.

As I got out of the Volkswagen, I saw thirty or forty dwarves dressed in overalls and hard hats exit one of the buildings and head toward one of the buses. I heard their guttural conversations drift my way, and slow to a stop as they reached the bus and more of them saw me.

It felt as if they all stared at me as they queued up to board the bus.

Okay, I'm out of place here. We've established that.

I wanted to see more of Magetech, and I was holding the hope that Mr. Lucas' uncharacteristic openness would filter down to the factory floor. Seeing the dwarves react to me made me second-guess that idea.

"Maybe I shouldn't be here," I whispered in a puff of fog.

I managed to shock myself by voicing such an unprofessional thought. I was still suffering from the aftereffects of my visit to the corporate office. I was expecting some evil premonition, some sort of nasty mana overload to raise the small hairs on my neck.

Fortunately, I didn't sense much of anything.

That made me wonder what was at the corporate office that made me react so badly. It couldn't be raw mana, considering what Magetech did here. I couldn't imagine there'd be *less* concentration here than downtown.

I took a few deep breaths, became a journalist again, and walked into the front office.

* * *

The name Simon Lucas was good for opening doors. Enough so that I had the sense that I was expected. After I showed my credentials and did a little strategic name-dropping, I soon had a bright-blue engraved visitor ID and a tour guide.

I was surprised that the foreman who got the job to show me around happened to be human—though he was as grizzled as any dwarf. "You keep that ID on you, boy, or security will hit you." He reminded me of an old shop teacher.

On our way to one of the factories, I got a glimpse of some of the security he was talking about. Not only were there double rows of razor-wire topped chain-link surrounding the compound, but they had some really impressive guard dogs. A Rottweiler is intimidating enough, but give one an extra two hundred pounds of muscle and an extra head or two, and you had a pretty good deterrent against industrial espionage.

My guide didn't need to tell me to stay on the path behind him.

The first building I saw was an assembly plant. We walked along a path, safely behind a thick sheet of glass. My guide expressed some pride in the vast space beyond which was filled with a forest of industrial robots undergoing strange repetitive gyrations. He explained that the line I watched was the ultimate in flexibility, the same robots that put together cell phones one day could put together wide-screen TVs the next.

The flexibility was necessary, since ninety percent of Magetech's production was retrofitting third-party electronics. Most of what this line did was disassembly of some brand-name device, insertion of Magetech's patented hardware, and reassembly.

The robots themselves were unusual. I could see glyphs engraved along the arm, and most of them sat inside a protective circle of some sort. I looked closely, and judging by the swinging gestures and unnatural glow, a few were actually casting some sort of spell over the finished products—HP laptops at the moment.

I peppered the guy with questions, and, fortunately he didn't seem to mind answering them. A lot of what I asked was a matter of confirming background details. I didn't bring up Nina's rumors since I doubted that would be productive at the moment.

However, I looked down and saw a trio of dwarves working on one of the robots whose glyphs glowed an unhealthy green and I asked, "You employ a lot of dwarves?"

He nodded. "They can work safely around hazardous mana levels."

I looked down again at the shop floor, and the robot the dwarves worked on belched a noxious looking cloud of green smoke. "If it's not safe down there . . ."

"How can we be up here?" He knocked on the glass. "One of our developments, mana shielding. All the radiation is confined inside this building."

I looked at the glass, trying to see what he was talking about. "I didn't know you could do that."

My guide laughed. "A lot of what we do here would be impossible without it."

"How's it work?"

"Trade secret—suffice to say it came from the study of dwarven mana resistance."

"I see . . ." So, perhaps there was more to the fact that Dr. Shafran had no dwarves willing to be examined.

He took me around to see a clean room where chips were etched and enchanted, and a few warehouses where boxes waited to be shipped across northeast Ohio.

Everywhere dwarves worked, they gave me the evil eye. My guide made sure to steer me away from any employees. Judging by the way they reacted, I couldn't tell if the foreman was trying to hide something, or if he was protecting me.

It was late evening when I parked at my condo, trying to tell myself to take a break. The story would wait until the morning.

Fate, the Oracle, or just plain old bad luck had other plans.

When I stepped out of my Volkswagen and saw the lights on in my apartment, I knew there was a problem. I don't leave the lights on, as a rule. And as I slowly walked toward the lobby, I didn't see Willie, the doorman, anywhere around.

Not a good sign.

I hit the speed-dial on my cell phone; it rang once. "Cleveland Police Department."

I had a couple of thoughts about who might be knocking around my apartment, and was checking on the first possibility. "Can you connect me to the Special Paranormal Unit? Commander Caledvwlch, please."

The phone rang.

I got Caledvwlch's voice mail, which was just as well. "This is Kline Maxwell. It's ten after eight on Friday, I'm at my condo, and if you're not waiting in my apartment, either I'm about to be jumped or the FBI is about to haul me in for questioning about your dead dwarf."

I pushed my way into the lobby, and I wasn't particularly surprised when a gentleman in a dark suit stepped up to me and said, "Mr. Maxwell, come with me, please."

I hung up.

My apartment was Fed central. Half a dozen dark-suited men were poking around every corner of my condo, and judging by the state it was in, they had arrived a few minutes after I had left to see Dr. Shafran. They had easily put a good two hours into trashing the place.

They'd opened closets, rummaged through drawers, and right now they were in the process of pointing various arcane charms at the walls and the furniture.

"And what can I do for you?" I asked as my escort unceremoniously deposited me on my couch.

"Hey . . ." I stood up, only to be pushed back down by another suit.

I looked up at them. "You know, some sort of ID would be nice, not to mention a warrant."

"Still as cooperative as ever, aren't you, Mr. Maxwell?"

The voice was familiar, but I couldn't place it until the speaker walked into the living room.

"Blackstone?"

He hadn't changed much. Hair a little grayer, but he still looked more like a math professor than a government agent. He reached into his breast pocket and pulled out an ID for me. I gave it a cursory glance.

" 'Counterterrorism?' New career track, or are you 'on loan' again?" Last time I saw him he was a semilegal spook working out of the euphemistically named "Threat Assessment Office." I'm not exactly sure what intelligence umbrella it worked under, but it was responsible for a fair bit of the cloak-and-dagger work around the Portal before the Feds got custody of it.

I guess it would have been too much to hope that the Feds winning that particular battle would put Blackstone out of a job.

"I have some questions for you."

I looked at the Feds ransacking my apartment. One of them found some dirty laundry I'd hidden and was busy dumping it on the floor, one dirty sock at a time. "I hope you have a warrant."

"We're here under authority of the Federal Special Administration Zone."

"Christ, Blackstone, that hasn't been used since the end of the blockade."

Blackstone shrugged and smiled. "I don't have to explain this to you, do I?"

What I said a while back, about repealing tax abatements, goes for extensions of executive power, too. Back in the chaos when the Portal opened, the federal government did a few crazy things—like ringing Cuyahoga County with tanks. In the midst of all that was an executive order that made the area within the Portal's influence a police state in the name of national security.

To my knowledge, it had never been tested in court, since the Feds never actually "occupied" Cleveland—Congress intervened before that happened.

I suspected that Blackstone was pushing things a bit.

"We're going to have a little talk," he said.

"Are we?"

"You're going to tell me everything you know about the dwarven operation."

I put my hand on my forehead and rubbed my temple. I could tell already that this was going to go really well. "Exactly which dwarven operation are we talking about?"

"You know better than to play coy with me. This isn't just provincial Cleveland voodoo involved here."

"Let me guess, it's a matter of national security."

"Let me spell this out for you. We know that there are humans involved in this ring. We know you had contact with Ossian Parthalán a few hours before he was assassinated, and that he sent you one package we know about. We've identified one cell in California, and just by coincidence we find that you've been out to the coast at least ten times in the past four years."

"Good Lord, Blackstone, my daughter lives there."

"And you've been a very attentive father."

"I don't believe this."

Blackstone sat on the arm of the couch, looking at

me. Behind him, one of the agents started methodically rummaging through my DVD collection, popping disks into a laptop he had placed on the coffee table. "Help me, Maxwell. I don't really think you're involved in this. But I have enough now to pull you into the system, and then you're not coming back out."

"What is it you think I know?"

Blackstone smiled. "I'm giving you credit for being a good reporter. You'd obviously tapped the dwarf as a source. All I want is what he gave you."

The hell you say.

A little voice inside me told me that Blackstone wasn't going to be satisfied with the truth. What I actually knew was rather weak justification for the kind of muscle Blackstone was flexing here.

Blackstone was an asshole, and I didn't doubt that he'd pull me in just out of spite if he didn't like my answers. I couldn't even come up with some convincing lie. I didn't know what I'd be lying about.

The guy probably had a truth-detecting charm on one of his entourage anyway.

Plan B; play up what I did know and stall for time.

I looked at the guys tossing my apartment and said, "They aren't going to find any more. He only sent one package."

"So why send it?"

"To back up the information he was going to give me. A sample of what Magetech was working on."

I paused. That was a guess, and I didn't like guessing in front of the Feds. But it sank in without much surprise on Blackstone's part. I took it as a silent confirmation.

"That explains your visit there today . . ."

I looked around and had another guess. From the behavior of the Feds here, it was pretty obvious that this salt was considered some sort of contraband. If I played Blackstone right, I might gain as much information as he did from this interview.

"If I'm guessing right—" I continued on with the assumption that if I qualified the statement as speculation it wasn't pure bullshit. "—a sample of what he was shipping to California."

Blackstone should never play poker. His satisfied expression told me all I needed to know about my speculation. "Go on."

I thought of the car with California plates in *Thor's Hammer.* "Did the zombie get to the car before you did?"

Blackstone frowned. "I'm asking the questions here."

"Uh-huh. A little interdepartmental dispute with the local cops? They decided it was their evidence?"

"That's not your concern."

"The locals tend to get possessive about murder cases, don't they?"

Blackstone leaned forward. "Shall we continue with the matter at hand, Mr. Maxwell?"

"What do you want to know?" I said in my most helpful tone. I found it an easier pose to make, now that Blackstone had confirmed a nagging suspicion of mine;

the suspicion that the Feds weren't fully cooperating with the local cops.

But then, what else was new?

"Let's start with the note. Who was Ossian Parthalán referring to? Why 'who' killed himself?"

Now there was an interesting gap.

"The way you were following our dwarf, I'm surprised you didn't have a tap on his phone—"

"Mr. Maxwell—"

"Apparently you didn't need a warrant."

"You are trying my patience."

"I'm cooperating."

"You're stalling."

You noticed. "Parthalán was hinting that the city government was involved. I never got to speak to him about it. He was killed before I got the chance. We were supposed to have a meeting the day he was killed."

"At the club?"

"No, the Old Arcade." I looked at him and decided to see how deep the schism between the Feds and the local cops actually went. "I found out he'd been killed when Commander Caledvwlch showed up and questioned me about it."

"What?"

"Maelgwyn Caledvwlch, head of the SPU. Special Paranormal Unit. If the dwarf's murder was part of a ritual, it falls into his jurisdiction—"

"Cut the crap. I know exactly who the damn elf is." He looked at a couple of the Feds who'd been watching our interchange. "I'm not even going to ask why we didn't know about this when it happened. I just want

someone to follow up and find out what else is going
on in the SPU we might have missed."

A pair of agents nodded and left.

"So, I take it this isn't a joint investigation with the
local authorities?"

"Maxwell, do you really think—" Blackstone shook
his head. "I don't think you realize how serious this is."

"Why don't you tell me?"

"You just told me that there were ties into the city
government. What makes you think the local cops
aren't involved?"

"Are you saying Maelgwyn Caledvwlch is dirty?"

"Good Lord—do you even remember how you met
him?"

Yeah, I did. It wasn't really a comforting thought. To
an extent, Caledvwlch's actions in the mess around the
Aloeus murder weren't his fault, they were proxy actions for a crooked cop he'd pledged fealty to—but the
law in this country doesn't make those kind of distinc-
tions and the reason Caledvwlch wasn't in jail right
now was primarily due to the DA's shallow investigation, and to the fact that, in the end, he handed the Rayburn administration the least politically damaging
scapegoat conveniently dead and unable to testify.

I could say for sure that the elf played by the rules,
but those rules were the ones he brought over from the
other side of the Portal.

"What did you talk to him about?"

I don't know if I was relieved or not when I heard
sirens approaching.

"Why don't you ask him yourself?"

One of the Feds searching my apartment stationed himself by the window and looked down at the street.

"What is it?" Blackstone asked him.

"Locals, looks like half the SPU."

"Shit." Blackstone looked at me accusingly.

I shrugged.

Blackstone shook his head. "Maxwell, you're either neck-deep in this, or you're incredibly stupid."

I didn't give him the satisfaction of telling him that those weren't necessarily mutually exclusive options.

Blackstone turned and walked over to the door of my apartment, just in time to confront a contingent of Cleveland police officers, Commander Caledvwlch in the lead. The elf towered over Blackstone, half his face obscured by the top of the doorframe.

"To what do I owe this pleasure?" Blackstone said.

"There is an ongoing murder investigation." Caledvwlch's voice was impassive as ever. "I am here to take Mr. Maxwell downtown for questioning."

"Mr. Maxwell is a material witness in a federal investigation."

"It seems we have a bureaucratic impasse, then." Caledvwlch pulled a cell phone out of one of the baggy folds in his suit jacket. "I will have to consult with the judge who issued the warrant."

"Actually," Blackstone said, "I think we're done here." He waved at his men, who started filing out of my apartment. He glanced back at me before he left. "I'll be in touch."

I'm sure.

Caledvwlch folded his way into the remains of my

apartment, followed by a pair of police officers. He looked at me with his shiny metallic eyes and said, "It puzzles me that men create rules only so they can twist them out of shape."

"I will admit that feudal fealty is a little simpler."

"I have a warrant," Caledvwlch said.

I sighed. "So you are taking me in?"

"Only to make a statement." He handed me a sheet of paper from within his voluminous jacket. It wasn't an arrest warrant.

"You're looking for the letter?"

"Any correspondence that might have come from Mr. Ossian Parthalán."

"I'm afraid Blackstone beat you to it."

He nodded, and I suspected that he wasn't surprised at all. "If you would come with me and make a statement to that effect?"

He led me toward the door, and the other cops stayed in my condo. "What are they for?"

"Simply making sure that your fallible human memory hasn't forgotten anything." The two cops picked up right where the Feds left off.

I'd known Caledvwlch for a couple of years, and if you'd asked me to predict what his office would look like, I would have probably envisioned something as austere, sterile, and functional as an operating theater in a Trappist monastery.

I guess I was a little off the mark.

He sat me in one corner while he folded himself behind a desk that seemed a little small for him. The first detail I noted was that all the furniture was wood, very little metal at all.

It made sense. Elves reacted badly to iron, not just in elemental form, but alloys to a certain extent. I don't know the medical or magical basis for it. But, while elves only seemed to be injured by iron that broke through the skin, every one I've seen was wary of being exposed to the metal.

And, apparently, Caledvwlch wasn't a fan of IKEA. The desk and the chairs were rich antique hardwood. The kind of furniture that graced a policeman's office of Eliot Ness' vintage. On the polished mahogany of his desk sat a trio of bonsai trees in brightly colored ceramic pots. In one, a figurine of a Taoist monk sat on a rock grinning at some private joke.

On the walls I saw an eclectic collection of art, mostly Asian landscapes in ink washes.

"Mr. Maxwell."

I turned back to face him. "You wanted a statement?"

"You keep appearing in our investigation. It is time I had a clear picture of why."

I shrugged. "I think we're investigating the same thing?"

"If that is the case, I would be interested in exactly how the dwarven enterprise of Magetech is involved." Caledvwlch chewed the word with some visible distaste. I couldn't help thinking that it was for my benefit.

"You have something against Magetech?"

Caledvwlch spread his hands across the desk. "The

dwarves are a noble race whose passage here was as perilous as our own. In the end, each of us chooses the paths we take. What connection exists between the dwarf Ossian Parthalán and the company Magetech?"

"I don't know. I was investigating Councilman Mazurich."

"And the material that Ossian Parthalán sent to you?"

"Salt."

Caledvwlch nodded, as if that was the answer he expected.

"Shall we review everything that happened since you received Ossian Parthalán's phone call?"

CHAPTER TWELVE

IT WAS WELL AFTER midnight before I was completely disentangled from the legal system, tired, unenlightened, and more than a little annoyed. I generally don't like being leaned on.

Right now, though, I was walking out of the Justice Center and just wanted to get home.

It had started snowing while I'd been sequestered with Caledvwich. The snow muffled sound. While the bars and clubs were just getting into gear a few blocks away, where I was the night was—for a moment—dead quiet. It was eerie the way the snow swirled around. And briefly, framed by the silence, I saw a reptilian silhouette eclipse the upper part of the Terminal Tower.

Somewhere, a traffic light changed, and the silence was broken as cars shot by on the street in front of me, throwing slush at me and at each other.

We had only thirty dragons or so in the Greater Cleveland area. I wondered which one I'd just glimpsed. They'd been keeping a low profile, especially since the Feds took over the Portal. They were a set of creatures that made the Feds really nervous—and while they had rights, they only had them under Ohio state law.

Most of them had comfortably integrated themselves into the local economy, and—as powerful as they were—I doubted any of them wanted to be a test case for some sort of Fed crackdown. I was sort of surprised to see one flying downtown, even this late at night.

I turned my attention to the street and looked for a taxi.

I was lucky; one had started slowing down and pulling over, even before I started waving at it. I figured I must have looked forlorn and a little lost.

The Justice Center was probably a good place to pick up fares, with people being processed out of the system at all hours, so I didn't think much of it as I opened the door and slid into the back of the cab.

"Shaker Square, please," I told the driver as I leaned back in the seat. The cabbie had the heat somewhere in the high eighties, and the snow that had dusted my clothes melted instantly, soaking me through. I wiped my forehead, unsure if I was wiping sweat or melted snow off my face.

Now Shaker Square is pretty much due east of downtown, which happened to be the direction the cab had been traveling down Superior to begin with when it picked me up. I didn't think much when the driver took a right turn right after Public Square. There were a number of ways to get there, and I had enough cash on me that I wasn't that concerned about being gouged.

It was the second right, immediately after that one, that made me suspicious.

"Hey? I said Shaker Square—where're you going?"

That's when I glanced at the hack license. "Samanish Thégharin," next to a picture of a broad, full-bearded face. Dwarven.

The cab continued turning, circling the Soldiers and Sailors' Monument in the shadow of the Terminal Tower, until we ended up westbound on Superior.

"Do you mind telling me what's going on?" By this point there was no possible route that would explain where we were going. My cabbie had a destination of his own in mind. This was not encouraging given the profile of Ossian Parthalán's kinsman that Reggie had given me.

"Look, why don't you let me out, I'll take the bus."

Mr. Thégharin ignored me, as if he couldn't hear me at all behind the Plexiglas partition. I reached for the door, but the handles were absent. I apparently was going wherever Mr. Thégharin wanted.

I thought about smashing one of the windows to make my escape, but there were some scary-looking glyphs etched in the glass, and I didn't relish finding out what they did the hard way.

Before I worked up enough panic to make the attempt, the Detroit-Superior Bridge loomed up in front of us. A mass of concrete and blue steel arcing over the Flats whose far end was hidden by layers of blowing snow.

Instead of crossing the bridge, my dwarf swerved right. If he kept to the street, he'd head down to the Flats, but he pulled over toward a forest of orange barrels and blinking sawhorses. It seemed as if he'd plow right into the construction barriers, but barely visible shadows emerged from the blowing snow to move the barriers aside and let the taxi pass.

I glanced behind me and saw the same barriers quickly replaced behind us. Then a tunnel swallowed us in darkness.

The Detroit-Superior Bridge was a Depression-era project, built when the city still had streetcars, so it was built with two levels. The upper deck was designed for automobile traffic, the lower deck for the streetcar traffic. The lower level was shut up and mothballed when Cleveland got rid of its streetcar system. Despite a long series of proposals, and one major renovation, the lower deck remained closed for several decades.

It wasn't until recently, with the rise of tourism, that any plans for using the space reached the construction phase. The Regional Transit Authority planned to expand its existing light-rail line from the East Side and downtown, moving west toward Lakewood and Rocky River.

The western link would cross the Flats using the existing lower deck of the bridge. All of which was still five to ten years in the future.

But construction had already started. And, as was the case for about half of construction work in this town, a dwarven company had gotten the contract.

The cab rolled through a dark tunnel, past two sets

of floor-to-ceiling chain-link fences that opened of their own accord. We passed pallets of rebar, concrete block, PVC pipe, and other items less identifiable to me.

Past the second gate, we pulled out onto the deck proper. It was a vast space, dotted by pillars marching off into the darkness. The far end was too distant for the headlights to make out, so it felt as if the half-finished railroad tracks marched off forever.

The cab rolled slowly down the center, between two pairs of tracks. Through concrete arches on either side, I could see the swirling snow obscuring the view of the Flats and the city.

Ahead of us, a group was waiting. A ring of squat figures was picked out in the taxi's headlights. They were dressed uniformly, as if they had all walked off the same job site. They wore brown coveralls, streaked with grime, heavy steel-toed boots, thick leather gloves, and hard hats. When they parted to let the taxi roll into the center of their circle, I saw that they all wore face masks or respirators.

I hoped the masks were more for anonymity's sake, rather than because of toxic particulate matter in the air.

The taxi came to a stop in the center of the circle, and the passenger door popped open for me. I didn't need a cue from my driver, Mr. Thégharin, to know what was expected of me. Despite my contrary streak, I am not completely self-destructive. I hadn't time to count, but there was a ring of about twenty dwarves circling this taxi. And, given the reputation they had for strength and martial ability—back home they didn't just *make* swords, after all—I doubted I could over-power any one of them.

Whatever was going on, I had a much better chance of talking my way out of it.

I stepped out of the taxi, and closed the door behind me. The taxi moved quickly enough that it almost knocked me over. It was through the circle, and the cir-cle had closed behind it all before I had completely re-gained my equilibrium.

The glow from the headlights receded as the taxi continued on its journey toward the west side of the Cuyahoga. As the artificial light receded, it allowed my eyes to register the flickering orange light of candles surrounding me. Heavy black candles as thick as my forearm, and about half again as long, placed around the inner circumference of the ring of dwarves sur-rounding me.

I turned slowly until I faced the odd dwarf out. This guy was dressed the same, but he wasn't part of the group ringing me. He was bent over, backing around the inner circumference of the circle, chanting some-thing quiet and guttural to himself as he poured some-thing white out of a small canvas bag. He was completing a circle that separated me from the others, and he was just now walking across the space where the taxi had left.

I glanced behind me and saw that he had already passed the half of the circle where the taxi had entered.

The bastard has good timing.

I walked toward the one spot where the circle was incomplete. I didn't know a lot about magic, but I knew breaking a circle was a bad thing. If I wanted out of this, I needed to step out before this little ritual was completed.

The dwarf in the ring directly in front of me reached for his tool belt and took out a small mini-sledge and hefted it while looking at me. I stopped, looked around at my four-and-a-half-foot-tall audience, and asked, "Someone tell me what is going on here."

The only audible answer was the continued chant of the dwarf pouring the circle, who took a few steps across my path to complete it.

The hair rose on my arms and the back of my neck. I could smell the energy released into the air.

Like hell dwarves don't do magic.

A solid blue arc whipped around the perimeter of the circle, close enough that the force threw me backward. I stumbled and fell on my ass, roughly in the center of the circle. All around me, the air crackled as arcs leaped up from the circle, forming a blue hemisphere of energy about twenty feet in diameter—ending just short of the ceiling above me.

My pulse raced. I couldn't see this ending well.

"Mr. Maxwell," spoke a vaguely familiar voice.

I lowered my gaze to confront the dwarf who had completed the circle. Apparently, he was on my side of the circle when he finished. He took off his mask and I could recognize him.

"Teaghue Parthalán."

He walked toward me, his face grim. "Abandon the path you follow, Mr. Maxwell."

I pushed myself upright. We both now stood on a

disk of concrete that seemed to hover in a universe of hazy blue. Nothing was visible beyond the barrier.

"Exactly what path is that?" I tried to keep my voice from shaking, and I wiped my palms on my trousers. I was still apprehensive, but the fact that Teaghue decided to talk to me was a little reassuring.

"The path the former brother of my clan had mind to set you on."

"It happens to be my job," I told him. It was my ornery streak speaking, and I counted it a victory of self-preservation that I didn't say the first five things that came to mind.

Teaghue shook his head and I had the odd impression that, wholly by accident, I had actually said the right thing. "You believe we do this lightly? But it has come to this. We must ask you to cease, for your sake as much as ours."

His attitude was not quite what I had expected.

"Is this a threat?"

The creases in Teaghue's face made his expression deep and impenetrable. His voice was cold. "It is a warning. A warning undertaken at great risk and no little expense. Ossian's misstep has drawn too much attention already. Should you suffer the same fate, the resulting chaos would be impossible to undo."

"Who killed Ossian?"

Teaghue stepped back and shook his head. "Do not ask that question."

I stepped forward. "Why?"

"You will draw *his* attention."

"Who?"

I was leaning over to talk to him, and with no warning, Teaghue struck me. His leatherwork glove hit the side of my face hard enough to knock me over. I fell back, spitting blood and cradling a broken lip.

"*Do not ask that question!*" Teaghue was obviously pissed, but there was an undercurrent there, one of very deep fear. I began to understand something—the dwarves were shilling for someone. It wasn't the dwarves who killed off Ossian, it was the Mr. Big who was running things. Ossian's attempt at contacting me made sense then; he wasn't turning against his clan so much as trying to get at Mr. Big.

I rubbed my mouth and looked at Teaghue. "If you tell me what's going on, I might be able to help."

Teaghue just shook his head.

I kept prodding. "Ossian must have thought so . . ."

"Ossian was a fool. Mazurich was a fool." Teaghue stepped up to me and grabbed my collar, and for the first time since we started the dialogue, I feared for my life. "And you are a fool, Mr. Maxwell. There are forces here you cannot contain and you would loose them on you and yours. The clans chose their path long ago, and turning back now would only destroy everything. Leave the authors of the Thesarch in the shadows."

"What do you mean?"

Teaghue backed to the edge of the circle. "We have done what good by you we can. Any further would do you ill." He muttered something and the blue around us dissolved, leaving me nearly blind in sudden darkness.

"Wait!" I said, getting to my feet again.

From a distance I heard Teaghue respond, "Abandon your path, Mr. Maxwell, it will only bring you sorrow."

Afterward, everything was quiet.

I stood and let my eyes adjust to the gloom. For a while it seemed that the rest of the world was reluctant to reveal itself. Slowly, as I listened, I started to hear the wind and blowing snow around the bridge, a distant siren, a lone car crossing the bridge on the deck above me.

When I could see well enough to feel safe taking a step, everyone was gone. The only sign of my strange interview was a white circle on the concrete, and a quintet of black candles outside its perimeter.

I looked at the circle on the ground and knelt by it. It echoed, on a larger scale, the circle drawn around the body of Ossian Parthalán. It was probably a stupid thing to do, but I ran my finger through the white crystals marking the circle, and touched it to my tongue.

Salt.

CHAPTER THIRTEEN

I TAKE A STEP *forward, naked, bleeding, and sliding on my own blood.*

I am thrown back as a quartet of horsemen erupt from the Portal. Upon the pale horse that tramples me, I see a skeleton wrapped with raw flesh stitched together with steel wire.

The figure of Death leans toward me, opens its mouth, and in it I hear the death rattle of Ossian the dwarf.

I turn and see the dwarf, spread-eagled and mutilated, lying on a vast mountain of salt. The dwarf's blood seeps into the grayish-white crystals, turning them orange, then crimson.

Live dwarves work at the base of the mountain, shoveling the bloodstained crystals into ore carts. They are all shackled to a large chain that is bolted to the base of a massive throne. I grab one and see the face of Teaghue.

"What are you doing?" I ask.

"It must be fed!" he says.

"What must be fed?"

The dwarf points his shovel at the throne.

*I look, and the goat-faced Devil looks directly at me. Reaching out with a clawed fist, he says, **"Behold the cost of defying me!"***

The Devil opens his fist and I see . . .

I sat bolt upright in my bed, my whole body clammy from the sweats, my heart racing. I didn't remember what I had seen. I didn't want to remember.

I think I knew . . .

My phone rang.

I turned and looked at the handset, sitting in its cradle. It was still dark outside, and the little red LED cast an infernal glow over the whole bedroom. It blinked slowly with the insectile buzz, giving me intermittent views of my apartment, still devastated by the law enforcement invasion last night.

I don't get premonitions, but I didn't want to answer the phone. I sat in my bed and stared at it as the clock next to it blinked 6:01 AM at me.

It stopped. I don't know why, but I'd been holding my breath.

I slowly exhaled. If it were important, they'd leave a message.

The way my heart was racing, there was no way I was getting back to sleep. I got up and stretched.

The phone rang again.

"Oh, hell,"

I reached down and grabbed it. "Hello?"

"Kline? Thank the Goddess. I've been trying to reach you—"

She sounded severely stressed out, but I wasn't in a

very forgiving mood. "Nina, it's six in the morning and I've only had three hours of sleep. Can this wait?"

"No, you're in danger. You can't let your daughter come to Cleveland."

"Look, me and my ex have dealt with that—"

"I've found out . . ." She trailed off.

"Found out what?"

"I can't over the phone. It's too dangerous."

"What's too dangerous?"

"Don't ask me any questions. Come to my house, where it's safe to talk."

"Nina, you have to tell me—" The receiver clicked and I was talking to a dial tone.

I rubbed my chin where Teaghue had hit me. I still tasted blood when I sucked on my lip. In Nina's protests, I had heard an echo of the dwarf: "*Do not ask that question.*"

What could be so dangerous that to even ask about it was threatening?

Given the past three days, I couldn't readily dismiss Nina's warning. I just thanked God that Sarah wasn't going to be showing up today.

However, I almost called Margaret just to make sure. The only thing that stopped me was the fact it was three in the morning on the coast. Calling now would take concerned parenting to a passive-aggressive extreme.

So I didn't call.

I should have.

Instead, I turned on the light and surveyed the damage. "*Real* glad you're staying home, baby," I whispered.

Between the Feds and the local cops, the place had been devastated. Every drawer and closet had been opened, the contents piled at random on the furniture and the floor. The furniture had all been pulled away from the walls, cushions removed and stripped, and the less said of the kitchen the better.

I was in as bad shape as my condo. I had slept in my clothes, which were dotted with dime-sized splatters of blood from my busted lip. I stood up and went into the wreckage of my bathroom, hoping for enough unmolested toiletries to clean myself up.

West 25th and Vega was probably a decent neighborhood before the Depression. Now it was just one of those odd urban corners of Cleveland that gentrification and economic recovery had yet to reach. Vega itself was easy to miss—it was a one-way street that sat right on top of the I-90 on-ramp. Nina's house faced the Interstate.

I would have thought a full-time staffer would have been able to afford better.

Nina's address wasn't as run-down as its neighbors. The windows had glass, the paint had been done in the last quarter century or so, and the wrought-iron fence around the property was intact and relatively new.

Squinting through the blowing snow, you could almost ignore its neighbors and imagine how it looked when this area was upper middle class.

She met me at the door and pulled me inside. She

looked as bad as she'd sounded on the phone. She wore jeans and a T-shirt, her eyes were red, her hair frizzy and yanked back in a severe ponytail. She looked more strung out than I felt, and I wondered if she'd had any sleep at all last night.

"I need to talk to you," she said as she pulled me into the house. I didn't get much of a look at the place. Victorian decor, lots of hanging fabric, lots of plants, the smell of incense.

"What about?"

"Shhh . . ."

She pulled me up a flight of stairs, past framed portraits of Buddha and Krishna, past a little statue of Shiva dancing, and into one of the upstairs bedrooms.

I stumbled in a few steps as she closed and bolted the door. She hung an amulet on the doorknob and said, "There."

Her voice echoed in the windowless room.

"Mind telling me what's going on?"

The room was empty. No furniture, no carpet, only a bare bulb in a light socket in the ceiling. Even the closet door was gone, leaving the closet an empty niche in one corner of the room.

On the hardwood floor was a large circle of glyphs drawn in a cursive feminine hand. "We should be safe in here," Nina said.

"Safe from what?"

Instead of answering, she pulled a tarot card out of her pocket and handed it to me. *The Devil* . . .

"What is this?" Fragments of my nightmare came to

mind, looking at the card. The massive stone throne, the dwarves chained to its base.

"Behold the cost of defying me!"

"The visions are worse," Nina said to me. "They keep coming. They're warning you . . ."

"Warning *me*? What do you mean?"

Nina grabbed me. "They're *your* visions. Now, you're seeing them yourself. I saw them first because I'm sensitive, and I work close to you."

I backed up and shook my head. "Whoa, Nina, I'm no seer. I'm the most thoroughly mundane man you'll ever meet. I normally don't even report on the stuff."

She stared at me, "You've seen them."

I swallowed and looked down at the card.

"The Oracle can reach anyone, and being exposed to high concentrations of mana can bring on a sensitivity . . ."

"I haven't been . . ."

Bullshit, Kline. The dwarf mailed you a package of salt intense enough to throw Kawata's spectrometer out of whack. That ring at the Nazgûl probably wasn't cornstarch, and you tasted a sample of what the dwarves were using last night, you Brainiac. God himself only knows what kind of power was flowing through Magetech corporate headquarters . . .

I must have zoned out because Nina was shaking me. "Did you hear what I said?"

"What?"

"You can*not* let your daughter come here. Not before the Tower falls."

The Tower? I hadn't seen that yet.

"Fine, fine." I held up my hands.

"What?"

"I've told you, it's under control. We've already postponed her visit."

Nina's face went white. "She *was* going to . . ."

"One o'clock flight this afternoon."

"So close . . ." She turned away from me and started shaking.

"It's all right, we bumped her trip."

She kept shaking her head. "No."

I put a hand on her shoulder. "It's all right."

She spun around and said, "No, it isn't. *Call her.*"

"What?"

"Call her and tell her not to come."

"What is this, Nina? What does my daughter have to do with it?"

"She won't be safe as long as he—"

She stopped talking and the only sound was the house creaking and settling around us.

"As long as who? What?" I looked around. "We went over this yesterday. You said you discovered something. What was it?"

She stepped away from me, shaking her head. "No." She looked up at the corners of the room. The creaking was getting worse. Small trails of dust drifted down from the ceiling. It suddenly began to feel very warm in the house.

Nina's muscles went tense and her eyes rolled back in her head.

"Nina?" I reached for her.

Bad move.

My hand touched her shoulder and I felt a shock as if someone laid a two-by-four across my face. I slammed all the way backward into the far wall, cracking the plaster and bruising my kidneys.

"Annoying little bitch."

The voice coming out of Nina's throat was deep, masculine, and somehow, familiar.

The room darkened as the single light bulb began to fail. The light turned red as the glyphs on the floor burst into flame. *"Maxwell is mine, and you cannot keep me from him."*

I tried to push myself upright, but I felt a spasm of pain in my lower back and my legs slid out from under me. "Who are you?" I managed through clenched teeth.

"You know who I am. I am the answer to your question."

"What have you done to Nina?"

"Only accepted her invitation."

"Show yourself."

The laugh was inhuman and soul wrenching. *"I will show myself to you soon enough, when you come begging to serve me."*

"Let her go."

The thing laughed again, and the room was plunged into darkness as the flaming glyphs died out. The light-bulb flickered back on in time for me to see Nina collapse on the charred protective circle.

"Shit." This time I managed to get myself up on my hands and knees to get over to her. She was breathing okay, and my rudimentary knowledge of first aid allowed me to find a pulse.

"Nina? Can you hear me?"

She stared straight ahead, at the ceiling. I shook her shoulder gently. No response.

"God damn it."

I pulled out my cell phone and dialed 9-1-1.

Not wanting to deal with the Emergency Room, I didn't tell the paramedics about literally throwing my back out. I watched, more or less helplessly, as they examined Nina, and carried her out to a waiting ambulance. I called Columbia, knowing full well I'd get her voice mail on a Saturday, and left a message for her about Nina.

Then I called HR at the *Press*, hoping they had the right emergency contacts for her.

I didn't even know if she was married.

I sat in the Volkswagen for a long time before I could get my head around what had happened. This wasn't just Mazurich and a dead dwarf. Somehow this was tied to me, and my daughter.

It took a long time for Margaret to answer the phone.

"Hello?" Her voice was cracked and hoarse, I could tell that I hadn't woken her up. I heard someone in the background. I heard her stage whisper to someone, "It's her father."

I felt the bottom fall out of my stomach. "Margaret? What's wrong?"

"Kline, my God, I was going to call you—I'm still talking to the police."

No.

"What's the matter?"

She was whispering again, "No, he's my ex-husband, and he's in Cleveland."

"Margaret, what's the matter? Is Sarah all right? What happened?"

"We had a fight, a bad one . . ."

"Is she all right?"

"I think so, but—"

"But what?"

"She ran away."

My hand was shaking. This couldn't be happening. We had safely dealt with it.

Margaret was still talking. ". . .while I was asleep. I thought it was all settled. But she took the car. I don't know where she went. The police are here."

I felt like Macbeth watching the trees walking toward the rampart walls. "I know where she went," I whispered.

"What?"

"Send the cops to the airport."

"I don't understand. I canceled the flight myself. She couldn't—"

"Trust me," I said. "She's going to try and come here."

Margaret suddenly sounded suspicious. "How are you so sure?"

"Because that would be the absolutely worst thing that could happen."

"Kline?"

"Get the cops to check the airport. If we're lucky, the flight hasn't left yet. You can't let her come here."

"Now you're scaring me."

You should be scared.

"I have to check some things on my end here. Call me immediately once you find anything, okay?"

"She didn't tell you anything, did she?"

"I wish she had."

"I'll let you know."

"Thanks."

When I hung up, all I could think about was the last image from my nightmare; the Devil's hand opening, revealing the bloody, broken body of my daughter . . .

CHAPTER FOURTEEN

I FOLLOWED THE AMBULANCE to St. Vincent Charity Hospital. I had a desperate sick feeling that I was somehow responsible for what happened to Nina. When I came in asking about her, they stuck me in a little waiting room filled with hotel paintings, a phone, a box of tissues, and a Bible.

Great . . .

I called the *Press* again, but they hadn't had any luck contacting Nina's family. They'd already left several messages, but her only emergency contacts were her parents, who lived in Minnesota.

Another émigré to the exotic mana-soaked shores of Lake Erie.

I didn't know much about Nina's background, but I could guess at it. Mana likes ritual and pattern, and has a habit of infecting, or adapting to, existing codes and patterns. Anyone who had studied magic or the occult before the Portal opened had a leg up. A lot of people came here because their old magical studies suddenly had practical applications.

Nina had probably gone through the obligatory New Age experimentation in college. A little tarot here, a little cabalism there, some Golden Dawn everywhere . . .

Made me think of the students Dr. Shafran complained about.

I sat in a plaid lounge chair, picked up the house phone, and tried to call Dr. Shafran. I figured if anyone knew what the hell I might be dealing with, he'd be the guy.

No such luck. Of course he wasn't in the office. And I ran his voice mail out of tape three times trying to explain what I wanted. At the end of the third message, I tried to get a grip on myself.

"Okay," I said to myself, "panicking won't help anything. Act like a damn professional."

If the guy wasn't at work on Saturday, I'd get his home number.

Easier said than done.

The guy wasn't just absent from normal directory assistance, even the people I knew in the phone company couldn't pull a listing for him.

In the end, I needed to call Quint anyway.

"What you got for me?"

"Kline, your doctor has a long file. You want the long version or the short one?"

I looked up at the clock and shook my head. "I have time."

Magetech wasn't a public company, but the pile of money Quint was able to trace was two zeros beyond what Mazurich had been hiding. Magetech had more patents than a Catholic schoolgirl convention, and the guy's name was on every one.

However, for someone researching the effects of magic on the world, Dr. Pretorious located himself safely outside its influence. He bought a house in a golf community south of Columbus about three years ago and secluded himself there. I had an address, as well as the market value of the residence—seven figures, and it didn't start with a one.

After Quint had worked backward through Pretorious' employment history, and a background check that the CIA would call anal, I asked him, "Could you do a quick look up of another doctor for me?"

"Name?"

"Dr. Newman Shafran, he works at Case Western."

"Hmm. You shopping around, Kline? These guys are probably too old for you."

"I'm just looking for a home phone."

Quint made a melodramatic sigh. "If you insist. Give me a moment."

I heard typing, then a muffled curse. "Can you spell that name for me?"

I did.

"Give me a moment." Quint muttered something unpleasant. As he muttered, a doctor walked into the room.

"Hold on," I said to Quint, who wasn't listening. I looked up at my visitor. "How is she?"

The doctor was an Indian man about ten years younger than I was. "Medically she's in no danger at the moment. I understand you were present during the attack?"

I nodded, lowering the phone. "Is she awake?"

The doctor shook his head, "I'm sorry. She's unresponsive."

"What's the matter?"

The doctor sighed. "There's no physical damage. She has suffered feedback from some magical event. I need the exact history of what happened—"

"Can't you transfer her out of the Portal's influence?" I asked. That was what they did with her predecessor when he was infected with semiconscious tumors that started sprouting little eyes.

"That's not a trivial treatment decision. Without analysis of the enchantment binding her, the effect of taking her out of a mana-dense area could be unpredictable. Can I have that history?"

I gave him what I knew, which wasn't much.

"Thanks." He put his hand on my shoulder, "We're doing what we can."

It didn't make me feel better.

When he left, I heard a small tinny voice say, "You bitch!"

I picked up the receiver, "Quint, you still there?"

"Tell me, Kline, are you just trying to make my life interesting?"

"Pardon?"

"Dr. Newman Shafran? Home number? The man doesn't exist."

"What, I've talked to him . . ."

"No phone, no credit report, address a PO Box. I can't even find the university records to match his doctorate."

"I don't understand. He works at Case. He's published scientific papers."

"Sure, dozens—but I swear he walks off the campus and ceases to exist. If I didn't . . ." he trails off. "I am such an idiot."

"What?"

"I was going to say, 'If I didn't know better,' but, of course I don't know better, do I?"

"Know what?"

"The man's an émigré from the Portal. Of course, no birth certificate, no paper trail prior to a dozen years ago. Hell, even his publications don't go back more than a decade."

"But he has a doctorate?"

"Threw me, too. This will be a little weird, you want me to keep digging?"

I shook my head, feeling a little uneasy about Dr. Shafran. I couldn't believe the man was from the other side of the Portal. He seemed way too much of the world I lived in. But all that was beside the point anyway. I didn't need to be going off on tangents. "No, Quint, leave it for now. There's another man who's more important. The name's Simon Lucas . . ."

When I left the cell-phone-free bubble of St. Vincent's, I had missed half a dozen calls. All from Margaret.

I called her back from the parking lot. Once I was in the Volkswagen, out of the snow.

"Where have you been?"

"The hospital, I had to turn off my cell—"

"Are you all right?"

"I'm fine, it was a coworker. Did they find Sarah?"

"Kline, our daughter has a future as a con artist."

I leaned back in the seat. "I was right, wasn't I?"

"The police found my car in the airport parking lot. She used her boarding pass—the one we thought I canceled."

"Thought?"

It turns out that my daughter was nothing if not resourceful. Margaret had, in fact, changed the flight dates. But she had done it via e-mail, and apparently Margaret had never bothered to set the password on her e-mail. Sarah was able to look through all her e-mail and pull up confirmation numbers and credit card info—enough to actually place a phone call to the travel agent last night, undoing Margaret's changes.

Apparently, doing everything on-line made it even easier for Sarah to impersonate her mother, since the agent had never actually talked to Margaret.

Once her boarding pass was valid again, all Sarah had to do was slip out early enough to make the flight. By the time the cops had caught up to the missing car, the plane had already been boarded.

I shook my head. "What is she thinking?"

"I don't know, Kline."

"You have the itinerary? Any layovers?"

"The cops already asked, no. It's a direct flight."

"What does she expect me to do? She has to know I'd put her right back on the next flight out, even if there weren't—"

I was about to say *"doom-laden prophecies."*

"Weren't what, Kline?"

"A . . . a teenage susceptibility to self-delusion and denial. She really should have known better."

"Something else . . ."

"There's more?"

"She unplugged my alarm clock." She paused, and when I didn't immediately grasp the significance, she elaborated. "If I hadn't gotten up at four to go to the bathroom, if I had slept in, I might not have been able to get to you before the plane landed. She'll be there in less than two hours."

I exhaled.

"Well our little con artist is going to be lucky if I don't get my own ticket next to her on the way back."

Of course, Murphy's Law being what it is, the weather had to screw things up.

I was lucky to make it from St. Vincent's to Hopkins Airport in under an hour and a half. What had started as a light flurry managed to turn into a full-fledged blizzard before I had completely merged onto I-77 South.

Ten minutes before my daughter's plane was scheduled to arrive, I was just one of hundreds of people staring out the windows at Hopkins International Airport. Like everyone else, I was watching the sheets of white pounding the tarmac, and explaining to a cell phone just how the weather had screwed up everyone's life.

"Nothing?" Margaret said.

"No," I told her. "Pretty much every outbound flight's been canceled. I think I'm going to be lucky if they don't divert Sarah's flight to Akron or Columbus."

"That bad?"

"Bad enough that all the hotels around the airport were booked solid before I got here. I was lucky to get the Tower City Hilton."

"You couldn't just put her up in your condo like we originally planned?"

"Not a great idea, right now. Long story."

"It's what you're working on, isn't it? Are you getting death threats again?"

"In any case," I said, changing the subject, "our daughter has to know that things aren't business as usual. I'm not going to reward her by pretending this is okay. She's going to a hotel with me, and back out once the weather is clear."

"You're right," I heard her sniff over the phone. "I just can't help thinking we might have been too hard on her. It isn't like Sarah to do this—"

I know. "Suite 1123, Tower City Hilton. I called in the reservation when I was fighting this crap on the freeway."

"Okay," Margaret sounded uncertain. "I still wish she could stay with you."

"She *is* staying with me. It's a suite, two bedrooms."

"Look, that hotel must be expensive at the last minute. You should let me pick up part of the bill."

"Don't worry, I can afford it. If anything, we should take it out of Sarah's allowance."

"Kline?"

"What?"

"I know you're angry, but remember, she wanted to see you."

I rubbed my face. My jaw still hurt from where the dwarf had slugged me. "I know."

"Call me when her plane comes in?"

"Sure."

I hung up and looked up at the flight schedule. Twenty-minute delay so far.

"Sarah, what the hell were you thinking?" I whispered to myself as the delay rolled over to forty minutes.

CHAPTER FIFTEEN

W HEN SHE WALKED out the gate, I think she almost seemed surprised to see me.

"Dad?"

I walked up to her. "I think you have a bit of explaining to do, young lady."

"I tried to call you."

"Uh-huh, so you resort to car theft and fraud?"

"She wasn't going to let me come!"

I frowned. "Don't take that tone." I took the bag she
was carrying. "Did you check anything? Do we need to
go to baggage claim?"

"No."

"Then come on, let's get back to my car before the
weather gets any worse."

She nodded and followed me through the terminal.
After a few minutes she said, "I was looking forward to
this trip for a year, then she said I couldn't go . . ."

"*We* said you couldn't go. Your mother does talk to
me, you know. We bumped your visit to January be-

cause you needed to cool your jets for baiting your mother."

"It wasn't fair after planning—"

I stopped and turned to face her. "Do you have any idea what you just did? This wasn't breaking curfew, or pushing your mother's buttons. You broke the law, young lady. If your mother and I were more estranged than we are, I would be counted as an accessory. The only reason you aren't on a flight back to California right now is because there aren't any. I'd take you to a Greyhound station if I could trust you not to bolt at the first rest stop."

"Dad?" she was starting to tear up.

I sighed. "You have no conception how disappointed I am in you right now."

The floodgates were open now, and she pulled out the A-bomb of emotional blackmail. "I just wanted to see you, Dad. It just got so bad I had to go."

Uh-huh, you have the mother from hell.

"Yeah, I'm sure." I put my hand on her shoulder. "Well, lucky for you, you're going to have about twenty-four hours to get over it before I can send you back."

By the time we got to the exit, I realized that Sarah was not dressed appropriately. She wore jeans, a short-sleeved blouse, and a little leather jacket that existed solely to be a fashion accessory.

I tried offering her my trench coat, and she just folded her arms and said, *"I'm okay!"*

But even as she shook her head, I could see her staring out the glass at the layers of white falling down on the parking lot. She probably hadn't seen snow in person since she was five.

"You really need to wear something heavier than that. Did you pack something?"

"I'll be okay."

I bit my tongue. I knew enough to realize how easily a detail like appropriate winter wear might have been lost in the midst of the apocalyptic decision for her to come here.

She looked up at me. "You know, I saw a fashion show on satellite and they had a designer here who makes these killer jackets. It moves, like it's alive, and it changes color to whatever you think of . . ."

Great, and how much does that cost? "Honey, I don't think we're going to go shopping. Besides, you couldn't take something like that back home. It wouldn't work outside the influence of the Portal, and if it's heavily enchanted, leaving the influence of mana would probably destroy it."

I pushed through the door into the blizzard.

"W–well. If I got anything l–like that, you'd keep it safe for me? T–till I came back?"

"I said we're not going—" I looked at her, and saw eyes red from crying. I couldn't be a hard ass anymore. "Sure, honey."

I told myself that she was going to be safely in my sight from now up until I put her back on a plane home.

"D–Dad?"

"Yeah?"

"Give me your j–jacket."

I set down her bag and pulled off my trench coat and draped it over her shoulders. Doing that made it sink in exactly how much my girl had grown. I didn't feel distant from her, since we talked on the phone at least every other day, but I only actually saw her a few times a year.

Giving her my jacket made me realize that she was only a hair shorter than I was now. She could easily be one of the college interns at the *Press*—or a hostess at the bar where the old men of the paper went to talk about the interns without causing a hostile working environment.

Sarah must have heard me sigh.

"What is it?"

"Just thinking about work." I picked up her bag and gestured toward the lot. "I'm parked over there."

"Oh, wow, is that a dwarf?"

I silently thanked God that her hands were too busy holding my coat on her shoulders for her to point. She was looking over at a taxi stand where a cab was idling, the driver waiting for a fare.

"Don't stare . . ."

It couldn't be, could it?

Cabs in this town were evenly divided between Jamaicans, Arabs, and dwarves—and no, I don't know why Jamaicans drive cabs in Cleveland, but they have since before the Portal opened. So we're at the airport, a dozen cabs lined up, of course there'd be dwarves.

It was pushing it to assume I really recognized this dwarf. No way this was Samanish Thégharin, I was just being paranoid . . .

Our eyes locked and I told myself that I had only seen a bad digital photo on a hack license. That and the back of his neck.

The dwarf in the cab smiled at me.

Shit.

"Dad, you were telling *me* not to stare."

The cab pulled away, without a fare. He seemed to make a point of driving right past us, as if Mr. Thégharin wanted me to know for certain who he was.

"Sorry, just happens that I know him." The sense of dread and urgency fell on me redoubled. I grabbed Sarah with my free arm and led her toward my car. It was an effort to keep from breaking into a run.

"*You* know dwarves?"

"Only a couple. I was just surprised to see him here." I tried to push the conversation away from Mr. Thégharin. "I know quite a few more elves."

"Yeah?"

"There're a few in the police department. They're an interesting bunch."

The drive back was agonizingly slow, because of the weather. Sarah was obviously disappointed. I guess, even under parental house arrest, she'd expected to at least *see* something of the mystic kingdom known as Cleveland, Ohio. And after all her planning, her first views were little more than swirling white and the occasional ODOT snowplow trying to keep the Interstate clear.

I was torn between thinking it served her right, and feeling sorry for her.

She made up for it by peppering me with questions, some of which I'm pretty sure she already knew the answers to. I guess it was her way of having a conversation with me, without talking about how she got here, or how much trouble she was in.

So most of the drive I spent answering questions about everything from the Portal to the local unicorn population.

"Fact is, most of the legitimate mages in town are employed by the government."

"So what do they do?"

"Mostly? They protect the public from the mages who aren't. There's a large black market around for all sorts of nasty enchantments. One of the priorities, ever since the Portal opened, is to try to keep a step ahead of the bad guys. From mass-producing protective charms to keep buildings and vehicles secure, to tracking down counterfeiters."

"Counterfeiters?"

"With the right materials, even a half-assed mage can easily make a physical copy of any small inanimate object. Such as a DVD or a twenty-dollar bill."

"There's a lot of that going on?"

"One of many reasons for a strain between the federal and local governments here. We're number two as far as IP piracy goes, right after China." I shrugged. "Fortunately, as long as the good guys catch the property before it leaves the Portal's influence, a forensic mage can detect the history of the material."

"What if it does leave?"

"Then you have a problem."

"I never really thought about that . . ." She looked out at the snow.

"Well the movies and TV shows don't usually focus on the run-of-the-mill stuff."

"What about monsters? Griffins, dragons, that sort of thing? Are there a lot around, do you see any?"

I almost winced when I thought about griffins. I shook my head. "There're only about thirty dragons around, and they tend to be too busy to accommodate journalists."

"What are they busy *doing?*"

"Nothing particularly sinister—not unless you're a left-wing Democrat." I looked across and saw Sarah's blank expression and elaborated. "Dragons are fundamentally capitalists. They're into money and power, and they're rather adept at acquiring it. They came through the Portal, set up shop, incorporated, and started buying companies."

"You're kidding."

"You're picturing a dragon sitting on a mound of gold and gems? These creatures are intelligent enough to know that a pile of stock portfolios and board memberships mean a lot more in twenty-first century America, even if they can only legally sign contracts and own property in the state of Ohio. They may be huge and menacing, and breathe fire, but an army of well-financed lawyers can be a lot more intimidating. And can venture a lot farther afield."

"You met a dragon, didn't you?"

I nodded. "Theophane. She bought out the top few floors of the BP Building."

"What was that like?"

"Intimidating . . ." I talked on for a while about my meeting with the dragon Theophane, two years ago. That was the last time my job had gotten me involved deeply in nonhuman politics. And while I kept my voice light, I couldn't help but be apprehensive.

That time, when I dug into the history of elves and the death of one supposedly immortal dragon, I almost got myself killed. And the mess that resulted ended up killing a half dozen others, including a fellow reporter, and Caledvwlch's predecessor as head of the Special Paranormal Unit—the latter decapitated by an eight-foot-tall stone gargoyle in the middle of my living room.

Not the best time of my life to be thinking about right now. The last couple of days held uncomfortable echoes, and it made me realize that I didn't want my daughter anywhere around here. Not now, maybe not ever.

Margaret was right.

Sarah was going back first thing in the morning, even if I had to drive to the Pittsburgh airport to get her out. As my paranoia worsened, I doubled back twice, just to make sure no dwarven taxicabs were tailing me.

When I finally felt safe, I took an exit and drove downtown on surface streets.

"Where are we going?"

"The Tower City Hilton."

Sarah frowned, squinting out at the office buildings flanking us. "I thought I was staying at your place?"

"You aren't vacationing, young lady. This is just to put you up until I get you on a flight back to your mother? Understand."

"But I thought, now that I was here—"

"Sarah, you didn't think, or you wouldn't be here."

She gave me the silent treatment as I checked us in. I didn't try to press her. In the end I was simply too relieved to have her with me, safe. The crap happening around me was just too threatening, enough so that I had the unprofessional urge to follow through on my threat to Margaret and book my own ticket back with her.

In the end, given the weather and the glut of outbound passengers, I was lucky to find one seat available on an outbound flight that was leaving anytime soon. I was really proud of myself when I found an 8:30 AM flight out of Akron. I reserved her a seat, somewhat fraudulently, with my *Press* AmEx card.

When I hung up, Sarah was leaning against the doorframe to her bedroom, staring at me.

"Dad, I'm sorry . . ."

I looked at her, and my dad sincerity detector wasn't quite working. I sighed. "You really need to think things out before you act, honey."

"You don't understand—"

"Sit down, Sarah."

She dropped into a lounge that faced me. "Dad—"

I held up my hand. "Let me give you the obligatory parental speech first." I leaned forward. "I'm not going to tell you that you aren't old enough to make decisions for yourself. That's the nature of the age you're at. This is the point where you make decisions that will affect the rest of your life."

"Dad—"

"Before you pull stunts like this, you need to decide if you're willing to live with the consequences. If your mother was the troll you make her out to be, it could have been a cop picking you up at the airport. Car theft, credit fraud, flight across state lines. Felony convictions don't make your life easier."

"Come on, Mom wasn't going to—"

"Call the police? Who do you think found the car at the airport? To be honest, if she went as far as pressing charges, I don't think I could blame her."

"Oh." She looked down at the carpet.

"For the life of me I can't understand why you seem to go out of your way to antagonize your mother."

"You don't live with her," Sarah said.

"No," I said, "and in less than a year you don't have to either."

"Dad, I feel as if she's trying to wall off a whole part of my life. Part of *me*."

"What do you mean? We talk almost every day—"

She slammed the arm of the chair she sat in and stood up, shouting at me. "Damn it, Dad! This isn't about that! It isn't about you."

I leaned back. I was speechless for a moment, allowing my ego to absorb the statement. Not that I was dad of the year here, but I had been thinking . . .

"What is it about, then?"

Sarah shook her head, and I could see the tears starting. "I'm sorry. This isn't your fault." She ran to her room and slammed the door.

"Sarah?" I walked up to the door. "What is it?"

I could hear her crying.

I hesitated a moment and opened the door. She was splayed out, facedown on the bed. I could hear her say something like, "I'm sorry."

"What is the matter? Why did you run away here? Is there something at home I don't know about?" At this point I was visualizing nightmare scenarios that had been forbidden territory until now. "Is someone abus—"

She raised her head, sucking in an offended breath. "My God, Dad!"

"What am I supposed to think?"

She flopped back down on the bed. "I was born here," she whispered.

"What?"

"Mom doesn't understand. This all is part of my life, who I am."

I sat down on the foot of the bed. "So you run away here?"

"Don't I have a right to know where I come from?"

"Maybe there's a better way to deal with that, and your mother."

She sighed. "Maybe."

I placed a hand on her shoulder, trying to comfort her. She shrugged me away.

"Can I have some time alone?"

"Okay." I stood up. "Let me know if you want to talk."

"Uh-huh."

Apparently, she didn't want to talk. After about fifteen minutes of quiet sobbing, the jet lag caught up with her and she started snoring. I went in and took her shoes off and threw a blanket over her.

I had no right to, but I felt a little like crying myself. Not happy news when you find out that you're not the epicenter of your little girl's world any more. For all my attempts to be practical and realistic, the fact was that I still saw her as a twelve-year-old girl.

It just never occurred to me that anyone could feel that sort of connection to this place. The whole situation seemed too new for this to be anyone's ancestral homeland . . .

Sarah was what, five years old, when the Portal opened?

Another five years, there'd be a whole generation that had been born since the Portal. What kind of point-of-view shift would that make?

Case was going to need another Dr. Shafran or three.

These were the thoughts running though my head when my cell phone rang, a little after seven.

"Maxwell," I barked into the phone.

"Well, you like to get your money's worth, don't you?"

"Quint? You got me something about Simon Lucas?"

"Mr. Lucas is a busy little beaver. He's one of those guys that get a one-dollar salary on the books and gets paid options up the yin-yang."

"Worth a lot?"

"I counted easily over 150 publicly traded companies where his investment is into eight figures or higher."

"150 . . ." I tried to do the math in my head, but it had been a long day.

"All seems aboveboard. Including his immigrant status."

"Immigrant?"

"Yes, another one from the other side of the Portal."

"Great. It seems that Magetech has been very good to people."

"Mr. Lucas seems to have done the best, though he doesn't seem to figure largely in any paperwork Magetech had filed with any government agency. This guy is easily the highest compensated executive in the state of Ohio."

Pretty good for someone who was only close to the top of the Org chart, and one of the only humans in the rarefied upper atmosphere of the Magetech hierarchy. All the higher executives, and the board, were dwarven.

Oddest of all was where Mr. Lucas listed his residence.

All his financial records that Quint had been able to access, including some tax forms released to the SEC, listed Simon Lucas' residence on Whiskey Island.

According to all the man's records, he resided in the middle of the dwarven enclave, where the mana was so dense that human beings couldn't work there without going mad . . .

CHAPTER SIXTEEN

I GOT MY WAKE-UP call at five in the morning, and I was relieved to look out the hotel window and see a clear sky. I figured we had more than enough time to make it down to Akron and have some sort of breakfast at the airport before I put her on the plane. I dressed quickly, skipping a shower and a shave, figuring to let Sarah have the run of a clean bathroom before we left.

Dressed, I steeled myself for a tearful argument and knocked on the door to her bedroom.

"Come on, Sarah. Wake up, we have a plane to catch."

She didn't answer me.

"Sarah?" I pushed the door open.

The bed was empty.

"Oh, no." I stepped in. She wasn't here. Neither was her bag. "Shit, you're kidding me. Sarah?"

I ran out and threw the door to the bathroom open. "Sarah?"

Nothing.

She wouldn't just walk out . . .

"Why not?"

How the hell could I be that stupid? She as much as told me that she was running away to Cleveland, not to her father. She'd done everything but come out and tell me she would bolt.

I ran out into the hall, dashing the hope that she had just stepped out of the room. I was in the elevator, halfway down to the lobby, when I realized that my car keys were gone.

Better and better.

I walked out of the elevator and through the lobby, looking for her. No sign. *Christ, she doesn't even have a winter jacket.*

I found the concierge by the Euclid exit. "Pardon me, did you see my daughter leave?"

"Pardon."

"My daughter, she's seventeen, blonde, probably wearing a leather—"

"Oh, yes, an hour ago, I directed her to the garage."

I ran to the garage, dialing the police as I went.

"Hello?"

Margaret yawned and I realized that it must be three in the morning on the coast.

"It's Kline," I said.

"Oh," she was too calm. She must have been too asleep to hear the stress in my voice. "Are you at the airport already?"

Yeah, she was expecting me to call, wasn't she?

I looked around, for a moment too numb to say anything. I was sitting on the rail where my Volkswagen had been parked. A pair of police cars was here, which was a bonus for your average runaway case. I was lucky in that I had one string that I'd pulled as hard as I could.

"Kline? You *are* at the airport."

"She did it to me, too . . ."

"What?"

"Right up to lifting my car keys."

"Oh, my God."

I shook my head. "I was an idiot. She came out and told me she thought she was missing part of her past—"

"Yes, you."

"No, Margaret, this isn't about me."

"What are you talking about?"

"She didn't bolt from the hotel because she was desperate to see me. She ran here because she has some weird idea that this city is part of her heritage."

"I don't understand what you're saying."

"She told me that she thought you were 'walling off part of herself.' I don't think she was planning to see me at all."

"Where would she go?"

"I don't know. Does she know anyone out here? Any boyfriends?"

"Kline?"

"This is serious. Our daughter has just stolen *another* car and now I have no idea where she could be going. She has to have left some sort of clue. Something on her computer, e-mail, letters, a diary?"

"What do you think—"

"I don't know what to think, but ransack her room and call me back when you find something— The police are here, I'll call you back."

"But—"

I cut her off as one of the strings I had pulled unraveled in front of me. Walking up the ramp of the parking garage, toward me and the two police cruisers, was the tall gangly form of Commander Maelgwyn Caledvwlch.

One of the hazards of name-dropping to a police dispatcher, the name in question might actually show up.

"Mr. Maxwell," he greeted me in his semi-Jamaican monotone.

"Commander Caledvwlch."

"I have become interested in your assessment of my priorities." He waved a long hand, encompassing the empty parking space and the pair of police cars. "I understand that your child removed your vehicle without your permission. But my understanding of human reasoning falls short when I discover that this requires SPU involvement. Can you enlighten me?"

I shook my head and put my cell phone away. "I got two answers for you, neither of them very good. Can we go somewhere private and talk?"

Caledvwlch took me to the back of a mostly-fiberglass minivan, which passed for an unmarked patrol car for the SPU elves. Not that any of them ever went undercover. It all had to do with headroom and iron content.

I eased into a seat with a groan and Caledvwlch managed to fold himself in next to me. I looked at him, the

alien angles of his face framed by a ruff of hair and con-
voluted pointed ears. He watched me with metallic eyes
with no visible iris or pupil. Behind the impassive expression I knew sat a sense of duty and fealty that made
a fourteenth-century Samurai look like an anarchist.

I didn't know how he'd react to a father who was just
freaking out and didn't know what else to do.

"The first answer," I looked at him. "Hell, it isn't one.
I know how police prioritize things in this town. Runaway—especially one an hour old—isn't going to make
it to the top of the list." I looked at Caledvwlch's face, no
reaction. "If I just let it go with my daughter swiping my
car, I'd be lucky if someone came and took a statement
within the next twenty-four hours."

"The human phrase, I believe, is, 'to light a fire under
someone's ass.'" He said it with no discernible emotion,
and I wondered if it was possible he was mocking me.

"I am part of your investigation, however tangential.
I just made sure everyone knew it."

Caledvwlch nodded and seemed to be lost in thought
a moment or two. Then he asked me, "There was an in-
cident, yesterday, with a colleague of yours."

I swallowed. I probably should have reported it to the
cops. "Yes, Nina Johannessen—"

"She is in a coma. Did you know that?"

"Yes, I told the doctors what I could . . ."

"She is a seer, correct?"

"Yes."

"Did she see something about your daughter?"

I looked at Caledvwlch as I wondered exactly how
much he knew. As usual, he didn't provide me any ex-

ternal clues. The elf would provide the play by play for the apocalypse with all the passion of a golf announcer.

"That was the other reason . . ."

I unloaded on Caledvwlch, probably the way any parent would unload on an available cop, even without any overt displays of sympathy. I didn't need his encouragement. I was prepared to hand everything I had over to him, however tangential, if it might have some distant relation to where my daughter might have gone.

I went over Nina's visions, the tarot cards, my nightmares, and how Nina said it was tied to my daughter. I told him about Nina's possession, and how whatever had taken control had the same voice as the Devil in my dreams.

"You should have reported that," Caledvwlch said quietly. "Possession of an unwilling victim is a first-degree felony."

"I know, but I called my ex after that, to check on Sarah, and that's when I found she'd slipped out of the house and got on a plane."

"You understand that you have just admitted to a criminal act?" Caledvwlch said. "At this time it is my duty to advise you of your rights."

"You're arresting me?"

"I am taking you to the station for a more formal questioning," Caledvwlch said. "A full statement now and I will not be prompted to take you in for failure to report a crime."

"What about my daughter?"

"Mr. Maxwell, as you informed the dispatcher, this is part of an ongoing SPU investigation."

* * *

Caledvwlch took me to an interview room only a few blocks away at police headquarters. While I'd suffered a few arrests in my career, I'd never been brought to the Special Paranormal Unit's interrogation room. Even when Caledvwlch "rescued" me from Blackstone, Caledvwlch just used a spare office to question me.

I didn't think it was a good thing that I now rated special treatment—and when a uniformed cop let me in, I was very glad that Caledvwlch hadn't felt the need to actually arrest me.

The room was constructed specifically to suit the needs of the Special Paranormal Unit, and those needs were, well, *special.*

First off, the room itself was designed like an operating theater, rather than a standard soundproof interrogation chamber—a cylinder with concave walls, with observers stationed behind one-way glass at the top of the room, looking down. The walls weren't layered in acoustical tile, but were concrete with gold symbols inlaid flush with the surface. When the foot-thick door shut behind me, the inlay formed multiple concentric circles ringing the wall from floor to ceiling.

In the center of the room was what looked like a dentist's chair. Looking at the heavy straps, I was rather glad that they didn't have me sit there. I got to sit at a more normal office chair that was one of a half dozen places at a metal table that formed a donut around the chair of honor.

When I sat, I said to Caledvwlch, "Nice setup you have here."

"Sometimes we must conduct difficult interviews."
He waved at a plainclothes human who had joined us in
the room. "Dr. Singh will be observing here, and may
have some questions of his own."

Dr. Singh was a bald, white-mustached Indian man.
He nodded a slight acknowledgment to me. I wondered
who he was. I guessed that he was a forensic mage of
some sort.

Caledvwlch sat down as well, "Shall we take your
statement from the beginning?"

"Well, I talked to Nina—"

"Ossian Parthalán," said Dr. Singh. "Begin with his
phone call."

"What?" I asked. "I went over this already, my
daughter—"

"From the beginning," Caledvwlch said.

I looked from one to the other. "This has nothing to
do with my daughter. It's the damn dwarves again.
Damn it, we need to find her. What happened with
Nina—"

"Mr. Maxwell," Caledvwlch raised his voice only
slightly, but it was enough to cut me down in my tracks.
The elf had held a gun on me before, but he had *never*
raised his voice.

Caledvwlch stared at me with those cold metallic
eyes, "This has everything to do with your daughter.
Now, *from the beginning*."

He didn't need to provide me with any more encouragement.

I ran down everything, step by step, since Ossian
Parthalán called me to question why Councilman

Mazurich shot himself. What scared me was when they had me back up and asked questions about my daughter.

"You received a call from California that evening," Caledvwlch said.

"Yes, Sarah." I repeated the conversation as I remembered it.

"Did she say anything odd," asked Dr. Singh. "Possibly about her trip here?"

I shook my head.

"Did she ever mention contact with anyone from Cleveland?" Dr. Singh frowned.

"No . . ."

Caledvwlch continued. "So you examined this envelope, describe what you found."

But Sarah . . . I looked at both of them and couldn't tell if I should push it or not. How the hell could my daughter be involved in some sort of conspiracy here. It didn't make sense.

"This is the first time you've been contacted by dwarves?"

"Yes . . ."

Unless it wasn't Sarah.

What if it was me?

Blackstone had mentioned a connection to California. *Thor's Hammer* had a car in the shop with California plates. Dr. Shafran had said that dwarves, unlike elves or dragons, would be able to travel beyond the influence of the Portal, and he had even mentioned California.

She clearly wanted to come to Cleveland for reasons

beyond visiting me. And Dr. Singh had practically re-peated my own question to Margaret verbatim.

Did she have contact with anyone from Cleveland?

What was it she said in the parking lot? *"You* know dwarves?"

"You took pictures at *Thor's Hammer?"* asked Dr. Singh.

"They were garbage . . ."

"Yes, from the mana saturation." Dr. Singh looked at me. "Have you erased those pictures?"

"No."

"May I see them?" He held out his hand.

I cued the pictures up on the screen and handed my cell phone over. Caledvwlch soldiered on while Dr. Singh looked at my mana-spoiled pictures. He grilled me on my visit to the *Nazgûl* and when I mentioned tak-ing pictures there, too, Dr. Singh looked up at me.

"Yeah, right after the others, just as useless."

Even as I recounted the story, I kept fixating on what Sarah had said.

"You know dwarves?"

It was exactly the way a teenager might phrase *"You* listen to hip-hop?" Or *"You* play video games?" All the inflection was on the bizarre concept that someone as old and out of touch as I was might have contact with something hip and new.

Dwarves?

What if Ossian Parthalán had more than one reason for contacting me?

Paranoia was running away with me. I had exactly zero evidence that my daughter had contacted any dwarves, ever. She was just upset. She'd come back within a few hours. All she wanted was to see this damn city . . .

Bullshit.

Even without the visions and Nina's collapse, I would have known that something was wrong. This wasn't how Sarah acted. Something serious had gone wrong with her life.

Caledvwlch walked me through my visit to Magetech, with Dr. Singh asking pointed questions about my blackout, and my catastrophic meeting with Nina. He grilled me on that, and on the subsequent arrival of my daughter, with no mercy. We went over what I remembered of each conversation over and over. Enough that I almost felt ready to break down the third time we went over my last drive with Sarah.

What kept me from losing it was the fact that Caledvwlch's questions about Sarah confirmed that he was operating under suspicions very similar to my own. He dwelled on her comments about the dwarf cab driver almost as much as I had.

When Caledvwlch drained me of just about everything I had, Dr. Singh stepped in. "You said you had nightmares, visions akin to what Mrs. Johannessen had told you about?"

"Yes."

"Describe them to me."

"What I remember . . ." I told him about Death galloping from the Portal, and the Devil enthroned above the dwarves.

Dr. Singh nodded and handed me my cell phone. "I

took the liberty of messaging these pictures to the Cleveland Police server. I think you might want to look at them again."

"Huh? They're just random . . ."

No.

They weren't random. My heart leaped in my throat as I recognized the landscape of my dreams. The swirling mirrored glass and mounted Death. The mountain of bloody salt twisted around Ossian's corpse.

What did Dr. Shafran say? *There's some slight evidence that such static is not wholly random, and is responsible for what some New Age victims refer to as the Oracle.*

"Your own visions, are they?" asked Dr. Singh.

I nodded, unable really to speak. I had scrolled to the last distorted image. In the final picture, the goat-faced Devil leered at me, holding something broken and bloody in his outstretched hand.

Oh, God . . .

It took a moment to notice, but the last picture had a date-stamp that placed it well after my shots at the *Nazgûl*.

I had taken a picture of the Devil while I was at Magetech.

CHAPTER SEVENTEEN

BY THE TIME CALEDVWLCH and Dr. Singh were done with me, it was already eleven. Caledvwlch and Dr. Singh disappeared into some authorized personnel only section of the SPU, cutting me loose in the lobby of Police Headquarters.

The first thing I did was call back to the Hilton in the vain hope that Sarah had come back while I'd been with the cops. No such luck. I did what I could to quiz the cops on the duty desk about where things were with finding my daughter, but somehow, once my daughter was involved, I had lost my ability to finesse information from people. The questions I pounded the cops with had all the subtlety of a kick to the groin.

"Do you know *anything?*"

Predictably, all I got were half a dozen ways to phrase: "Go home, we're working on it."

That, and the fact that no one had spotted my car yet, was all I got. As I calmed down, I was rational enough to be thankful that they didn't have anyone escort me out.

I walked outside, squinting in the daylight, and called for a rental car. I didn't want to deal with any more taxis, though the dwarf in question was nowhere in sight. I sat on a bench outside the police station, feeling worse than useless.

Damn it, Sarah, how could you do this to us?

As if cued, my phone rang. It was an unfamiliar number, but a California area code.

"Maxwell," I answered.

"Kline."

"Margaret?"

"Where are you?"

"Outside the police station waiting for a rental to show up. Where are you?"

"I'm with William Jackson. You don't know him, but he's the father of one of Sarah's friends."

"You found something?"

"I don't know. But she talked about Cleveland, and magic, with Beth, William's daughter. They actually talked about rites and rituals, and a lot of other stuff I don't understand. It scares me."

Christ, Sarah . . .

"They talked about forming a coven. Beth had hidden all these books about the cabala, the seal of Solomon— That doesn't make any sense, does it? They live in California."

"There's probably more of that going on there now than there was before the Portal opened. The Portal is the best recruiting tool these New Age types have ever had."

I kept remembering the pamphlet, "God's Plan or The Devil's Handiwork?" and Club *Nazgûl*. I've worked in this town enough to know the taxonomy of mages better than the pamphlet's author. I knew that a wiccan coven was spiritually on a completely different planet than a Satanist.

Somehow, when it was my daughter, I didn't find the thought at all reassuring.

"She was planning this for a long time," I said.

Of course she would want to go to a college around here. She was one of those people who wanted to be on Dr. Shafran's waiting list. My daughter wanted to be a mage. "Does Mr. Jackson have any idea where Sarah might have run off to?"

"No," Margaret said, "but Beth has had a history of trouble. She broke down when we confronted her."

"What did she say?"

"They were 'practicing,' they wanted . . ." Margaret broke up, couldn't go on.

"They wanted what?" I asked. "Were they going to move here?"

A male voice came through the phone, "Mr. Maxwell? I'm Bill Jackson, Beth's father."

"Yes, thanks for helping my wife—ex-wife," I rubbed my temple. "What did Beth tell you?"

"They wanted to emigrate."

I dropped the phone.

That had never occurred to me. Even though that

was the reason for the Portal, to travel between here and Ragnan.

For all the people that came through to our side, at least two of our own went the other way.

Even though the Feds tightened up immigration to our side of the Portal, thanks to an elimination of the worst price gouging by the city, there wasn't a shortage of people who had decided they didn't want to deal with this particular universe anymore.

Given the narrow aperture, it was rare to ever hear anything from our ex-pats again.

No, it didn't make sense. She'd need a passport, over two grand for passage . . .

And she turned eighteen next year and wouldn't need to have us sign off on a passport, or even tell us about it. If she was a student here, she might just buy a ticket with student loan money. Hell, Visa practically threw free credit at college students. And, when it came to that, over the past two days my daughter had shown no reluctance to steal credit card numbers.

Why?

Why would she want to abandon her mother, me, the entire planet, for a place that was literally medieval? I didn't know a lot of what was currently going on on the other side of the Portal, but of what I did hear, the words egalitarian, progressive, tolerant, and democratic were just the first on a long list of descriptive terms that did not apply.

Maybe I was just close enough to see the warts.

"Mr. Maxwell."

I dug my phone out of the snow with numbed fingers. "Yes, sorry."

"Margaret said you wanted to know if they had talked to anyone from there?"

"Cleveland? Yes."

"Beth says that someone visited their coven circle—a couple of times. A short old man, she thinks his name is Parthalán?"

"Parthalán." I whispered.

A pair of cars drove up in front of me. The first car was a sky-blue Solara. The driver got out and approached me. "Mr. Maxwell?"

"Mr. Maxwell?" Jackson echoed in my ear.

The driver walked up, keys in hand. "I'm from Enterprise—"

"I have to go," I said into the phone, "but do me a favor and ask Beth for everything she remembers about Mr. Parthalán."

"I hope you find Sarah."

"So do I," I said as I hung up.

"This is Dr. Newman Shafran, I'm not in right now . . ." I was getting sick of the doctor's voice mail. I decided that once I was done with Teaghue Parthalán, I was going to Case to hunt up the professor in person.

I sat in my rented Solara, parked about halfway up a cross street, just in sight of *The Dwarven Armorer*. The suit of plate still stood posed in mid-stroke, making me wonder how often Teaghue cleaned the salt off of it.

Shafran's voice mail beeped at me.

"Dr. Shafran. This is Kline Maxwell, and I need to

know *exactly* what you've heard about dwarves going to California."

I hung up.

"*Parthalán,*" I whispered.

He knew. He had to have known. It didn't matter if the dwarf that visited my daughter's coven— *My daughter's coven? Wrap your long-distance parenting head around that one.* In the end it didn't matter if that dwarf was Ossian, Teaghue, or some dwarf as yet unnamed. It strained coincidence to the breaking point to believe that it wasn't all connected.

Teaghue was the one dwarf still living who had made an effort to contact me. Even if it was a half-assed attempt to frighten me off a story.

I intended to return the favor.

My timing, however, sucked.

Before I'd even opened the door on my Solara, a trio of black Chevy vans shot by my car, skidding to a stop in front of Teaghue's shop, splattering gray slush all over his front display.

The doors slid open before they had fully come to a stop, and a dozen men in full Kevlar riot gear poured out of the two leading vans. As they rushed the building, I saw the letters "FBI" emblazoned in bright yellow across their backs.

Above us, a helicopter swooped down and started circling so low that I swore I could feel the downdraft from the rotors.

Ahead, beyond the vans barricading the shop, I heard the sound of wood breaking, then a small explosion. I couldn't see much past the vans, but white smoke began drifting up from the building. The door on the last van slid open, and Blackstone stepped out, talking on a cell phone. He stepped around the rear of the van, looking past the three vans at a commotion I couldn't quite see.

"You bastard."

In the best of times I didn't like Blackstone. Now he was stepping all over the one lead I had to where my daughter might be.

I jumped out of my car and started running toward him. I can honestly say I had no clue what I was planning to do when I got there. Events made up my mind for me, just before I reached him.

Something exploded out of the scrap heap next to Teaghue's shop. I saw a flash of motion, and then something large flew toward me, Blackstone, and van number three. I dove, knocking Blackstone out of the way, as a V-8 engine block slammed into the front driver's side of the van. The entire front end of the vehicle crumpled inward in a shower of safety glass. The whole van rocked back on its tires, the impact driving it back a foot or two.

"What the—" Blackstone started talking, spitting slush out of his mouth. I couldn't hear the rest of what he said, because gunfire erupted from every corner around me. It came from inside the building, and from all three vans.

The focus of all the gunfire was another zombie. The same wire-sewed flesh that had been in my nightmares. Like the thing that had wrecked *Thor's Hammer*, it was wearing a trench coat. It could have been the same one.

While bullets slammed into and through the thing's body, it picked up a wheel rim from the debris around it. It threw the rim like a lethal Frisbee, catching one of the armored Feds full in the face.

Blackstone had completely forgotten about me. He pulled himself up behind one of the vans and grabbed a walkie-talkie. *"Use the phosphor rounds! Burn the thing!"*

Phosphor rounds? That sort of thing was military ordnance, not standard SWAT equipment, even for federal counterterrorism units.

The gunfire stopped and I was able to hear a hollow *thump*. The sound was followed by a glowing trail that ended in zombie-boy's chest cavity.

The trench coat went up like a sheet of flash paper and the skeleton stood there, backlit from inside. The smell was horrible, like a cannibal hibachi grill.

However, zombie-boy wasn't easily discouraged. It actually reached inside itself, fished out the glowing round, and threw it back toward the building. Its throw was short and I could see several half melted wires dangling from its throwing arm.

Several more *thumps*.

I glanced back at the building, and saw a short silhouette climbing out of a window on the side opposite the scrapyard.

"Teaghue!"

I didn't even wait to see if anyone paid attention to me. I got up and ran.

CHAPTER EIGHTEEN

TEAGHUE RAN STRAIGHT for an alley, and I was right behind him. Above me I heard the helicopter.

I dodged trash bins and old tires as he led me behind several old industrial buildings. In the half minute or so it took me to catch up with him, I had time for one main thought.

The guy makes weapons for a living and is strong enough to coldcock me bare-handed. What do I do when I catch up with him?

Answer? *Fight dirty.*

Teaghue ran up a frost-covered pile of broken concrete, and jumped onto a chain-link fence ahead of me. He managed to grab the twelve-foot-high fence almost halfway up. He started scrambling faster than anyone with his length of limb had a right to. I ran up the concrete after him, knowing I had no hope of scaling the fence or making it over the barbed wire on top.

So, instead, I reached down and grabbed a chunk of

concrete the size of a two-liter bottle. It was so cold it numbed my fingers.

I brought it down as hard as I could on the back of Teaghue's right hamstring.

He cursed something vile and guttural in his native tongue as he slammed into the fence. I brought my concrete-laden fist up into where a human kidney would be.

"What are you doing? You misbegotten bastard!"

He was hanging only by his hands now, scrambling to get a foothold. I jumped up and struck him on the side of his head.

He fell off of the fence, rolling, stunned, facedown, at the base of the pile of concrete. I fell down on him, before he could recover. I put my knee down in the small of his back and stopped with a jolt that sent the concrete sailing from my hand.

It had become slippery, mostly from my own blood. At this point, I didn't feel much from my gore-stained hand as I wrapped it in Teaghue's hair.

"Tell me where my daughter is."

"You don't know what you're doi—"

I slammed his face into the ice.

"Tell me where my daughter is!"

"You can't— *He* will kill us."

I pulled back on his hair while holding the back of his neck with my opposite forearm. *"I'll kill you."*

"No," Teaghue sputtered.

I slammed his face down again, hard enough that my wrist made unpleasant noises. I ignored the spasm of pain and repeated, *"Tell me where my daughter is!"*

"*He* has her!"

"Who?"

"The one I cannot name!"

"*Don't fuck with me!*" I was shaking, and if I had a gun, *I would* have killed him.

"No, he knows when you speak of him. There's no protection here. None. A thought could bring him—"

Teaghue choked and sputtered. I felt his muscles tense, and he began bucking against me as if he was having a seizure. I let go of his head, and he began slamming his own face into the pavement.

"Teaghue!"

I got off of him and rolled his body over. His back arched and he started groaning. The atmosphere around us darkened.

A bolt of energy arced from Teaghue to the fence, and I could smell an awful mixture of static and brimstone.

Teaghue sat up facing me. His eyes were open, but they were dead and sightless. His cracked lips smiled and he opened his mouth to speak in a voice that was too familiar.

"*Good help is so hard to find.*" Teaghue laughed, spraying gobbets of blood and mucus.

"What have you done with my daughter?"

"*If they hadn't tried to warn you, this all would have been much less unpleasant.*"

"What are you? Where is my daughter?"

"*She is quite safe, and quite unaware of what is happening.*" Teaghue laughed again. "*But, Mr.*

Maxwell, when I come to ask something of you, it would be good to remember what I am capable of."

Still grinning, Teaghue reached up to his face. Before I realized what he was doing, he had hooked his fingers into the orbits of his skull. His laughter quickly turned to screams.

"Great work, Maxwell," Blackstone fumed as a medic taped my injured hand. "Tell me one thing, did you save my life just so I could witness how you screwed up my investigation?"

Another set of medics was busy zipping Teaghue's remains into a body bag.

"Blackstone," I said, "my daughter is missing."

"Yeah," Blackstone watched them take Teaghue away. "And you think this helped her? What the fuck do you think you were doing? You, of all people, ought to know better. Corner a suspect with no backup, no kind of protection. Not even a goddamn rabbit's foot. You're damn lucky he didn't kill you."

I rubbed my bandaged hand. "Yeah, lucky."

"If you're not careful, you'll make me think you took him out on purpose."

"Blackstone, can we cut the crap? Am I disappearing into your little federal black hole? Or am I free to go?"

Blackstone paced around me, his shoes making sucking sounds in the slush. "As much as I'd like to put you on ice for the next decade or so—I think the people we want are going to try and contact you again." He waved over a couple of suits. "So I'm letting you go with an escort. Special Agent Francis, and Special Agent Levi," he indicated the two new people.

"Mr. Maxwell," they both said in unison. If it weren't for the fact that Francis was black, they could have been clones of each other.

"Follow him to his hotel room and sit on him." Blackstone turned toward me. "And don't worry about your apartment, we have a few agents keeping an eye on it for you."

I sighed.

"Oh, if you're wondering about local police," Blackstone handed me a sheet of paper, a copy of a fax stamped with a time early this morning. "I made a point of getting all the paperwork nice and tidy. We trump Caledvwlch's little circus of sideshow freaks."

I handed the warrant back and looked at my new federal baby-sitters.

My federal escort took me back to my hotel room. It was about this time that I had the sick realization that I hadn't called Margaret. There's only one thing worse than having to tell your ex-wife that your daughter might have been kidnapped—and that's not being the first to do so.

"How could you not tell me!"

Margaret was hysterical, and I wasn't doing the greatest job of keeping my own composure. I stood in the bedroom while my bookend Feds stood in the suite's living room doing a lousy job of pretending not to overhear us.

"What was I going to tell you? I had evil premonitions—"

"There are FBI agents in my house!"

"I know, they're here, too."

"Why would someone take Sarah?"

"We don't know for sure that anyone's taken her."

"Bullshit, Kline. You're a terrible liar." There was a pause. "I'm coming down there."

"Margaret, I know how you feel—"

"I want my daughter back! I'm getting on the next flight."

I rubbed my temples. "I don't think the FBI will think that's a good idea."

"Fuck the FBI."

"Please, Margaret, they're trying to find her." I almost choked on the phony sincerity of that line. I knew, intellectually, that Blackstone was trying to find Sarah, if only because of her tie to his investigation. But I didn't believe in it any more than Margaret did. "They're going to want you to stay there, in case they try and contact you."

"What if there's no ransom? If it's some psycho predator? You have black mages and Satanists—"

"I don't think that's what happened."

"How the *hell* do you know?

I swallowed. "I think they're trying to get to me."

"They? Who *are* they?"

"I wish I knew." I looked off into the living room. Francis, the black one, caught my gaze and quickly looked away. "But I think they're trying to blackmail me."

"Kline, if anyone hurts her because—"

"You should probably keep your phone line clear."

"In case they call," she said flatly.

"Or Sarah," I said, exhausting every remaining fragment of optimism.

She hung up.

I sat on my bed and stared at the receiver. I don't know what I expected . . .

We used to be married; shouldn't we be able to comfort each other?

I felt empty, used up, and helpless. I didn't know if my daughter was alive or dead, and there wasn't anything I could do about it. Worse, what I *had* done only seemed to have made things worse.

Margaret was right. Sarah was gone because of me, and if anything happened to her . . .

"Mr. Maxwell," Special Agent Levi stepped into the bedroom doorway. "Are you okay?"

"What do you think?" I slammed the hotel's receiver back on the cradle hard enough to set my hand and wrist hurting again.

"Can we get you anything?"

"No," I snapped.

As he turned away, I got a better grip on myself. "Hey—"

"Yes."

"Sorry for the outburst," I told him. "Not your fault."

"No problem, you're entitled." He shook his head. "If I thought that dwarf had taken one of my kids—believe me, I know where you're coming from."

"You have kids?"

"Six and nine."

"Around here?"

Levi shook his head. "A little too crazy for my wife, I'm out of Pittsburgh."

"Oh, been gone long?"

"Too long. I was hoping to be back for Christmas," he shrugged. "Doesn't look like it's going to happen."

He must have noticed my odd look.

"Oh, *I* am Jewish, my *wife's* a good Irish Catholic. We had to give our mothers grandchildren just to keep them from killing each other."

That made me feel guilty about my own divorce. Did Margaret and I have any issue that compared to that? Maybe Sarah was justified in wanting to be rid of both of us.

"Well, I hope you get back for your kids,"

"Me, too."

"And on second thought, can you order something from room service? I just realized I haven't eaten anything all day."

"Sure, what do you want?"

I lay back on the bed, groaning as the muscles knotted in my back. "Doesn't matter."

CHAPTER NINETEEN

I SPENT THE NEXT few hours running through every conversation I had with Sarah, trying to figure out exactly when I should have known, at what point I could have intervened to prevent this.

Damn it, Margaret, didn't you notice something? I wasn't there, you saw her every day.

Yeah, that was really fair, especially when it looked as if my daughter was enticed into something because she was *my* daughter.

Hell, if I wanted to backtrack blame, we could go all the way back to when the Portal first opened. At the time it had seemed reasonable that I would want to stay and cover the story of the millennium—and with every passing year, hindsight told me that it was Margaret who had been the reasonable one.

The times I wanted to feel better about the divorce, I told myself it was inevitable. I was too work-centered for the marriage to work. When I was being honest, I told myself that I had just let it happen. It had been what I really wanted, Margaret and Sarah far enough away that I could concentrate on what I was doing without worrying about them. Jump into my career full tilt, guilt free, and my only family concerns the periodic phone call . . .

Payback's a bitch.

Just waiting was killing me. I knew that I wasn't the first father to go through this, and that this wasn't the FBI's first experience with kidnapping, but it felt all wrong to me. They should be out there *doing* something. I should be out looking for my daughter, not waiting here for some sort of contact that might never come.

Besides, I doubted that I'd receive any contact while the Feds were baby-sitting me.

"I'm not doing myself any good," I whispered to myself. If I couldn't do something productive, I should do something distracting. I got out of bed and opened the door. Agent Francis was flipping through a magazine.

"Mr. Maxwell?"

"You think one of your guys at my condo could bring me my laptop? I should probably try and get some work done. I have a column due tomorrow."

Francis nodded. "If the forensic team's done with it, I don't think that will be a problem." He picked up the phone.

"And I think I left some of my notes on the coffee table."

"Sure— Hello, this is Francis, I'm with Mr. Maxwell.

Yeah, he wants a couple of things from his condo if you're done with them . . ."

With my hand wrapped up, I was reduced to a two-finger hunt-and-peck. That was okay. That was the speed my mind was working at. I was lucky that what was due was an op-ed piece rather than anything hard. I just wasn't mentally up for that kind of fact-checking at the last minute. My notes from home might have a feature story on Mazurich buried in them, but I wasn't up to digging it out.

Instead, I fleshed out a half-written piece about the rising star of Gregory Washington and his apparent inevitable ascension to the mayor's office. It was only eight hundred words, but it was close to midnight before I finished it.

At least Columbia will be happy.

I e-mailed the story to her.

I almost logged out, but I saw an unfamiliar e-mail address in my inbox.

Thinking it was news of my daughter, I opened it.

"Someone wants to help you. Midnight at the Superior Viaduct."

"What?"

I glanced at the clock by my bed, and the digital numbers flashed 12:00 at me. "Great timing," I whispered. "Maybe tomorrow . . ."

I looked back at my laptop, intending to respond to the offer of assistance, letting them know I wasn't going to be able to attend any clandestine midnight meetings . . .

The e-mail was gone.

I tried to find the window on my desktop, I searched through the inbox, and the trash, and even tried downloading messages again, but it was gone.

The message didn't exist, but I knew I had read it.

"Shit."

"You okay in there, Mr. Maxwell?" Levi appeared in my doorway. The agents must have switched shifts.

"Yeah, I just deleted something by accident." What was I supposed to do? Tell the Feds about it? And what if the guy contacting me was gun-shy? If someone really had help to offer, could I screw that up?

Then again, what if I imagined it?

Right now I couldn't even prove that I had been sent anything. It could easily be fatigue catching up with me, granting me a little wishful thinking. I'd only seen it thirty seconds ago, and it was already too easy for me to dismiss it. Why should anyone else take it seriously—

Give it a break, you just don't want to tell them.

I *was* sure that I had read the message. And going to the trouble of sending me a self-erasing e-mail strongly suggested that the sender only wanted to deal with me. Given what I was involved in, it was likely that I hadn't been looking at an e-mail, strictly speaking. The more I thought about it, the more likely it seemed that it was some sort of disguised enchantment, made up to look as if it was a normal e-mail. Mages had managed to send me messages that way, through electronic channels. It allowed some layer of camouflage—the mage can cast something on a server, or a switch box, or even wire conduit and the communication can go off at some preset time when the caster is nowhere near the site of the spell or the recipient.

The message had said midnight but didn't specify a date.

So I had two options. Either the proposed contact was past and I was SOL, or the instruction was a general communication protocol, and any date I visited the site at the specified time, something or someone would present itself. It was easy enough to set up some standing enchantment that would reveal itself at the specified time.

Twenty-four hours.

If there was even a fraction of a chance, I was not going to allow Blackstone's little army to screw it up. My daughter was a lot more important than his investigation.

"You should get some sleep," Levi told me through the door.

"I know." I yawned. Fatigue was finally starting to win over stress. Besides, I needed to get some rest if I was going to lose these guys and get to the Superior Viaduct for this meeting.

I shut off my laptop and tried to sleep.

CHAPTER TWENTY

I LOOK, AND the goat-faced Devil looks directly at me. Reaching out with a clawed fist, he says, **"Behold the cost of defying me!"**

The Devil opens his fist and I see the image of my daughter, Sarah. Her body is naked, battered, and covered in gore.

"Dad," she manages to whisper.

"No." I run toward the Devil, but he pulls his clawed hand back and Sarah is gone.

"Show me to my adversary."

I begin to object, I don't know who the adversary is. But then the mists clear, and I see a tower hovering over the city, greater than any skyscraper.

"There!" I point.

A booming, inhuman laugh resounds. **"Your service will be rewarded."**

The Devil rises from his throne, and walks toward the tower. Moments later, after losing sight of the Devil, the tower begins to crumble.

* * *

"Sarah!"

I sat bolt upright in bed, plastered with sweat. Heart racing.

Daylight filtered through the drapes. And for a moment I allowed myself to relax. Then I heard the noise.

It came from the living room of the suite, a high-pitched electronic whine. It twisted and vibrated, and found just the right frequency to set my teeth on edge. My skin felt prickly, in a sensation that was becoming all too familiar.

I got out of bed, calling, "Agent Francis? Agent Levi?"

I slowly pushed the door open.

The two Feds were nowhere to be seen. The shades were all drawn, so the only light was a blood-red glow from the television. What was on the screen was no normal broadcast. Somehow, despite all the redundant data transmission and all the built-in filtering, the television was picking up pure mana interference. The image was twisting and surreal, faces melting into a flaming blood pudding.

"Agent Francis? Agent Levi?"

One face emerged from the chaos on the screen, the goat face from the tarot, and my dream.

"Look upon my face."

Not a great idea, but I couldn't help myself. I locked eyes with the Devil-image and felt a shuddering wave of vertigo as the hotel room was wiped away by flames and blood as the Devil took my throat and pulled me into his presence.

He threw me to my knees and I faced the ground, coughing blood and staring at dirty brown soil.

"Behold, Mr. Maxwell."

I got to my feet and gasped. I was in a vast floodlit chamber, obviously underground. Behind me were vast spaces with unfinished walls, but in front of me the stone—the salt—was carved into incredible pillars, vaults, and arches.

Statues climbed over each other, toward the ceiling, and—like a cathedral—central to it all was a vast rose window that glowed with stained glass.

"The salt mines . . ."

"The lair of the dwarves."

I stumbled forward through a vast Gothic doorway. Before me was a great hall, with benches to seat hundreds. It was empty except for a single high chair next to an altar at the opposite end of the hall.

"Sarah!"

I ran toward her. She sat, eyes closed, hands folded in her lap. I almost reached her before a clawed hand yanked me back. *"No. Do not wake her."*

"What have you done?"

"Me? Nothing."

I reached for my daughter.

"Her conscious mind could not bear the sea of mana she sleeps in here. Should she wake, she would go mad."

"What do you want?"

"What you want, Mr. Maxwell. Publish your tale. Make public the dwarven trade in the substance of mana itself. Let it be known that they traffic it beyond

the shores of the Portal. Tell how your politicians profit . . ."

"Give me back my daughter."

"Do your job well, and she will be safely returned."

What the hell kind of blackmail was this? What kind of ransom? I didn't understand. Still, "Give me my daughter first."

The Devil chuckled and grabbed me by the shirt. *"Show some good faith, and I might."*

The world turned red and bloody again. I looked into the Devil's face and his eyes began to glow at me. *"You also know the cost of defying me . . ."*

The Devil's eyes became bright white, too bright to look at. My eyes watered and I shook my head.

"Mr. Maxwell?"

Someone was holding me down and I tried to push him off as the light went away.

"What the—" I looked around and the Devil was gone. Agents Levi and Francis were there, and the man holding me down and shining the light in my eye was a paramedic.

"Are you okay, Mr. Maxwell?" Levi asked.

"Yeah, I'm fine." I looked up at the medic, "What happened?"

"You had a seizure," said the medic. "For about fifteen minutes you were completely unresponsive."

I sat up. "I'm fine now," I said despite the fact that I suddenly felt dizzy.

"I think we need to take you to the clinic for observation."

"Is that necessary?" I looked over at Francis and

Levi and their expressions told me all I needed to know. Whatever they had seen was severe, and the growing pain in my back told me I'd been doing more than lying around.

Levi looked over at Francis, "I'll go with him. You stay here in case there's some attempt at contact."

Attempt at contact? Boy, did you guys miss it.

They took me to the Cleveland Clinic where I spent a good part of the afternoon suffering through a series of uncomfortable and unnecessary tests. After which they deposited me in a private room, with Agent Levi stationed outside.

Great . . .

I needed to get out from under the FBI's thumb if I was going to have a chance to follow up on my phantom e-mail. I needed to think of something.

The problem was, all I had was a hospital gown and one of those stupid little bracelets. I don't know where my clothes had gone, and I didn't even have my cell phone. It took me a while to come up with even a stupid plan.

Fortunately, the clinic provided me with a phone.

"You're shitting me," Reggie said.

"Can you do it?"

"You're making me an accomplice."

"That isn't an answer."

"Damn it, you going to give me something for my byline out of this?"

"How 'bout my notes on Mazurich's secret slush fund. You can go to town."

"Christ, you *are* desperate. I'll be there in fifteen minutes."

It was fairly simple as escape plans went. Which meant that there were probably way too many things that could go wrong. Fortunately, I didn't have too long to dwell on it. By the time I had gotten the window to my room open, and brushed the snow off of the sill, I could hear Reggie's voice outside.

"I want to see Maxwell. I brought him a change of clothes."

"You'll have to leave that with me," said Agent Levi.

"Come on, how long has he been wearing the same stuff—"

I ran back to the bathroom, which was right next to the entryway. I wedged myself in the shadows, trying to be invisible, as Reggie walked into my room.

"Hey, Maxwell!" Reggie walked into the room and repeated, "Hey!"

With the bathroom and the front door open, I could just see Levi, sitting by the doorway. A paper grocery bag sat next to the chair. I had to smile when I saw that Reggie had scrawled "Kline Maxwell" on it in permanent marker.

"Hey," Reggie said, "where is he?"

Levi got up and walked into the room. "What?"

I watched him from behind as he looked at Reggie, then the bed, then at the open window. While his back was turned, I dashed out, grabbing the grocery bag.

"What the hell," I heard Levi say as I took the first turn I came to.

I tried not to run as I looked for a place to slip out of view. There were orderlies, nurses, and doctors, but everyone was in the middle of doing something, and no one yet seemed to have the spare time to notice me. Before any of them did, I saw another bathroom in the hallway, and I slipped inside.

Just like Reggie had said, the bag held a change of clothes. The fact that they were Reggie's clothes didn't really matter to me at the moment. The sleeves were short and the waist was loose, but at least the sneakers fit. Ratty as they were, he had even had the sense to bring a winter jacket, stocking cap, and gloves—all bearing the logo of the long-absent Browns football franchise.

I waited until the hallway was quiet, then I slipped back outside.

I took a very circuitous route to the parking garage, and found Reggie waiting for me in an idling Lincoln Town Car. He threw the door open for me and said, "You owe me."

"Yeah. I know."

He drove off, back toward downtown.

"There's one more thing," I said.

"Of course there is."

"I'd like to borrow your car."

Reggie gave me a withering stare for a moment. Then he said, "Of course, why not?"

CHAPTER TWENTY-ONE

SANITY WOULD DICTATE that I lay low until midnight and my anonymous meeting. I managed to do that for nearly an hour. Then I broke down and started driving along the west side of the Cuyahoga. I wasn't clear on everything that was going on, but I was clear on where it was centered.

Whiskey Island.

What I would do when I got there was an open question. However, it was clear that Magetech's strings were being pulled from there. And if my demonic visitor was to be believed, my daughter was kept somewhere out there, in the mines.

As I turned away from Edgewater Park, on to Whiskey Island Drive, I was able to see the Cleveland skyline beyond the wooded confines of the dwarven peninsula. Whiskey Island was flanked to the right by the skyscrapers a mile away on Public Square, and on the left by the dark twisting clouds above the Portal.

Whiskey Island stabbed right between the two features as if it were a conscious metaphor for the division between the two worlds.

After passing through the Shoreway underpass, I paralleled the long-disused Conrail tracks that used to serve the port and the salt mines. I passed chain-link fences that were sagged and rusty, a few bore warning signs that I had never seen before. Big red letters "Fe" covered half the sign. Text in English warned "High Iron Hazard."

The English words were accompanied by a script that I believed was elvish.

Lots of things had occupied Whiskey Island at one time or another; nineteenth-century Irish immigrants, a defunct Coast Guard station, volleyball courts, a marina, the salt mines, of course . . .

And the Port Authority once ran an iron ore pellet terminal here. Decades of use probably saturated this area. I would not want to be an elf right now.

I shook my head. It was as if fate itself conspired to isolate the dwarven enclave.

The road got worse, the asphalt deteriorating the farther west I went toward the tip of the peninsula. It finally degenerated into a gravel track ending at a gateless chain-link fence. At one point I could have driven all the way to the largest marina on the Great Lakes—but that didn't exist anymore.

I got out of the Lincoln and looked around. I hadn't expected the way to be completely clear; I was at the back door, so to speak. All the traffic and new construction was concentrated on the southern edge and the western tip of the peninsula. The road I was on, like the train tracks, was mostly abandoned.

However, if my memory of my research was accurate, the salt mines were on the opposite side of the tracks from the old pellet terminal. At one point, they might have been visible from where I stood, but high concentrations of mana had some interesting effects on vegetation.

Past the chain-link, and the train tracks, stood a grove of trees whose twisted and gnarled trunks could have clung to the land here for a millennium. Could have, but didn't. This was one of a few areas where dark old-growth forests seemed to have erupted overnight, post-Portal. Somehow the twisted patterns of mana allowed centuries-old roots to climb over fifty-year-old train tracks. In one place a trunk as wide as the Lincoln grew through the open doors of a derailed boxcar.

The woods hid the southern sky, the naked winter branches as dense as any canopy. The only sound: my feet crunching gravel and the ominous creak as wind from the lake shifted the branches around me.

While the road was fenced off, the chain-link was in bad repair and showed no obvious wards. A man-sized gap was in the fence opposite the Conrail tracks, and led to a dirt trail that headed off where the road used to go.

"Okay, Kline, does this make sense?"

Yesterday I had chased a dwarf to his death. I had good reason to believe they held my daughter. Chances were they wouldn't be pleased to see me.

But Teaghue said that "He" had her. I didn't need to be a brain surgeon to figure out what demonic manifestation the late Teaghue Parthalán was referring to. Both in his last words and in the circle his fellows constructed for my benefit on the Detroit-Superior Bridge.

Add to that the image from my nightmares; the dwarves chained to the demonic throne, mining the massive mountain of salt . . .

"What are you doing?"

"It must be fed!"

However badly things went with Teaghue, I had a gut feeling that I might find some ally among the dwarves. Or at least some source of information.

That's how my rationalizations went as I slipped through the fence. Despite that, the fact was cold logic should have dictated that this was as dumb a move as chasing Teaghue had been.

A few steps past the fence, and the trees had me surrounded. I had to keep checking to make sure the path was still visible behind me. Enchanted woods had a habit of closing up behind people.

This one didn't seem to mind leaving me an escape route, though after a hundred feet, the path twisted around enough to make me lose sight of the fence and Reggie's car.

I stopped a moment.

This was one of the places in the area that no one had managed to map accurately since the opening of the Portal. All I had was some general geography. I was on a peninsula about a mile long, ranging from a third to a half mile wide. The western end, where it met shore, and where I had come from, had been the industrialized part, the east end had never really been developed and only had an abandoned Coast Guard station.

I was pretty sure that I was roughly in the geographic center, which would put me due north of the salt mines and the dwarven settlements.

However, the thick woods around me encouraged me to stay on the path, which kept going east—as far as I could tell.

I kept an eye to the right, looking for a clearing, or any passable way toward the mines. However, to all appearances, the plant kingdom had been completely triumphant. The Conrail tracks were totally overtaken. I saw railroad ties, and the rails themselves, embedded in large trunks ten, twenty, thirty feet up. Roots embraced and seemed to consume large fragments of concrete and asphalt. Corrugated steel poked out of snow-covered earth, only visible because the undergrowth had shed its leaves for the winter.

I knew the area I was in was way too small to really become lost, but even in a space less than a mile square, I knew it wasn't safe to brave these kinds of woods. They tended to be larger on the inside than they were on the outside.

The light started to fail. Looking up, I saw the dappled white fragments of sky turn grayer. Another storm front moving in from the lake.

As if in response to my thought, thick white flakes began to drift down through the twisted branches above me.

"Fuck," I whispered, and my breath fogged around me.

In response I heard something rustle.

I froze.

The woods stayed silent around me. I couldn't tell if the sound I'd heard came from behind me or ahead of me.

I took a step.

Something crunched the gravel on the path behind me. It wasn't my foot.

I started moving. I tried to be quiet, but I could hear my shadow picking up the pace to match me. My heart raced, and the trees themselves seemed to feed into the sense of panic. I wanted to run, but I tried to reason with myself, *the point was to talk to someone, right?*

I wasn't Indiana Jones or James Bond; there wasn't any way I was going to free my daughter by stealth or force. The only thing I could do was to convince someone to hand her over. I had to talk to someone.

Now was as good a time as any . . .

I turned around and stood my ground, facing the last turn in the path behind me.

My stalker stopped moving before he came into view. If I listened now, I could hear his breathing heavy and deep. I could just see a wisp of his breath emerging from behind a tree.

I sucked in a breath, calmed myself, and put on my best journalistic game face. "Come on out, I just want to talk to someone."

I heard weight shifting on the gravel path. It sounded bigger than a dwarf. More like several.

I took a step forward. "Kline Maxwell, *Cleveland Press*. But, I think you know that, don't you?"

Something rustled again, a noise that took me a moment to identify.

"Come out and talk . . ."

Wings.

It came out, but it wasn't a dwarf, or even several dwarves. It leaped into the path in front of me, springing on feline haunches that were sized more for a Clydesdale, and stared me down with the head of a raptor that should have been extinct for a few hundred thousand years.

The griffin let out a screech that could probably knock lesser avian dead out of the sky.

Unlike a lot of critters that came out of the Portal, this was not something you could reason with. It was a wild animal. Most had a healthy fear of humanoids. However, this one was too hungry, too pissed, or just too nasty to be fazed by me.

It reared, and I did the only thing I could. I dove into the woods.

It wasn't quite the sanctuary it seemed.

I left the path, and the trees seemed to open up around me. Suddenly the stand of trees that seemed so closed in that a dwarf couldn't pass through widened to the point where a man could fully stretch his arms between the massive trunks.

While that meant I could run, unimpeded; it also meant that a pissed-off griffin could follow me. The only thing that kept me alive was the fact that the trees were just close enough to prevent it from pouncing or taking flight, and its bird-clawed forelegs were more designed for tearing prey apart, not chasing it.

That meant that I could barely keep ahead of it while running flat out. My only hope was to find some cover before I hit a clearing, or the water.

I hit all three at the same time.

After running through the unnatural woods for ten minutes beyond the point where I should have reached the edge of the peninsula, I broke out of the edge, somewhere on the northern shore. I faced a clearing stacked high with mountainous piles of dismantled steel machinery. A scrap heap a few dozen orders of magnitude beyond the piles next to *The Dwarven Armorer.*

I ran between stacks of girders too tight for my pursuer to follow. Behind I heard a screech and a rush of feathers. I could feel the griffin's hot breath on my neck as I wove deeper into the rusty iron maze.

I saw its shadow fly across the slice of sky visible above me. I leaned against a slab of metal and hyperventilated. My lungs burned and my legs felt like rubber.

You're a genius, Kline . . .

I closed my eyes and shook my head. At least I had my bearings again. I was standing in the last remnants of the Hulett ore unloaders—skyscraper-sized mechanical dinosaurs, four of which had dominated the pellet terminal for a good ninety years during the last century. They had been obsolete for a few decades when the Port Authority decided to dismantle the beasts— four of the six left in existence.

In the constant tension between redevelopment and preservation, redevelopment had won. Unfortunate, since political wrangling over this spit of shoreline, and the subsequent opening of the Portal, meant that the Port Authority never got to expand the docks here, losing even the existing facilities.

But the bones of this industrial fossil rested to the east of the old pellet terminal. So once I was clear of griffins, I could follow the shore and get back to the car. The shot of adrenaline from my confrontation was just what I needed to come to my senses and realize my limitations.

I waited a good twenty minutes until I was sure the griffin had given up on me. Then I tried to backtrack, which turned out to be less simple than it sounded.

I wove back through the maze of iron, toward what I thought was the edge, and I faced a dead end—a slab of iron an inch thick, dotted with rivets the size of my fist. I couldn't even see around it.

I turned around and worked my way back, and realized I had no idea which way to go. I stood at the intersection of five paths that wove through the ocher piles of iron, my feet sinking into thick, red slushy mud. My footprints led down four of the paths, in both directions.

"*Shit.*" My voice came out in a puff of fog.

I looked at the piles of scrap and saw figures spray-painted on the pieces. I had ignored them, at first. Just ID numbers, probably left over from when the Historical Society had plans to reconstruct one of these monsters on another site.

That was right, as far as the white numbers went.

However, someone had also sprayed red and orange paint on the girders, marking arcane glyphs that actually hurt my eyes when I stared at them.

That couldn't be good.

I swallowed, and started to get the same creepy sensation I had gotten around Magetech. There, things seemed to hide beneath the reflections; here, it was as if something ugly hid under the pattern of rust flakes on the iron beams.

If I had my cell phone, I would have tried to call Dr. Shafran for advice. The little I knew about mazes like this, they usually forced you through the center in order to get out.

The problem was, like ancient Crete, there invariably was something nasty in the center.

However, I didn't have much choice but to play along.

I followed the path that wasn't graced by my footprints. I slogged between twisted iron walls that tried to claw their way into my brain. I forced my gaze down, focusing on the path ahead of me. Every heartbeat felt as if the walls would close in and squeeze the life from me, even though in my narrow focus, the path became wider.

Each intersection, I could see one path that did not yet have footprints. Each time I took that fork.

My socks were wet, and every step I had the nasty sense that something was reaching up through the mud and touching the soles of my feet.

"And I was worried about the woods . . ."

I slogged on, following the logic of the untraveled road. The weight of the metal around me became a heavier and heavier pressure on the back of my mind.

Until I came to a dead end.

"Fuck!"

I looked up, and the sky itself was gone. I was in a cavern built of iron scrap. I could see, but the ruddy light was sourceless and nothing cast a shadow. When I turned around, I saw no footprints in the mud behind me.

"Shit. Are you out there?" I shouted. The words hung in the air, echoless. "Someone show themselves!"

The light in the air appeared to pulse. I was breathing hard, the air burning my lungs as badly as it had after I'd run from the griffin. Vertigo gripped me, the dizzying sensation that the world around me was dropping into free fall.

"I want my daughter!"

The glyphs spray-painted on the metal walls around me began to glow. It became harder for me to breathe, the air as thick as the mud swallowing my ankles. I tried to shout again, but the words came out as a wheeze.

The sourceless light slowed its pulsing, dimming to invisibility, leaving only the glowing glyphs surrounding me. The sense of falling continued and I was tumbling in a void, my muscles locked, unable to breathe, only able to see the burning glyphs that were like hot brands stabbing into the back of my skull.

*   *   *

Voices spoke a guttural language other than English. Somehow I understood the unseen speakers.

"The journalist."

"Yes."

"He must not be here."

"He is here."

"Who does he serve?"

"Who do we serve?"

"He has cost us too much."

"We have cost him too much."

"Can he do what we cannot?"

"He will or he will not. Those who look cannot find him here."

"He will return."

"When it is done, and all is lost—or won."

I sucked in a breath, shocking myself awake.

I was behind the wheel of the Lincoln. I was parked on some residential street somewhere. The sky was dark and it was just beginning to snow. I turned the key and the clock on the dash told me it was 10:30.

"What the hell?"

I had blacked out again. It was either another mana overdose, or it was some dwarven security system, or a little of both. I should probably count myself lucky coming through unscathed. I hoped to God I hadn't endangered my daughter.

No, the demonic bastard wants me. He needs the leverage . . .

I gripped the steering wheel, trying to calm down. Then I realized where I was.

The dwarves were trying to give me a message.

I was parked in front of the late Council President Dominic Mazurich's house. And on the passenger seat was a key on a St. Christopher key chain.

CHAPTER TWENTY-TWO

LET IT NEVER BE said that I can't take a hint.

Whatever was going on, I was getting the feeling that even if the dwarves weren't exactly on my side, they weren't on the side of my daughter's kidnapper either. Whoever was hiding behind the tarot Devil was at odds with the dwarves themselves.

"What are you doing?"

"It must be fed!"

Perhaps it was Magetech itself. It wouldn't be the first time a corporate entity took on its own life and started cannibalizing its workers and founders.

Whoever or whatever it was, the dwarves were afraid of even referring to it indirectly. And given what happened to Nina and Teaghue, they had good reason. But it was clear that they didn't serve that master willingly.

So I made the assumption that I had been parked here to push me in the right direction.

I walked up the driveway to Mazurich's side door and tried the doorknob. Locked.

I looked for any obvious wards. I didn't see any, but if this was the house key, the St. Christopher medal was probably keyed to them. Even so, once I unlocked the door I stood and waited.

If any neighbor called the cops, or a warded alarm was tripped, I might get away with misdemeanor trespass if I was outside the house when they showed up. I gave them enough time to show up.

They didn't.

I let myself into Mazurich's house. I gagged a little. Death still clung to the air in here, as if an evil rot had sunk into the walls.

I stepped into the darkened house, unclear exactly what I was looking for. I left the lights off. The glass may not have attracted attention, but I wasn't about to press my luck. I let my eyes adjust until the glare from the streetlights outside was enough for me to navigate by.

I left the kitchen and entered the living room. A sectional couch, coffee table, not much else. Family photos crowded the mantel. Nothing out of the ordinary.

My foot crunched glass.

I knelt down and picked up the remains of a picture frame, a partly torn photograph fell from it. I set down the frame and picked up the damaged picture.

It was a digital shot, the strange ghosting marked it as probably coming from one of the first post-Portal cameras. Given the date on the back, and the subject matter, probably a prototype.

The picture showed Mazurich, Dr. Pretorious, a cluster of dwarves recognizable from their portraits at Magetech HQ, and Mr. Simon Lucas. The tear in the photograph split Lucas in two, and there was a heel print in the center.

I suppose that once suicide was the obvious cause of death, the cops stopped bothering with evidence. And the Democratic party machine, which drove most everything in the county, might have discouraged any close examination of the council president's connection to Magetech.

However, to be fair, I might just be a lot more comfortable with that kind of conspiracy.

I placed the photo on the mantel and headed upstairs.

Mazurich's house made me uneasy. It wasn't squeamishness as much as the look I was getting into Mazurich's personal life. I knew how much money this man had collected from Magetech. Even if the money was sheltered and hidden, one would expect to see some of that in the man's home. What someone chooses to spend money on is one of the keys to their character.

Mazurich hadn't done much of anything. It was almost as if he hadn't changed anything in the house since he separated from his wife. The impression came from the fact that every room seemed to have broken patterns. Pictures on the wall that formed lopsided, unbalanced designs. Matching end tables in a child's bedroom, but with no bed between them. Throw rugs on the wall-to-wall carpet arranged around furniture that wasn't there. Chairs facing blank walls . . .

I knew many, many people who put too much of themselves into their work. I counted myself among them. People whose residential address was little more than a place they went to go to bed. Their homes became shells. This felt worse.

Could a house be worse than soulless?

I wondered if I was suffering from the aftereffects of my ill-fated trip to Whiskey Island.

The master bedroom was the scene of the suicide. Here, the smell of death was the worst. Even though I could see that crime scene cleanup had been through here. The mattress was gone from the bed, leaving the naked box spring, and a large square of the wall-to-wall carpet had been cut away, baring the hardwood floor. In the streetlight glow from the window, there seemed to be a darker spot on the wood. Ink-black and shiny.

I stepped forward and the stain was gone. Some odd reflection, that's all.

Why am I here? What am I looking for?

I saw the bullet hole. It went into the wall above the headboard. Around it, the wallpaper had been stripped baring the plaster. More attempted cleanup.

I stepped forward and suddenly saw the wall spotted with gore, tufts of hair, shiny bits of—

I stumbled back and the vision disappeared.

"Okay, that wasn't the light."

I walked backward from the bed frame, toward the door. My heart raced.

The mana from the Portal used the environment around itself as an organizing principle. The patterns could be chemical, like the crystalline structure of the salt under Lake Erie; or ritual and cultural, like the New Age occultism that Nina had practiced. It could be geographic, such as in the mystical woods that had enveloped the North Chagrin Reservation; it could be architectural, like innumerable churches, or the maze the dwarves had made of the Huletts' remains.

Patterns could also be emotional, and psychological.

Such as this house, the mind of Mazurich, and the way he had killed himself.

The door slammed shut behind me.

"Shit." I whipped around and grabbed the knob and tried to pull it open. It was shut fast by something more powerful than the latch.

Something laughed behind me.

I turned around, back flattened against the door.

"Only the damned follow me here." Mazurich's voice was little more than a whisper. He sat above the bed, hovering above the box spring where the missing mattress must have been. Blood flowed from his mouth, turning his chin and the front of his shirt a glossy black. His skull was shaped wrong, and when he moved, I could see that it was because of a massive crater in the back of his head.

He turned his face toward me and stared into my eyes. I couldn't look away. I knew the face. I had interviewed him innumerable times. I also knew he was dead, and the specter before me couldn't be him . . .

Just an image conjured up by the Portal.

"W–why did you kill yourself?" I tried to keep my composure. It wasn't easy.

Mazurich laughed again. When he lifted his head, I could see through his mouth to the wall behind him.

"You know, Maxwell. You'll join me in hell soon enough."

I shook my head, no.

"You will do His bidding, even if you fight Him."

"Who is he?"

"He has an infinity of names: the morning star, the bringer of light, the father of lies."

"He has my daughter."

Mazurich laughed.

"You are already lost."

"No," I whispered.

"You will give your soul for what He will promise you."

I screwed my eyes shut and clenched my fists. I tried to anchor myself against the fear. "What the hell are you?"

"What you will become."

"No," I shook my head. "You're the mana-animated guilt of a poor bastard that couldn't accept the decisions he made."

"You cannot fight Him."

"No," I whispered. *"You* couldn't."

A chill wind blew through the room, making my bones ache. For a moment I could actually feel my heart stop.

I opened my eyes, blinking, and the phantom was gone. No specter, no blood, and even the smell of death seemed to have receded.

The morning star,

The bringer of light,
The father of lies,
Lucifer,
The Devil.

Mazurich was a good Catholic, and if that's really what Mazurich thought, I could understand how he might end up killing himself. I was shaken myself as I backed out of the bedroom.

What if the authors of that evangelical pamphlet had a point?

When I got back to the car, it was after eleven and I had another meeting to go to.

CHAPTER TWENTY-THREE

THE SUPERIOR VIADUCT has an interesting history. It was one of the first rail connections between east and west across the Cuyahoga River, and one of the first moving bridges marking it as a precursor of dozens of drawbridges that would rise, fall, and swing across the river.

Nineteenth century trolleys crossed an arched stone approach toward a swinging iron trestle that would carry them west. The operation lasted only a quarter century or so, surviving at least one fairly significant disaster where a trolley plunged into the river, eventually to be replaced by higher, more modern structures at the beginning of the twentieth century.

The iron trestle of the bridge was shortly sold for scrap. But the arched vault of the eastern approach has remained for close to a century, a bridge to nowhere. Like the Huletts, it is one of many odd artifacts in the city that are subject to periodic debates that swing between development, restoration, and apathy.

With the viaduct, there was a brief development de-bate, but since the Portal opened the pendulum had swung solidly toward apathy. However, as far as meet-ing places went, it was probably the most public aban-doned structure you could find—a raised open-air deck cutting through the heart of the eastern shore of the Flats.

While the East Flats were a little less hard core than the West—a fetish club like the *Nazgûl* wouldn't fit in with the restaurants and comedy clubs that clustered on this side of the river—the area was still choked solidly with people at quarter to midnight.

It reminded me why I haven't gone clubbing for over twenty-five years. I don't know what was worse, the five-mile-per-hour traffic, or the twenty-something pedestrians who believed that sidewalks were only a suggestion.

Fortunately, I still reached my destination ten min-utes early. I parked Reggie's Lincoln by the barriers at the eastern end of the viaduct. I stepped out of the car and was just far enough away from the chaos and noise around me to hear my feet crunch in the snow.

The night was clear and cold, the only cloud was the fog from my own breath. The deck of the viaduct arced away from me, over the Flats, to dead-end at the river. Blocking my path, on the other side of the traffic bar-rier, was a tall chain-link fence. It had a gate, but it was padlocked.

I stood at the gate and looked at the deck. It was cov-ered by a layer of snow, silver and unmolested under the glow of the full moon.

It looked like I'd got here first.

I wasn't about to break in. I could see a frightening array of wards scribed on the top rail of the fence. I didn't know what any of them might do, but I wasn't about to find out the hard way. I wasn't going to help Sarah by inflicting random curses on myself.

I stood by the gate and waited for my anonymous e-mailer to show himself.

I waited.

I checked my watch five times, each time sure that I'd been stood up, or that the phantom e-mail had really meant *only* last midnight.

However, every time, my watch told me that even less time had passed. It didn't feel possible. The ten minutes to midnight seemed to stretch to twenty. Everything seemed to crawl around me. Even the fog of my breath seemed hesitant.

By the fifth time I suspected there was something more going on than my impatience. My watch read 11:58:49, and I was convinced that I'd been standing here for way more than eight minutes.

I looked at the seconds and waited for the 49 to change to 50. And waited. In my head I counted to ten before the LCD winked over to 50. I counted fifteen to reach 51.

I looked up from my watch and realized that it wasn't just a wayward timepiece. The noise from the Flats was wrong, octaves lower than it should be, I couldn't pick out anything recognizable as a human voice, and everything was muffled and nearly subliminal.

Down the street where there were people, I could see movement, but barely. I looked down and kicked the snow at my feet, and saw it hang in the air for a short eternity before arcing slowly back to merge with the slush at my feet.

I looked back at my watch.

11:59:03.

I counted a full twenty seconds before the number flipped to 04.

Almost at the same time, the air around me rang with the sound of a gigantic bell. The sound was undistorted, and felt so close that I could picture myself right next to Quasimodo as he pulled the rope.

In front of me, of its own accord, the gate in the fence opened.

I looked around and all I could see of the world had stopped. The people at the end of the street showed no visible movement. By them, a glowing cigarette butt hung in midair where a leather-clad biker had thrown it toward the gutter. The Harley he rode was caught in mid-spray passing the college kids, the slush frozen in the air, halfway toward them.

There was another resonating bell sound, the gong vibrating the fillings in my back teeth.

My watch still read 11:59:03.

Something told me it was slow.

I expected it to be awkward to move, but whatever enchantment gripped me must have compensated for little things like air resistance, acceleration, and gravity. Whoever this was, he wasn't minor league.

I passed through the gate and walked across the

snow-covered deck of the Superior Viaduct as the bell tolled again. Three down, nine to go.

Whatever distorted my sense of time began operating on my sense of space as well. The world around the deck of the viaduct began to twist, the moon coming impossibly close, and the neighboring Cleveland skyline receding into the far distance. The Flats below sank into a deep abyss while the river widened to rival the lake, swallowing the western shore.

The bell tolled four. And the air, cold and razor clear until now, began to spontaneously form mist, wrapping itself around me as I walked. The air became heavy, humid, and slightly warm.

Five.

I slowed my walk, because I knew that the viaduct dead-ended before the river, and I couldn't remember if the raw edge was fenced off or not. I didn't want to step off the end by accident. It felt as if I had easily traversed the length of it already.

Six.

Much longer than I expected, I couldn't trust my sense of distance anymore. If I was where I thought I was, I'd be midway across the river by now.

Seven.

I couldn't see my feet, or much of anything other than gray mist and a fuzzy glowing orb in the gray that showed where the moon must be. I could feel that I had left the snow cover. My feet fell on naked concrete. Or stone.

"We're not in Kansas anymore." The mist soaked up my words without the slightest echo, almost to the point where I thought I didn't actually hear them my-self.

Eight.

The path I was on tilted upward and became un-even. I almost stumbled until I realized that I had come to a stairway. My heart was racing, my body was half convinced that any moment I would find the edge and take a fatal tumble into the river.

I had to tell myself that there were less grandiose ways to kill me off.

"Yeah, unless this is another hallucination."

Nine.

Pushing away unpleasant thoughts of bad trips and hostile illusions, I climbed the stairs. The mist began thinning almost immediately. After a few steps, I could see the moon clearly again.

Ten.

I stepped upward, out of the mist, and saw the moon eclipsed by something I had never seen on the Cleveland skyline. A cylindrical tower bisecting the swollen moon, with a height rivaling some of the tallest buildings downtown. The stairs I climbed, still shrouded in mists, weren't straight, but spiraled up the side of the tower, whose base seemed to have a foundation in the mists themselves.

Even though I had never actually seen it, the tower was familiar.

"Show me to my adversary."

Eleven.

I finally stepped completely out of the mist; setting my feet on the first visible stone stair climbing up the edge of the tower. As I did, the mists themselves fell away.

I gasped.

There was no sign of the stair I had climbed to arrive here, or of any structure below the last two steps I had trod. The stair and the tower were anchored in nothing, suspended midair above the Cuyahoga River, about seven or eight hundred feet above the Superior Viaduct. The Cleveland skyline spilled out below me.

"The FAA has to love this thing."

I climbed up another quarter turn around the side of the tower and came face-to-face with a pair of ebony doors thirty feet wide and almost fifty high. An alien script wrapped every inch of their surfaces, glowing a blackish green in the moonlight. The hairs rose on the back of my neck, and the power here was thick enough for me to smell it in the air. It was like breathing hot static and adrenaline.

Twelve.

The bells came from inside the tower, and at the stroke of twelve, the huge doors swung out in front of me. They moved slowly, which was good because I needed to step out of the way to avoid being pushed off by them. Sidestepping the opening doors gave me a good look at how massive they actually were—the things were thicker than I was, and I needed to lose weight. Four-and-a-half feet thick at the base. The doors to this place took up more cubic feet than my entire condo.

I stood there at the entrance to the phantom tower as the doors completed their transit. Beyond was a massive hall that seemed to take up half the volume of the entire tower. Cylindrical walls shot away on either side, cased in marble, and hung with rich tapestries. Massive Gothic pillars formed concentric circles a third of the way in, reaching up to support vaults to a vast domed ceiling whose ribs at this distance seemed spider thin—though they probably rivaled the doors for sheer mass.

Thick rugs covered a flagstone floor arranged in a complex pattern that might have had some mystical significance. Iron sconces held torches illuminating the center space, and heavy chains suspended a vast iron chandelier—another object bigger than my whole condo—over the center of the room.

Sitting on the floor in the center of this vast room was the largest dragon I had ever seen.

The doors shut behind me before I fully realized I had walked inside.

"Welcome to my home, Mr. Maxwell. I am called Hephaestus."

Hephaestus was gargantuan, even for a species known for its size. A wall of reddish flesh, scaled and ribbed, towered over me even from a hundred feet away. His chest was almost as broad as the entry behind me. His forelegs, folded in front of him in a near catlike pose, were thicker and longer than my entire body and ended in clawed hands that could probably bat my Volkswagen around like a wad of tinfoil. Massive wings draped behind him, obscuring half of the huge chamber from me, and, perched on a towering serpentine neck was a triangular saurian skull that was the size of an Escalade.

His coloring ranged from a pinkish coral near the center of his chest, to a crimson so dark it was close to black along his spine and wings. He stretched his forelegs, and I could feel the movement in the stones beneath my feet.

"Come to me, I would talk to you."

I had only ever had one extended conversation with a dragon before. They tended to be solitary creatures, interacting with maybe one or two human proxies. They also were attracted to power, in its various forms, whether it be raw physical strength—which Hephaestus obviously had in spades—or the more intangible aspects such as wealth and knowledge.

Since they interacted with human society here, most concentrated on the purest distillation of power that we could provide—money. If you dug into the list of all the billionaires resident in Northeast Ohio, I would bet that once you dug behind all the shell companies and legal fictions, six of the top ten would have wings, claws, and little whips of sulfur smoke trailing from their nostrils.

"Unique home you have here,"

"Thank you," Hephaestus said. His booming voice had all the subtlety of a chainsaw being thrown into a wood chipper, but I could catch an inflection of pride. *"Not many have had the honor of an audience here."*

"It is impressive," I said, stopping about twenty feet away, which seemed a safe radius from any idle gestures. Also, with Hephaestus' head so far above me, it was about as close as I could get without tilting my head at an angle too unnatural for conversation. "And well hidden."

The floor shook as Hephaestus let loose with a rumbling bellows sound that, if I hadn't heard a dragon laugh before, would have scared the shit out of me.

Even so, I still backed up a step.

"Amusing choice of words, Mr. Maxwell. Hide? Indeed!" He lowered his head, circled his neck around me, and rested his chin on a clawed forefoot. I turned around to keep eye contact just as my gut began to realize that I was suddenly completely encircled by a wall made of dragon.

An instinctive step back and I was leaning against the curve of Hephaestus' muscular neck. I could feel his pulse in the small of my back, like a coal miner trying to pickax himself out of a hopeless cave-in. *"I do not hide, Mr. Maxwell. I merely make my home where men do not care to look."*

"Forgive my ignorance, but I've looked at this patch of sky every day for the last few decades, and I haven't seen this tower of yours. It's rather large to miss."

"Suffice it to say that, until tonight, you have been looking beside this spot, not at it. Most men have not trained their eyes to look in this direction."

"I seemed to walk it okay."

"When led, Mr. Maxwell. You could not see where you were going, could you?"

Despite the fact that Hephaestus spoke with a sonorous tone that vibrated my sternum and made Barry White sound like a castrati, I could swear that there was something almost impish in it. As if he took great pleasure in showing off his sky castle.

"No, I couldn't." I looked around. "Is this something like the Portal. Have I walked into some other reality?" I calculated my question carefully. The Portal had been a construct of another dragon, one named Aloeus. That was a fact that wasn't general knowledge, mainly because I wasn't able to get the details into print without having the story pulled by the forces that be. And while I had yet to write my book on how I found out that particular tidbit of information, I was pretty sure that Aloeus' handiwork was known among most of the nonhuman community. I also knew that if the elves could be defined by their reticence, dragons were almost as surely defined by their pride.

As I expected, bringing up Aloeus' handiwork encouraged Hephaestus to elaborate on his own. *"So close to understanding that you impress me. Like, but yet unlike. The Portal is simple, a hole in the wall, nothing more. No grace, no finesse. This, the creation of Hephaestus, is much more than that. A pocket of space that did not exist before my thoughts of it. A place that was not, but now is."*

My host was gracious enough to allow the implications of that to sink in. Could someone—something—create a whole universe from scratch? "How big is this place?"

"As large as suits my fancy at the moment."

"You didn't come through the Portal, did you?"

Again, the booming laughter came. The pressure made my skull ache as Hephaestus' neck vibrated behind me. It confirmed a suspicion that had been brewing ever since I walked in and saw him. There are not that many dragons in northeast Ohio. They might be secretive, but they also tend to stand out in public. A single appearance is enough to register deeply in the public psyche, especially for someone whose job is to cover the local news—"fuzzy gnome" or not.

The fact that Hephaestus was a new face to me, made me suspect that he did not come here through normal channels. At least that was more probable than the Feds suddenly loosening up the flow of nonhumans through the Portal.

"Astute you are, Mr. Maxwell."

I looked up at the tower above me; at the torchlight; the candles in the chandelier; at the tapestries I could see beyond the dragon's bulk, all of which could probably be titled "The Death of St. George" in one form or another; and it impressed me that exactly none of the twenty-first century seemed to have touched this place—

Other than myself.

"Jesus Christ, did you just *move* this place?"

"You are indeed worthy of my attention." Hephaestus lowered his clawed hand so his head hovered before me. *"Though it would be more accurate to say that I altered its orientation relative to various planes of existence, rotated its axis somewhat closer to that of your world."*

I stood there in silence for a few long minutes. I rubbed my face and realized that I hadn't showered or shaved in the past two days. My hand was shaking, and with the initial shock of meeting the dragon here wearing off, reality—such as it was—began to sink in.

"Why did you bring me here? Your message said you could help me. I need to find my daughter."

"Indeed, the predictable mortal concern for progeny."

His breath was hot, wet, and smelled of brimstone. His face was barely three feet from me—closer than I'd ever want to be.

"Can you help me?"

"In return for your help."

"What do you want?"

Hephaestus uncoiled from around me and sat upright. On his haunches, wings unfolded, his neck coiled almost to the chandelier. If it was possible, it was even more intimidating having his SUV-sized head sixty feet above me than when we were face-to-face.

"Mr. Maxwell, we have a common enemy."

Of course, I asked the obvious question. "Who is it?"

"I will not speak one of his names here, suffice it to say he has many of them." Hephaestus waved a clawed hand, and a line of torches lit along a stairway that spiraled along the inner wall of the chamber, behind the ranks of pillars. I hadn't noticed it before, and because it was a human scale, much too small for Hephaestus, I wondered if it actually had been *there* before.

I turned back around, and Hephaestus was gone.

"What the—?"

A human voice, a *familiar* human voice, came from

behind me. "Perhaps more the correct question might be *what* is it?"

I turned around and faced one of the last people I expected to see. "*You?*"

"Me," responded Dr. Newman Shafran, and the thick accent couldn't quite hide Hephaestus' glee at my surprise.

CHAPTER TWENTY-FOUR

"COME, COME," Dr. Shafran took off a pair of thick round bifocals and used them to gesture toward the staircase leading up the wall. "To answer the question foremost in your mind, I am the Dr. Shafran you have known, and he is I." He looked at me with a glint in his eye, "as we are both the dragon Hephaestus."

That helped answer why Quint couldn't find a phone number for Dr. Shafran. The good Dr. Shafran might well cease to exist when he left the Case campus . . .

For once I had trouble coming up with a coherent question. "How, why . . . ?"

Hephaestus chuckled. "Please, let me take you to my library."

I followed him up the spiral staircase.

"To answer your concern, this mortal shell is propelled by my spirit which, along with the rest of my body has, in the terms I used earlier, rotated on its axis to be behind myself." He turned and smiled at me.

"Is there a real Dr. Shafran?"

"Oh, why be needlessly complex? Dr. Shafran is as real as you. Allow a scholar his alias."

We circled around the vast chamber once, and we were barely a quarter up the side of the wall. "Why do it?"

"What shocks you more, Mr. Maxwell? That I show such duplicity, or that I demean myself as much as to wear a man's shoes?"

I didn't know how to answer the question. The last thing I wanted to do was say anything that could come across as insulting. If anything, Hephaestus had managed to convince me that he possessed powers way beyond anything I had ever seen. I tried purposeful misdirection again. "I have seen remote-control golems before, gargoyles and undead—yours is the most real—"

Dr. Shafran touched me and the physical contact was enough to stop me talking. "Because it *is* real, Mr. Maxwell. This is my flesh." He let me go. "A gobbet of it, anyway."

We continued up the stairs as he talked. "Why should I reduce myself so? Because I can. To disguise the person of one's flesh so is beyond the means of any of my peers and it pleases me to do what others cannot. And it gives me an eye with which to view the men of your world. It allows me to watch, and to see . . ."

"See what?"

"The aforementioned enemy."

We continued to trudge up the stairs, and I began to see what looked to be an opening to the upper portion of the tower.

"What about my daughter?"

"Patience. You will see that our desires are one."

He led me upward and eventually we walked into a room that was as vast as the entry hall, the walls lined with shelves that held an endless supply of books ranging from simple scrolls to giant metal-clad volumes as tall as I was. The room smelled of incense, dust, and old paper. From the expression on Hephaestus' face I could tell that I was looking at a hoard as great as any pile of gold.

He walked over to a long table where a book was already open. He looked down at it and said, "Do you know much of the history of your sister land across the Portal?"

The Cliff Notes version of what I knew went something like this:

There's a realm of magic, elves, dwarves, fairies, and dragons. In the midst of this land enters mankind—i.e., my own kind, only scruffier. They found a land called Ragnan that slowly gobbles up everything around it. Among other things, the fact that men weren't immortal gave them a tactical advantage—they didn't care nearly so much about dying.

Ragnan becomes an authoritarian regime—human only—led by a god-king called the Thesarch, who seemed to have more authority than your average Pharaoh. He was helped in part by the fact that he was at the apex of the mana pyramid and could muster spells that could waste entire cities.

The last Thesarch was named Valdis, and he seemed particularly nasty and long-lived. Many of the nonhuman societies surrounding Ragnan crumble before Valdis and his enchanted human armies.

Then, a dragon named Aloeus throws a monkey wrench into the works by blowing open the Portal, opening the way between here and there. Out pours a tidal wave of magic and refugees, and—among other political maneuverings—Aloeus manages to broker a deal that has the Ohio National Guard send a unit of armor and air cavalry through the Portal.

Valdis had a blind spot, not seeing the unenchanted, thoroughly mundane troops as a threat. Apparently, no one had shown him that things could be blown up very well without any mana at all. So, thanks to Aloeus, Mayor Rayburn, and the governor of the great state of Ohio, a coup ended the reign of the Thesarch, and started a rat's nest of political ramifications on our side of the Portal that was still working itself out.

So far, so good, from Hephaestus' point of view.

But there was more to it.

There always was.

"The explosion of the nation of men across the continents took generations in mortal eyes," Hephaestus opened a large atlas, showing alien lands in scripts I couldn't read. However, as he turned the pages, it was clear what was happening as the maps became dominated by a single color. "But for most immortals—dragons, elves—the pace of change came too fast to react. I watched many die."

"What about dwarves?"

"Mortal as well, but they lacked man's ability to master mana, and fell too often before it."

"I know of Ragnan's conquests—"

"Do you know of her ally?"

"Ally?"

Hephaestus walked over to a dark grimoire, bound in black leather that seemed to show remnants of facial features in the grain. He drew it off the shelf and placed it on the table between us.

"Not all immortals fought the Thesarch's rise."

Hephaestus opened the book and flipped though pages of arcane symbols until it opened on a full-page illustration. I wasn't really surprised to see—sitting on a stony throne, before a background of fire—the Devil from the tarot card.

"Shit . . ."

Mazurich, or what was left of him, was right. What I was dealing with was Satan himself. Or, at least as close a manifestation as the Portal could conjure up. The reign of the Thesarch was based on a literal deal with the Devil.

Or *a* Devil.

Appearance aside, Hephaestus wasn't describing Judeo-Christian metaphysics. He described a race of beings, few in number, older and more powerful than even the dragons. Beings that were so much of the mana they swam in that they often could forgo a physical form. The mana itself was a sense organ for them, making them near omniscient.

Demons and angels . . .

Their limited physicality, at first, made them little more than shadows in the conscious world. Creatures of dream and spirit, little known and little seen.

Until one of their number discovered a vulnerability in the mortal mind, a vulnerability that allowed him to cohabit the brain and the senses of a man—to give himself form . . .

And lust . . .

And desire . . .

"The vulnerability was two-way," Hephaestus said. "Its spirit could infect the body of a man, but it, in turn, became infected with the basest material drives."

"This thing allied with the Thesarch?"

"This thing *was* the Thesarch. It fed its human host with unimaginable powers, and in turn, human armies slaughtered immortals whose existence might drain the font of mana it now wanted solely to consume."

"Couldn't someone stop it? Others of its kind . . ."

"Were the first to die, consumed in rituals to extend the life of the first Thesarchs."

"But Valdis was killed . . ."

"And it infested the neighbor most convenient to it." Hephaestus shook his head. "Valdis was a host, nothing more. The latest in a long line."

"But the Thesarch was overthrown over ten years ago . . ."

"Do you know how long that is to ones older than I?"

Valdis, apparently, wasn't the only one who was surprised by machine guns, rockets, and high explosives. Our demonic spirit saw in the National Guard hints of powers that had never been conceived within the boundaries of Ragnan. So, instead of taking the mantle of Valdis' successor, it found someone anonymous to take it on its way to the other side of the Portal.

Why settle for one world, when two were available? And one was so much more interesting.

I shook my head.

"As powerful as this thing is, it can't live without mana, can it?"

"It is almost mana personified. It is as if you asked: 'Could matter exist without mass?' "

"Then how can it expect to take over this planet? The portion with mana is geographically infinitesimal."

"It has patience, and servants."

"What do you . . . ?"

I remembered my vision, the mountain of salt, the dwarves shoveling it while chained to the Devil's throne.

"They're smuggling salt."

"Spreading mana," Hephaestus said. "Every ritual that frees the mana trapped in those crystals, will leave some to sink into the earth. Every time, pulling the boundaries of the Portal outward."

I nodded, "He's holding the dwarves by the short hairs. They're living in what's got to be the place where he has the most powerful influence."

"And he's using them to spread that influence."

Patient bastard . . . "What do you think I can do?"

"I've been watching for his reappearance." Hephaestus folded his hands. "He is vulnerable on this side of the Portal while it is mana-poor. Until now, I was unsure that he was even here. Now I am." Hephaestus caressed the spines on one of his shelves. "Originally, I intended to shut off the Portal itself."

I swallowed.

"But the geology beneath your lake means that there may be enough mana to self-sustain now," Hephaestus frowned. "So I must change tactics. If these plans are disrupted, along with the distribution of mana, he may not be able to recover. Merely publicizing what is happening, the dwarves' smuggling ring, may be enough to cut him off from the mines, and weaken him enough to be defeated."

"You said you'd help with my daughter."

"Agree to this, and I can open a route to wherever she is. After which, you should both leave the area, go somewhere free of his influence."

I nodded.

"Do you agree?"

"There's one problem, Hephaestus."

"What is that?"

"That is exactly what he wants me to do."

I had managed to leave the dragon speechless.

CHAPTER TWENTY-FIVE

I FOUND MYSELF back at the Superior Viaduct and Reggie's Town Car with little sign that anything had happened at all. It was four in the morning, and I only had my footprints going toward the end of the bridge and back to show that what I'd witnessed was more than hallucination.

It actually helped my sense of reality that my footprints passed through a locked and warded gate.

"What now?" I asked the chill night air.

Hephaestus/Shafran might be a powerful ally, but I didn't trust him entirely.

Actually, I didn't trust him at all. The dragon, like all dragons, was in it for himself. The fact that he so offhandedly mentioned shutting down the Portal was testament to that. That wasn't just shutting down the economic engine for the whole region. That would be condemning hundreds of thousands of creatures—including his fellow dragons—to death.

Someone about to throw away that many lives

wasn't really that interested in Sarah. No way I could trust him to come though on any sort of promise to rescue my daughter. As far as I knew, there was only one being who had that power.

I let myself back into Reggie's car and pulled away into the Flats.

Before I quite realized where I was going, I found myself on I-77 heading toward Columbus. I think I was moving faster than I was able to think. At least faster than I was able to rationalize. The one thing I did know was that I was the only person I could trust to have my daughter's interests at heart. Not Hephaestus, not Blackstone and the Feds, and certainly not Old Scratch, the force behind what seemed to be going on.

And what was it that seemed to be going on?

Smuggling for one. The dwarves were mining salt out of their caves under Whiskey Island, salt that apparently was something akin to magic plutonium, a mana battery so rich in the energies coming out of the Portal, that it allowed the dwarves themselves to play against type and actually cast spells. A mineral potent enough that the Feds were worried about it being smuggled out of northeast Ohio.

If the salt allowed spell-casting of any sort outside the direct influence of the Portal, no wonder Blackstone and company were so panicked. Federal policy number one regarding the Portal was containment. There wasn't any nightmare scenario, from rampant counterfeiting to terrorism, that couldn't be made worse by mixing magic into it. In theory, given the plans and enough mana, a mage with the proper incentive could reproduce a nuke.

The idea that kind of power could spread elsewhere, not just domestically, but overseas, would give a lot of people in Washington sleepless nights.

That's not even addressing the political problems if nonhumans decided to leave the state where they had legal recognition. A dwarf might pass without much notice, but a dragon?

That was the first part of it . . .

Then there was Mazurich, who orchestrated placing the dwarven clans in the place they were currently exploiting. Nothing about his history implied anything other than a working-class alliance that would have made sense just about anywhere with any immigrant population. Mazurich became a dwarven advocate . . .

But somewhere Old Scratch got involved. I wasn't sure exactly when, but from Hephaestus' history I saw two possibilities. Old Scratch must have been drawn to the area of the salt mines from the start. Coming through the Portal to this "mana-poor" world, the way the salt mines apparently became a mana battery would have drawn his attention as soon as he arrived.

So he found the dwarves in residence, and somehow took over, infecting them as he had the rule of the Thesarch.

Or there was an even more sinister possibility—

If Old Scratch comes here very early, as Valdis is falling, or perhaps even before, he might be responsible for Mazurich's deal for the dwarves. Perhaps his intent was to have a captive population, tied to the mines, the labor needed to refine and distribute the mana he wanted spread across this new planet.

If Mazurich discovered this, that one of his greatest humanitarian achievements was at the behest of the Devil himself, the guilt may have driven him to kill himself.

This piece fit everything that had happened to date, except possibly the most important part, from my point of view—

Why did Old Scratch want me to run an exposé on the dwarven operation?

From every indication, he wanted me to blow the whole story wide open. Hephaestus wasn't the only one who was dumbfounded. I couldn't see any angle that made sense. All I knew was that whatever was going on, Old Scratch was manipulating things so I would make the situation public.

Then there was item number three . . .

Magetech.

It was part of the story, but beyond the financial conflict-of-interest story about Mazurich, I didn't know how.

It was becoming imperative that I know the whole story, because without it I was not going to know what was motivating Old Scratch. And I knew that, until I found out what the Devil wanted, I wasn't going to have much hope of getting my daughter back.

There were three sources I knew to go to for information on Magetech. The first, Magetech itself, had an evil effect on me the last time I visited. I had a feeling that it was a dangerous place, and the simple fact that it was saturated with mana meant that it was probably a hangout for Old Scratch himself. And, if I was avoiding concentrations of mana, directly approaching Dwarf Central at Whiskey Island was flat out, not to mention that—if I took Hephaestus at his word—it was Old Scratch's base of operations.

Last was a Dr. Pretorious, who had moved to Columbus, safely outside the influence of the Portal—also safely out of reach of Old Scratch.

It was after dawn when I had reached the southern outskirts of the state capital, and pulled up to Pretorious' house. Nothing much distinguished it. It was one large house in a development full of large houses. The only thing that might have marked it as odd was the fact that every window was shaded from the outside world. Even the vast windows marking the great room were shrouded.

In addition, the driveway up to the three-car garage was covered by an unbroken layer of snow. I began to worry that the doctor wasn't home.

I got out of the car and trudged through the snow up to the front door. I didn't see any sign of life. I rang the doorbell, and got no answer. I leaned on the button, listening to the electronic chimes inside the house.

Nothing.

I pounded on the door with little hope. "Dr. Pretorious? Dr. Pretorious?" My words came out in puffs of fog, and I began doubting that I had the correct house. I was going off of memory for the address. All my notes were in the hands of the FBI at the moment.

For a few seconds I wondered if Blackstone had beat me here . . .

"*Dr. Pretorious!*"

I tried the door itself.

Unlocked.

I let myself in, not knowing what to expect.

The smell hit me first, before my eyes adjusted. Food rotting, feces, ammonia . . . The heat was jacked so high that breathing the fetid air was like trying to suck air through a wet towel—a towel that'd been used to clean up the bathroom at a strip club. A cheap strip club.

As my eyes adjusted, I began to see eyes, dozens of eyes. Pupils reflecting light back at me. I froze when I heard something growl. I hyperventilated, thinking of all the nasty goblins, gremlins, and little beasties that crawled around dark places. I had to tell myself that I was too far from the Portal for that sort of thing, but I still held my breath until I could make out the feline outlines that went with the demonic eyes.

Cats. Just a shitload of cats.

"*Fuck,*" I said, half relieved, half angry at myself. The word was enough to send about half the eyes scurrying deeper into the darkness.

I closed the door behind me, and stepped carefully around debris on the floor as I felt around for a light switch. I found a panel of three on the wall, only one of which worked. A light came on over the master staircase.

"*Holy shit . . .*"

The house was only ten or fifteen years old, cost a few million . . . In three years, Dr. Pretorious had managed to completely destroy it. Cat shit was everywhere. Wallpaper was stained and peeled off of yellowing walls. The carpeting had been shredded, the fibers pulled up into random piles all over the floor and the stairs.

The cats orbited me, staring, none closer than about fifteen feet. None of them seemed to be hurting for food, and the floor was scattered with empty cans and empty twenty-pound bags of cat food.

Deeper in the house I heard a television turned to Fox News or CNN. I could hear some talking head discussing trade relations with China.

I stepped carefully around the crap on the floor and headed toward the sound of the television. "Dr. Pretorious?"

The cats followed me, mewing and occasionally hissing if I passed too close. One that had been concealed under an empty pizza box lying in my path suddenly appeared in front of me, back arched, spitting, then jumped me. I had to bring my foot up to deflect it back toward the ground.

It shot away, and I escaped with a slightly unraveled sock.

I flexed my bandaged hand. Just being in this atmosphere was probably going to give me an infection. It was bad enough here having exposed skin. An open wound . . .

The den was actually worse. Lit only by the television, I saw a massive leather couch that looked as if it had had a losing argument with a rototiller. There had been built-in bookshelves, but most of the shelves had collapsed, spilling their contents on the floor, allowing the books to be shredded in a giant improv litter box.

There was someone watching the television, seated in a wheelchair. He looked about two or three times as old as his portrait. Hair uncut, beard unshaven, skin pale, spotted, and deeply lined.

"Dr. Pretorious?"

The old man continued to stare at the news.

"Dr. Pretorious?"

"Is it time already?" he whispered. His voice was cracked and brittle, as if he hadn't spoken in a long time.

"My name is Kline Maxwell, I'm from the *Cleveland Press* . . ."

"Is the seal broken? Have you seen a pale horse?"

Shit, the guy's lost it. He's nuts.

"I wanted to talk about Magetech."

He turned toward me, and his pupils were wide and cloudy with cataracts. I doubted he could see anything. "I don't talk about that."

"You were a scientist, you helped found the company."

He shook his head violently. "I don't talk about that." He stared at the television again. He switched to another news channel where a Republican Senator from North Carolina was talking about an upcoming Supreme Court nomination.

I looked at him, and the television, and asked, "What are you looking for?"

"A sign. A sign he is coming."

"Is he part of Magetech?"

He was quiet for a long time, before he said, "I didn't know." He turned toward me. "Tell them I didn't know."

Filthy as the floor was, I knelt down so I could be on the same level as he was. "If I'm to tell them, I need to know your side of the story."

"I don't talk about that."

"Because you're afraid of him."

"He will come, for all of us."

"Let me know what you did." I reached out and touched his shoulder. "You've been beyond his reach for three years."

"You don't know anything."

"Then tell me."

CHAPTER TWENTY-SIX

IN FITS AND STARTS, it came out.

Early on, Mazurich understood that someone needed to reconstruct the physical infrastructure of the city, or any political gains made by Mayor Rayburn and the statehouse would be hollow. Roads, buildings, sewers, those were all immediate, and led to the alliance between Mazurich and the dwarven immigrants.

Beyond those first steps was the creation of Magetech.

Shortly after the first city contracts were signed with the dwarven clans, and before they had found a homeland in the mines under Erie, Mazurich was approached by another immigrant from the Portal. Simon Lucas had been one of the growing numbers of human immigrants to come from Ragnan.

While Mr. Lucas was new to our world, he had an excellent command of English and some compelling arguments. Cleveland was in danger of becoming simply an extension of Ragnan. Science and technology couldn't be allowed to retreat in the face of the Portal. On the contrary, the disciplines developed in this world, in the absence of mana, could be used to create an understanding and manipulation of mana beyond anything imagined in Ragnan.

Mr. Lucas persuaded Mazurich, especially as it became clear that, like the dwarven contracts to maintain the roads, it had been left to local companies to solve the problems in the technical infrastructure, the interference of magic in everything from the communications signal from cellular phones to digital cameras.

Mr. Lucas helped arrange the settling of the dwarven clans under Whiskey Island, and in turn the dwarven clans, rich with funds from city construction contracts, invested their funds with Mazurich and the new Magetech start-up.

Mazurich bought several technology companies that had been collapsing under the stress of the Portal. And he brought in Dr. Pretorious.

"The engineers and programmers studied our technologies, how to make them work. I studied mana . . ."

A lot of mana.

Dr. Pretorious was probably exposed to more mana than any human in history. He had free access to the product of the dwarven mines for his experiments, and over a period of seven years studied how to use it in an industrial setting.

"Infused into alloys and crystals, wires and circuits—the basis for self-perpetuating machines, enchantments that replicate with no human intervention. Mana concentrated to the point it sustains its own creation." He stared at the television. "We conceived of things that could make the heavens tremble and the stars fall from the sky. We manufactured means to open the gates of hell itself . . ."

"Simon Lucas."

"The Devil himself," Dr. Pretorious said. "I don't talk about that."

"You need to tell me, what is he trying to do? What does he want?"

He continued to stare at the TV, as if he could actually see it. I looked at it and saw coverage of a winter storm in Chicago, headed toward us. The color seemed off . . .

On the bottom, the scroll blurred and started repeating "I don't talk about that . . . I don't talk about that . . . I don't talk about that . . ."

All around us, cats began crying. The feline wail became louder and louder, as if we were suddenly in the midst of hell's own choir.

"The sign," whispered Dr. Pretorious.

The picture on the television blurred into a mass of swirling color, splattered blood, and laughing half-fleshed skulls.

I shook my head. "No, we're not close enough to the Portal."

I heard shattering glass from behind me. I turned to see a pair of shadows walk into the den. In the ruddy glow of the television I saw raw flesh, stitched over bone with steel wire.

"I've been waiting for you," said Dr. Pretorious as he turned his wheelchair around.

"What are they?"

"Our children," he said, facing the two zombies. One reached for the old man, and I did what was probably one of the top ten dumbest things I have ever done.

I grabbed for the zombie.

Not only that, since I'm right-handed and obviously wasn't thinking, I grabbed its wrist with my injured hand. The words "bad move" are an immeasurable understatement.

My grip sank into rotten flesh, and I could feel bone and wire—and touching the wire was like touching a high-tension line. The creature didn't even need to shake me off. When the metal cut through the dressing on my hand, and touched skin, I felt a resonating blow of energy rip through my body. It tore through me with such force that, for a moment, it was as if my perceptions had been blown free of my flesh. I could see my own body fly backward though the air and slam into the remains of one of the bookcases.

I blinked away phantom images of shattering Magetech and Death from the tarot . . .

Zombie One grabbed Dr. Pretorious by the neck and lifted him out of his wheelchair.

The other one headed toward me.

I tried to push myself upright, but my hands slid on books and cat feces and I couldn't do much more than push myself a little backward. I heard a strangled gasp from Dr. Pretorious. Then the other one grabbed me by the shoulders.

Again, terrible forces flew through me, twisting my vision outside of myself.

Then the impact of a window snapped me back to the here and now. The window gave way around me, the heavy drapes entangling me were the only thing keeping me from being flayed alive by flying glass.

I landed, stunned, in a snowdrift, in front of the house.

Every move I made sent daggers of pain through my arm and my back, but I scrambled to get free of the drapes wrapping me. As I did, I heard the sound of sirens coming closer.

I pulled the drapes free of my face and my upper body, and saw my zombie, framed by the window. Steam rose from its raw flesh as it climbed out of the window, toward me. The sunlight reflected off the metal wrong, as if the metallic stitching holding this thing together was reflecting back a completely different light.

The air around it was blurry and out of focus, as if I was looking at a heat haze around it. However, I suspected it was more from the concentration of mana powering this thing, than from any mundane energy.

I half crawled and half rolled out of the drapes, and managed to push myself to my feet. In that time, the zombie was already halfway toward me, and the other one was climbing out of the window.

This cannot be happening in Columbus . . .

But it was clear. Magetech had managed to encapsulate the forces flowing from the Portal, and create a self-powering magical effect. Those things were radiating mana, almost as if they were Portals themselves, spewing magical radiation enough to interfere with the doctor's TV.

I made a limping dash toward the Lincoln, barely ahead of the zombies. I reached the door just in time for the first police car to skid to a stop at Pretorious' cul-de-sac.

"*Freeze!*"

I stopped moving, even though I knew that the cops weren't shouting at me. I heard one of them say, "Holy shit." And the undead twins shifted their attention to the police. Two uniformed cops took position on the other side of their patrol car, and started firing.

Bullets tore away chunks of flesh and clothing, but otherwise didn't impress the two zombies. One of the cops tried to call something in on the radio, but I could hear the mana interference from where I was.

I dove into the Lincoln.

These bastards might have unnatural speed and strength, but the physical tensile strength of flesh, wire, and bone had to have limits.

"Sorry, Reggie," I muttered as I shifted the Lincoln into gear.

Now we were a little more evenly matched.

I fishtailed in the driveway, pointing the nose at the two zombies, and beyond, at the police car. The cops were backing away, reloading, and the zombies were almost at the patrol car itself.

I floored it.

The wheels whined and spun in the snow under me, and for a moment I thought I wouldn't move at all.

Then the tires bit through to pavement, and the Lincoln shot forward, the momentum carrying it across the snowy lawn.

At the last minute, as the zombies turned back toward me, I spun the wheel hard left. Across the snow that had the effect of turning the car sideways without any slack in its forward momentum.

I sandwiched the zombies between the passenger sides of the two vehicles. I heard screeching metal as all the glass on the passenger side shattered. And the upper half of one of the zombies flopped through the front passenger window.

As it reached for me, I shifted into reverse and floored it. The rear right tire screeched on pavement, and I could smell melting rubber as the Lincoln and the patrol car began rotating counterclockwise.

It grabbed my sleeve as I frantically shifted in and out of reverse, trying to unlock the Lincoln from the patrol car.

The rear window shattered, as Zombie Two broke through.

I floored the accelerator in reverse, shooting backward into the cul-de-sac, trailing the rear passenger side fender of the patrol car.

I slammed the brakes, and Zombie Two fell backward off the rear of the car. I hit the accelerator again, and the Lincoln bumped up twice as I rolled over the zombie with front and back tires.

The other one was pulling itself in through the passenger window. I shifted into drive and floored it, over the other zombie, sideswiping the patrol car again. This time the force of the impact tore Zombie One loose.

I pulled the Lincoln to a shuddering stop as three more patrol cars shot down the street toward us.

Fortunately, the battle was over. The zombies were still moving, but their limbs were shattered to the point that no one was in any danger unless they came within biting distance.

From behind me I heard a bullhorn fighting static.

"Step—bzzt—of the car, kee—bzzt—in sight!"

I didn't need to hear what they were saying to understand it. I stepped out of the car and, without anyone asking, knelt on the ground, and placed my hands behind my head.

The first two cops only paid me nominal attention; they were more interested in the impossible piles of dead things that were squirming in the middle of their subdivision. As I waited, I watched cats jumping out of Dr. Pretorious' house, running away from the carnage.

It took about four hours for the Columbus cops to process me. The guys were nice enough about it; I'd saved two of their guys from the *Night of the Living Dead* road show. However, I still was witness to a murder, and I'd committed God only knows how many moving violations in someone else's car with no actual ID.

Thankfully, while Reggie was pissed, he wasn't pissed enough to tell the cops I'd stolen his car. So they fingerprinted me, took a few mug shots, and took my statement.

The statement was the longest part, and I probably wasn't quite as forthcoming as I should have been. Not that I was actively untruthful, I was just preoccupied as I began to understand Old Scratch's motives.

Hephaestus was half right. . .

I told the cops how I borrowed the Lincoln because my own car had been stolen. By my daughter. Which was the subject of another police investigation. Yes, I'd seen those zombies, or a zombie like them, involved in another break-in at an auto shop in Cleveland. They could contact Commander Maelgwyn Caledvwlch of the Cleveland Police for more details.

I left out everything about my meeting with Hephaestus, because I didn't know how deep Old Scratch's lines of information went, and the more I thought about it, the more I became certain that the old dragon was the only real bargaining chip I had.

All in all, I was busy marking time until Blackstone showed up.

He didn't disappoint me.

He marched into the squad room where a Columbus detective was interviewing me, leading a small army of Feds. He waved his ID around like a club. "Okay, Maxwell, you're coming with us."

My detective stood up. "Sir, we're in the middle of an investigation here."

"Not anymore."

"I need some authority—" The phone on the detective's desk began ringing.

"That would be your chief."

The detective answered, "Yes. Yes. But—yes. Okay. I will"

Blackstone waved at me. "Good Lord, Maxwell. What the hell were you trying to do?" He turned toward the detective as the man hung up. "You'll coordinate with Special Agent Thompson here," Blackstone waved at one of the interchangeable Feds. "He'll collect all your case files and arrange transport of all evidence."

Looking beaten, the detective nodded.

"Come with me," Blackstone said to me.

I stood up. "You really know how to make a good impression."

Blackstone grabbed my arm. "This isn't a game."

"You think I don't know that? It isn't *your* daughter."

Blackstone hustled me out of the police station.

CHAPTER TWENTY-SEVEN

BLACKSTONE THREW ME in the back of one of their vans and we drove off back toward Cleveland. Blackstone sat in front.

After a while, when I had firmed up my plans in my head, I asked, "I guess it would be too much at this point to let me go under my own recognizance?"

"Maxwell, I hope that's just your sorry attempt to be funny."

I stared out at the freeway, where the snow was already becoming heavy. "What do you want, Blackstone?"

"I want you to go to your hotel room and *stay* there."

I shook my head. "No. Not that, what's your goal here? What is your ultimate mission . . . ?"

"Do I have to spell it out for you? We need to bottle up this dwarven smuggling operation, shut it down."

"And beyond that?"

"We're the first line of defense between the things released by the Portal, and the rest of the country."

"Why don't we pull over at the next rest stop?"

"Christ, Maxwell, you think—"

"We need to talk."

Blackstone looked at me, then at his driver. After a moment of thought Blackstone told him, "Do it."

Blackstone led me away from the idling van until we were standing next to the main building of the rest stop. The snow was heavy enough that the Interstate was invisible from where we stood, and the noise from the idling van was nearly inaudible.

"What?" Blackstone snapped, his voice coming out in a puff of fog.

"Look, I know you've been trying to keep a lid on the Portal for a long time. But you saw what happened in Columbus. The genie is out of the bottle."

"If we get a handle on this type of trafficking—"

"Those things were self-powered. This goes beyond the dwarves and their magic dust. There's a technology out there that could let *anything* walk free of the Portal and go *anywhere* . . ."

"I'm not an idiot, Maxwell," Blackstone said. "I saw that mess. What are you getting at?"

"What if you could do more than shut down the dwarven operation? What if I could hand you the company responsible?"

Blackstone laughed. "You have an inflated sense of your investigative prowess. You think I don't *know* where this is coming from? You think I can just walk in the lobby on your say so? Your friend Dominic Mazurich wasn't the only politician paid off by

Magetech. Unless you can give me something ironclad, I don't think we need to go on."

"What if you had someone inside, who would give you everything?"

"Define 'everything.'"

"Evidence against the dwarves, testimony against Magetech, and the specs on their research."

"Did Dr. Pretorious tell you something?"

"Are you interested?"

"What are you asking for?"

"Twenty-four hours without an escort."

Blackstone stared at me. "How do I know you're not bullshitting me?"

"You don't. But am I asking too much?"

"I'll give you . . ." Blackstone looked at his watch. "Until nine AM tomorrow morning."

Not quite twenty-four hours, but I wasn't about to push it. "Okay," I said. "Now, does someone have my clothes from the hospital?"

Blackstone was as good as his word. By three, I'd gotten my own clothes, my wallet, my cell phone, and the keys to my rental car. Once I was back in my rented Solara, I scanned through my messages.

Three from Margaret, two from Reggie, one of which was mostly profanity, and one from Dr. Shafran asking if we should meet again.

Yes, I thought, *we should.*

But not before I met with someone else.

First, I called Margaret back. For the most part I let her cry on my shoulder since that meant I didn't have to go into much detail over what was happening here. I kept it short and vague—the Feds were still waiting for some kind of contact, and I was about to call someone who might know something about Sarah's whereabouts.

By then, I had driven around to the West Side technology park where Magetech housed its corporate headquarters. I didn't want to actually walk into their buildings again—a blackout would be a bad thing at this point.

I pulled my Solara to a stop in the parking lot of a small windowless bar that looked as if it predated the technology park by a few decades. The place was called "Slapp-Happy's" and looked as if it had just opened for the day.

I walked in and glanced at the television over the bar. The zombies had made the national news. I saw CNN running pictures of Dr. Pretorious' development. The video only started going funny when they approached one of the zombie parts or the battered remains of Reggie's Lincoln.

Great . . .

I didn't need to hear the audio to see where the story was going to go. The idea that the weird stuff in Cleveland was no longer completely confined would burn through the national news like a California brushfire. Paranoiacs like Blackstone would suddenly seem a lot more credible . . .

I was beginning to understand the point of the zombies.

The point was what was airing right now through one of Magetech's electronic satellite filters.

I took my cell phone, but I made a point of walking back to the pay phone nestled back by the bathrooms.

From there, I called Magetech.

Ten minutes later, Mr. Lucas slid into a booth across from me. "You look surprised to see me, Mr. Maxwell."

I shook my head and drank my club soda. "No, it's just your appearance is so . . ."

"What?"

"Mundane."

"How should I look, Mr. Maxwell?"

"I think we both know what you are, Mr. Lucas. Can we skip the pretense otherwise?"

"You have me at a disadvantage."

"I don't think so." I sipped my club soda. "I want my daughter."

Mr. Lucas leaned back in the booth. "I am sure she is quite safe."

I nodded. "I'm sure. She wouldn't be worth anything to you otherwise." Lucas stared at me, and I could see the hint of the Devil in his expression. Though I was probably imagining it.

"It took me a while to figure out what you wanted," I continued. "What you were trying to do with me. Sure, use me to sacrifice the dwarves and—posthumously—Mazurich. But why threaten me to do something I would have done for you with the right information? But that's how it works. I agree and you might let me see her, but it isn't over then, is it? You want an advocate, someone in the media. You'll hold her hostage as long as you think I'm useful . . ."

"Mr. Maxwell, why are we holding this conversation?"

"Your plans are coming together nicely. Spread the mana and you spread your influence. The dwarves were nickel and dime, weren't they? You don't need them anymore. Magetech has gone beyond the mines, hasn't it? You have the means to create mana now, and how better to spread that as far as possible than to have it fall into the hands of the U.S. government?"

"Mr. Maxwell—"

"You want Blackstone to take it over. You want all of this in the hands of DARPA and the DoD. Who else would exploit it quicker, farther, and with no regard to cost. They'll spread the mana for you faster than the dwarves ever could."

"—I don't think we need to continue."

"But I want my daughter back," I said as Lucas stood up, "and I have something you want."

Lucas stopped and turned toward me. "What?"

"Information." I sipped my club soda and waited. My heart was racing. Deals with the Devil were a little out of my league.

He looked me up and down. "Shall we accept for a moment, your premise?" He slid back into the booth. "Hypothetically, shall we decide I am the fiend you believe me to be? That I have access to your missing daughter? Fine, Mr. Maxwell. But I might point out that such a fiend would easily be able to detect falsehood."

I'm counting on it, Old Scratch . . .

"Might I assume that, for all of Magetech's advancements, it has not been able to uncover the central mystery of the Portal itself? How it formed, how to form something like it?"

"Make that assumption."

Thank you, Mr. Lucas, but that is pretty self-evident. You had to use the Portal to come here, and if you could create them at will, nothing would stop you from opening new ones wherever you wanted, and spilling Ragnan's mana all over the planet.

"So the dragons kept at least one secret from you."

Lucas didn't look happy. "*You* have this knowledge?" he snorted at me.

"I know where it is." I swallowed. I was reaching the most dangerous point of the conversation. Even now, I was second-guessing myself, but I made a point of remembering my vision. Death, the Devil, and the Tower crumbling to earth. I was *meant* to do this.

"Where?"

"It is in the possession of a dragon named Hephaestus."

"*Hephaestus?*" It wasn't just a look anymore. I could feel Lucas' emotion, in waves of force coming off of him that rivaled what I felt when I touched the zombie. I had to concentrate to avoid losing focus and falling into some new nightmare visions. "Where did you hear this name?"

I had expected a reaction, but this was more than I had hoped for. "You know him, then?"

"*He has chosen to be my adversary, and for that I will suck the power from his marrow.*" He reached over the table and grabbed me. The power came off him in searing waves. It tore into me, timed with my pulse, carrying with it images of fields strewn with skulls, pyres the size of small cities, dragons falling out of the sky, and the endless march forward of the Thesarch's army.

"You are Valdis," I whispered.

"Show me to my adversary."

"My daughter," I croaked. "Bring me my daughter and I will show you to his doorstep and lead you inside."

He let me go. And slowly the power drained back into its human shell. "Beside this prize, anything else you might give me is less than nothing. Give me this and you shall have your daughter."

I nodded. "Forgive me if I don't trust you. I want my daughter first."

"You try my patience."

"But you know I'm telling you the truth. Give me my daughter back, and I will give you what you want."

Lucas nodded. "I see that you believe this to be true. So I will do as you ask."

"Bring her to the Superior Viaduct tonight at five minutes to midnight."

"Remember, though, she will be hostage to your continued intention. I expect you both to accompany me to Hephaestus."

I nodded, not trusting myself to speak.

Lucas left me at the booth, and I had to sit and calm down for several minutes. I desperately wanted a drink, or five, but a clouded head was the last thing I needed. I was about to betray someone, *something*, incredibly powerful, and the last thing I needed now was to tip my hand.

When I felt calm enough, I walked back to the rear of the bar and called Dr. Shafran.

"Yes," he answered his line this time.

"It's Maxwell. We do need to meet again. Tonight at midnight."

I spoke with him another ten minutes, hoping I was doing the right thing.

Sarah, I'm going to get you back, baby.

Whatever I have to do.

CHAPTER TWENTY-EIGHT

*"***S***HOW ME TO MY ADVERSARY."*
I begin to object, I don't know who the adversary is. But then the mists clear, and I see a Tower hovering over the city, greater than any skyscraper.

"There!" I point.

A booming, inhuman laugh resounded. ***"Your service will be rewarded."***

The Devil rises from his throne, and walks toward the Tower. Moments later, after losing sight of the Devil, the Tower begins to crumble.

The image of the crumbling tower haunted me as I sat in my rented Solara, waiting for Lucas and my daughter. I was plagued with the recurring thought that I didn't know what I was doing. Desperation was driving me to risks I never would have contemplated before.

I was playing with my daughter's life, and I didn't know if I could go through with it. All I had to validate my decision was a hallucinatory vision, one that may have been open to interpretation.

As people have said to me before, the Oracle is a bitch.

Outside the car, the snow was getting worse. A blizzard moving down from Chicago, combining with lake effect, cut down visibility to about twenty yards. Occasionally, the wind would pick up and it would drop to nil.

Ahead of me, the twin cones of my headlights aimed toward the bridge, fixing on the gate. Caught in the beams, the snow moved sideways.

The clock on my dash read 11:49.

"Show, damn you . . ."

Slowly, a twin pair of headlamps became visible in my rearview mirror. They approached and came to a stop behind the Solara. I couldn't even make out the outlines of the vehicle.

Bracing myself, I stepped out of the car, and walked back toward my guest. The wind bit into my exposed skin, the flying ice like an army of tiny pikemen charging my skin as if it was a fleshy Bastille.

As I walked around behind the Solara, I started to see the vehicle that had driven up behind me. A Volkswagen Beetle.

My Volkswagen Beetle.

"Sarah!"

I ran to the car, sliding in the treacherous footing. I almost fell face first into the side door as I clawed through a layer of ice to find the door handle. I pulled the door open, wrenching my bandaged hand, and showering myself with fragments of snow and ice.

I stood by the open door, dumbfounded, staring into the idling car.

It was empty.

The clock on the dash of my Volkswagen read "11:54." As I watched, it flipped to "11:55."

"Mr. Maxwell?" came a voice from behind me.

I spun around to see Simon Lucas standing in the halo of my Volkswagen's headlights. The snow swirled around him, but didn't seem to touch him.

I backed away from my car, slamming the door. "Where's my daughter?"

"She's safe, Mr. Maxwell, I assure you."

"You were supposed to bring her."

He smiled at me with a stare that burned into every organ in my body. "I decided I should provide you with an incentive to avoid any second thoughts."

"No." This couldn't be falling apart on me now. "That wasn't the deal." I ran at Lucas, a move that beat me grabbing the zombie for dumbest move of all time.

"You do not dictate terms to me."

I didn't see him move, but there's a good chance he didn't. One moment I was running toward him. The next I was bouncing off the windshield of the Volkswagen. The windshield spider-webbed below me as my right elbow smashed through. Briefly all I was aware of was the pain streaking up my arm. It was so intense that somehow I missed the moments where I rolled off the hood onto the snow-covered street.

I blinked, and I was on my knees. Spitting snow as

I held myself up with my left arm. My right arm, clutched to my chest, was shooting pain so bad that I still couldn't focus on where I was, or what I was supposed to be doing.

I blinked, and the snow seemed to be slowing its fall.

"Do not presume. No servant is too valuable for me to destroy." I heard footsteps walk around in front of me. A pair of shiny leather shoes stepped into my field of vision. They were unmolested by snow or salt. As were the legs of the sharply creased trousers above them. *"On your feet, Mr. Maxwell."*

I pushed myself unsteadily up, one-handed. The pain in my right arm became more concentrated and localized, and I realized that something had dislocated or broken in my elbow. "Fuck."

"You pathetic little man. You think that is the limit of pain?" Lucas walked around me, not seeming to be completely in the world. *"With a thought I could place you in torment for a thousand years, focus your existence on a single eternal moment of agony."*

It was easy to see why this guy, as the Thesarch or as Simon Lucas, could command so many people. How the hell could you fight something like this?

"You offered me something I desire. You live now, your daughter lives now, only to provide this to me. Tell me."

I glanced through the window of the Volkswagen. Snow had just started blowing in through the broken windshield. The clock on the dash read "11:57."

"You want to find Hephaestus, and his hoard of knowledge, you only need to wait."

"I have no taste for riddles."

"The Portal to his lair will open at midnight." I looked up at the snow, which had near frozen in the air.

"Portal?"

"How do you think he hides from you so well?"

I received an inordinate amount of gratification from the surprise on Lucas' face. It had been a strategic omission on my part, partly because I had been trying not to give much away when I thought I had some chance of Lucas bringing my daughter.

The other part is I didn't want Old Scratch here to have too much time to prepare. The bastard might hold sway over every crevice that held mana, but if he wanted to pass through a Portal, everything I had learned told me that he had to do it in person.

And as I expected, his first impulse was not for a face-to-face.

The Simon Lucas who faced me, untouched by snow, was not Old Scratch. Lucas nodded at me, folded his arms across his chest, and shimmered briefly.

Then he was gone.

"Lucas!"

The unmoving snow was silent around me. I leaned back against the Volkswagen and unzipped my coat enough so I could slip my right arm in for some support. As time slowed around me, and the endless minutes crept along, I got a sick feeling that I might have lost my daughter, that I had done something to make Lucas doubt me . . .

But at "11:59" according to the Volkswagen's dash, a shadow fell out of the sky. Something huge and bat-winged passed over me, and thudded on the roof of the Volkswagen, shaking it back on its shocks. I stumbled away from the car, turning, half expecting to see Hephaestus before me.

My new guest wasn't quite that big.

"Your service is rewarded," it said from on top of the Volkswagen. It was twice as tall as a man, even seated on its haunches. It had the head of a goat—but a goat that was a carnivore. Fangs curled over its black lips, and its chin was streaked with blood. Its skin was reddish purple and bristled with black hair that became denser as it grew down from a near naked chest, to become a shaggy pelt down its hooved legs. *"Few mortals are privileged to meet my flesh."*

I backed up as the Devil extended a leg to step off of the car.

"I thought you didn't have a physical body."

"I desire one, so I have one." It drew its claws across the side of my car. They effortlessly pierced the skin and tore through the quarter-panel. *"Should I be confined to the proxy senses of my servants? What is my power if I cannot taste the blood of my sacrifices with my own tongue?"*

It looked down on me with eyes that were now completely inhuman.

"Better to sup on Hephaestus' soul."

Around us, the snow had frozen in midair and the mist from my breath hung unmoving between us.

Inside the Volkswagen, the clock flipped over to "12:00."

The bell tolled one, and the gate opened in front of the Solara.

"Now, show me to my adversary."

CHAPTER TWENTY-NINE

THIS TIME, THE WAY was harder, and time seemed to progress even slower. The snow had drifted up to my knees in places and my legs burned with the cold. My breath fogged, and I could feel it freeze on my cheeks.

And with every step, I felt the presence behind me. A massive weight I could sense, as if it was about to envelop me. A heat that offered no warmth, the sound of a heavy breath that smelled of carrion, the sound of muscle and skin moving. But when I looked behind me, I saw nothing. Some enchantment hid the demon from my sight.

I only looked behind me once. He corrected me by drawing one of his claws across my back, one of the same ones that had cut through the skin of my Volkswagen. My clothes were nothing to it, and it cut, burning, through to my shoulder blade. The wound wasn't disabling, but it hurt like hell, and the wind found another stinging patch of skin to attack.

As the blood froze on my shoulder, I heard a whisper in my ear.

"Do not turn again. Do not show you are followed."

I didn't even nod. I just trudged forward.

"Good."

It may have been my imagination, but I could feel the desire from this thing behind me. This close, I couldn't escape the sense of a black sucking need that seemed to overwhelm even the waves of power that surrounded the thing. It was as if I was leading the personification of lust, in just about every depraved connotation that word had. The kind of lust that made child molesters and serial killers seem civilized.

I knew this thing behind me had come from the Portal, and was just another in a long line of immortal entities to take up residence in my city. I knew that its physical presence was a self-creation, almost certainly modeled on the belief and customs it found here. It probably found that—like the ritual-imbued position of the Thesarch helped amplify the power of mana— taking a predefined demonic role was a shortcut to even more power . . .

I knew all this.

But when my feet found the first of the stairs, I knew in my heart that what followed me was the Devil himself. I was walking a path to certain damnation and I didn't know how to stop.

Even though the passage to the base of Hephaestus' tower took an eternity, we came upon the great ebony doors too soon for me.

The tower struck twelve.

The doors remained shut.

I could feel the fury rising behind me. The power of it passed me in waves, and I could almost see it wash against the doors. I thought I could see a tint of blood-red ripple across the black-green script.

It happened again, and it wasn't my imagination.

Waves of glinting red washed across the script in pulsing waves, emanating from the base, where the doors met. Behind me, I heard a laugh. *"The great Hephaestus hides behind his walls like a child."*

Visible now, he stepped past me, to face the giant onyx doors. On them, the script now glowed a pulsing red. With wings outstretched, the demon was almost as large as the doors themselves.

"I've come for you, dragon. And I will not be denied."

The script glowed a solid red, as if the door's core had become molten. Something urged me to back down a few steps.

"Your wards do not deter me," it said as it reached out and touched the door. The demon's touch unleashed a holocaust. Balls of flame erupted from the door, and instead of blowing outward, wrapped themselves around the demon, shrouding him in a fire burning red, then yellow, then white. The air filled with the smell of roasting flesh as the demon's skin began to blister and peel.

The demon laughed.

It kept laughing as more fire erupted from the door, sheets of flame and energy pouring into the spot where the demon stood. The flames were so hot that I could smell my own hair burning, and my eyes watered to look at it.

I backed down a few more steps.

Still it laughed.

The demon's flesh roasted away, leaving a carbonized skeleton that soon disappeared under the heat of the rippling fire. Still the flames enveloped the demon, erupting from the doors faster and faster.

Still the laugh.

The door slowed, sputtering, the script fading from white-hot to a dull red. Before it stood a pillar of fire in the shape of a demon. The flaming image stretched its arms, and from the flames came a voice.

"So like a dragon, to focus on the body."

I don't think it spoke English anymore. I don't think it "spoke" in any real sense.

The flaming arms embraced the door. I heard something sizzle and pop, and long cracks crawled across the glowing script of the doors, the cracks glowing hotter and emitting steam. The doors groaned and screamed as if they were living things.

I took cover flat against the stairs before the doors imploded in a shower of gravel, smoke, and red-hot ash. For a moment the entrance to the tower was wrapped in an impenetrable cloud. As it settled, the fire was gone, replaced by a demon form made of crackling red-hot onyx. Enchanted alien script still glowed on the surface of the stone, but the words somehow had become disturbing, obscene.

It flexed a new onyx claw.

"I think I like this better."

It stepped though the smoking hole that had been the grand entrance. I took the stairs upward, slowly, until I could see the great entrance hall. The onyx demon walked into the chamber spreading its arms and wings, facing upward.

"Show yourself, dragon!"

"DEFILER!" The nonword screeched through the tower, tearing directly into my brain. The force of it caused the great pillars to crack. Then, arcs of green twisting energy burst from the pillars, converging on the demon. The whipping tendrils buzzed and hissed with power so dense I needed to lean inward just to stay upright. My singed hair danced with static.

The script on the demon's skin now pulsed green as the tendrils danced across the surface of its body, pulsing in time to the buzzing energy. More tendrils exploded from the surface of the wall, blowing free plaster and marble, leaping from pillar to pillar, to slam into the onyx creature.

The demon groaned as the buzzing became a roar. Its back arched, as the substance of its body began to shake. The black-green glow pulsed more intensely as the tendrils, whipping and dancing, pulled the thing off its feet. The demon, body shaking and whipping around with the tendrils of energy, rose until it was in the center of the great room.

For a moment, it seemed as if Hephaestus was about to win.

Then the onyx demon froze in the midst of its seizure. The green tendrils of energy suddenly seemed to stretch and vibrate like elastic bands. The green in the demon's skin faded, and began pulsing red. The red leaked from the script carved in its skin to bleed into the suddenly taut, linear bands of energy connecting it to the walls of the room.

When the red reached the walls, the walls exploded. A cascading disintegration of fire, stone, and smoke, that rolled counterclockwise around the inner surface of the chamber tearing off every finished surface, crumbling stairs, burning tapestries, and imploding pillars. The force of it blew me back, rolling across debris, causing blinding pain in my shoulder and arm.

I blinked the pain and smoke out of my eyes and found myself facedown at the edge of the tower stair, looking down through blowing snow at the faint image of the Cuyahoga River.

I slowly rolled on my back.

The great entry hall had been blown apart. The interior had been razed to the outer stone walls, the great pillars blackened stumps, every surface steaming, the floor blasted, cracked and covered with ash.

If anything, Old Scratch seemed even bigger.

"Tasting your flesh will please me."

"OBSCENITY!" The sense of the word shook the tower to its nonexistent foundation.

The ceiling erupted. The arching dome collapsed, shedding blocks the size of large SUVs to crash into the floor around Old Scratch. The demon knocked some of the stones aside as they fell, sending one smashing through the skin of the tower wall to tumble into an imperceptible infinity between us and the Cuyahoga below, into a dimension I couldn't point out.

Something screeched from above, and the dragon Hephaestus flew down out of the descending rubble, flames belching forth to fill the room below him. The great lizard fell through smoke, and rubble and the burning remains of the library above. The wings of the dragon stretched from wall to wall in the remains of the great hall.

Hephaestus reached down into the pool of fire with taloned hands and scooped up the demon's body and slammed it into the floor. As the flames cleared, I could see the crater formed by the blow. In it, I could just see the remnants of crumbled bat wings.

Hephaestus slammed the demon down again.

Even though I saw a black leg snap completely off, I knew that Old Scratch wasn't beaten. Couldn't be beaten.

As if it sensed my thought, the demon started laughing.

Hephaestus brought the broken remains of the demon up for another blow, and the demon's arm shot out impossibly far, impaling the dragon's chest. Gouts of blood sprayed from the wound as the demon dug into the dragon's body.

A spasm racked the giant form, and Hephaestus crashed to the ground. The impact shook the floor, and as I looked up, I could see great cracks forming in the edifice of the tower itself, as if the dragon was part of the building's structural integrity.

Hephaestus' grip went slack on the demon, and the onyx creature, broken, humpbacked and laughing, attached itself to the dragon's wounded chest like a twisted lamprey. It wasn't even a laugh anymore, it was more a perverse childish giggle.

"Oh, yes. Such a feast. I shall wear this flesh."

The area around the wound began glowing red as the demon burrowed, spreading blood and gore. Above everything I could hear the fabric of the tower split and crumble.

Hephaestus' great head lay on the ground, and it shifted slightly to focus one gigantic eye on me. And, I could swear I saw the dragon smile, right before the great body vanished.

"What?"

The demon, suddenly alone in the center of the tower, tried to stand, but its body was half formed, fleshy and larval.

"Brace yourself, Mr. Maxwell." Dr. Shafran ran toward me, diving. He grabbed me and we rolled off the edge.

Suddenly in free fall, I tumbled under the tower. Dr. Shafran was gone and the wind whipped by me as I fell toward a river I knew I'd never reach. Above me, the great tower fragmented, the upper stories falling. For a moment it was exactly the image on the tarot card.

I felt more than heard the demon's voice, *"No!"*

The tower itself began twisting, the broken remnants turning in on themselves, the space it occupied whirlpooling in on itself as if everything was being sucked through a cosmic drain. The whole edifice folded into nothing.

Something swept by me and a clawed hand bigger than I was scooped me out of the air. Something twisted, and Hephaestus and I were flying over a normal Cleveland skyline.

A draconic chuckle shook the fillings in my teeth and made my injured arm ache.

"And he said I focus too much on the body."

CHAPTER THIRTY

M Y DESPERATE PLAN had worked better than it had a right to. It had relied too heavily on Old Scratch's weakness—a desire to dominate that went beyond any reason. I had been betting that giving the demon the chance to defeat a longtime enemy would preoccupy it, and it wouldn't consider the fact that, if Hephaestus created a Portal to a private retreat, it could just as easily close it.

However, almost everything had gone like clockwork. I had led him to Hephaestus' doorstep, and my strategic revelation of the tower's nature caused Old Scratch to show up "in person" without giving the bastard the time to consider the possible consequences. Arrogance and overconfidence led the way from there to Hephaestus' doorstep. And while the dragon's continued assault on the demon's physical body might not have been effective in terms of damaging his adversary, it was a pretty damn good distraction, preventing Old

Scratch from picking up on the fact that he was in the middle of a trap, and it was closing shut on him.

It helped that I had told the dragon what was coming when I phoned him in his Dr. Shafran form.

As we flew through the biting winter air, I screwed my watering eyes shut.

There was only one major flaw in the execution of my plan.

"*Sarah . . .*" I whispered.

My arm hurt as the dragon laughed again.

"Damn it! I lost my daughter!" I spat at the gigantic creature that dragged itself through the air.

"You believe I do not honor my agreements?"

Hephaestus rose above the Cleveland skyline, dodging downtown skyscrapers and the federal building as he aimed toward the Erie shoreline west of the river.

"What are you doing?"

Hephaestus laughed again, as the ground below whipped by faster than I could make sense of it. The dragon aimed like an arrow right at a spit of land that stuck out paralleling the shore.

As we shot by it, I saw a cluster of dwarves by the roadside look up toward us. Ahead and below, on the icy surface of the lake, something appeared, a sphere unfolding from the same nameless dimension the tower had been sucked into.

"Wait, I can't go——"

We hit the sphere, and the wind ceased. Our motion had stopped, and we were no longer flying over the lake. We were in a cavern, a familiar one . . .

A vast floodlit chamber, a vast space of unfinished

walls leading toward a carved building formed into incredible pillars, vaults, and arches. I could study the statues this time, and I could see dwarven bodies twisted into all forms of obscene agony.

"This was his cathedral."

Unlike my vision, the space wasn't empty. Dwarves crowded around the front stairs of the facade, facing us. They all stared at Hephaestus as he set me on the ground.

I looked at the dwarven faces, and saw fear.

I limped forward.

One of the dwarves stepped forward. I recognized Samanish Thégharin, my cab driver. "You cannot be here."

"My escort says otherwise."

"A human cannot live in these halls," Samanish grabbed my jacket. "Leave for your own sake, and before his wrath comes down on us all."

I pulled away. *"He is gone."*

"What?" Samanish's eyes widened.

"The one you will not name. The one whose existence poisoned the mana in these halls. The one who dedicated this hall to himself."

"I am here for my daughter." I started walking toward the great Gothic arch ahead of me. After a moment the dwarves parted in front of me. As I closed, I could see the facade crumbling. The statues seemed to dissolve into powder, the stained glass fading and flaking into gray dust.

Hephaestus must be enjoying himself.

I could feel the mana around me, subliminal, at the

corner of my awareness, like at the Magetech complex. This time, there was no foreboding to it, no evil weight . . .

Perhaps that was as good a sign as any that Old Scratch was gone.

I stumbled forward through the vast Gothic doorway. Before me was the great hall, its benches filled with hundreds of dwarves watching me. Obscene decorations crumbled around us as I limped up the aisle toward the high chair next to the altar.

As I reached the chair and reached for my daughter, the altar crumbled.

"*Sarah!*"

She yawned and stretched, blinking. "Oh, shit, Dad?"

"Are you all right?"

She looked me up and down, eyes wide. "All right? Dad? What happened to you?"

"Let's get you home." I led her out of the cathedral with my good left hand.

Not one of the dwarves moved as I took her out of the cathedral, which was in the midst of becoming little more than another unfinished cavern. "What's happening, where am I?"

"You might not remember it, but you were kidnapped."

"*What?*" she gasped as we walked through the doorway. Ahead of us, past a semicircle of dwarves facing the remnants of Old Scratch's cathedral, the massive form of Hephaestus sat on his haunches, arms folded.

His great Escalade-sized head nodded down toward us on the serpentine neck.

"Do I not keep my word, Mr. Maxwell?"

Sarah shook her head. "Oh. My. God."

"Thank you," I said. "I owe you."

Hephaestus snorted. *"Nonsense. You provided defeat for my adversary of an aeon. The books are balanced."*

"It's talking to you," Sarah whispered.

"And it is a pleasure to meet you as well, Miss Maxwell."

Sarah gasped and grabbed me. It was all I could do to keep from wincing when my injured arm moved. "It's okay," I said through clenched teeth. "He's a friend."

"Shall I take you from this place, or do you prefer to walk?"

I looked at the dwarves surrounding us and swallowed. "Perhaps we should go."

I took a few steps forward, and Samanish Thégharin stepped between us and Hephaestus. I stared down into his wrinkled face and felt my good hand ball into a fist. "This isn't a good idea," I told him. "I'm taking my daughter."

"Please," he said. "Forgive us."

"Just let me go——"

He rested a wrinkled leathery hand on my arm. "We saw what happened to our greatest benefactor. Mazurich's death is the shame of all our clans. We did not want you to follow him. Ossian, Teaghue, they tried to push you off the path He was driving you down. It cost us, and we found it cost your daughter as well." He looked at Sarah. "This wasn't our intention, but when He saw we tried to influence your father, He made us take you."

I removed his hand. "It's over now. I just want to take my daughter home."

"You've broken the chains binding our clans," he said. "Honor demands we repay you."

I looked across at the dwarves. All I could think was, what a damn mess. Even if I didn't break the story, it was probably too far gone for anyone to stop. Samanish Thégharin thought I delivered them from bondage, but I doubted that anyone beyond the people in this cavern would accept what they had done under that bondage. I looked around and thought of the trials, the scandals, and the innuendo that would decimate these clans.

Will you thank me then?

Fact was, I don't always love my job . . .

"Is there anything we can do?"

"Yes, actually, there is . . ."

EPILOGUE

ON TOP OF EVERYTHING else, dwarves make good medics. I had a decent cast on my arm as I dove Sarah back to our hotel. She started apologizing profusely when we passed the remains of my Volkswagen. I told her, honestly, that all that mattered to me was the fact I got her back.

I called Margaret and had the pleasure of handing my cell phone over to Sarah. I didn't even wince when Sarah started going on about how her dad was friends with a dragon.

I called St. Vincent Charity Hospital, and was relieved to find out that Nina had come out of her coma. I had hoped that with Old Scratch's influence gone from the local ether, she might wake up, but I hadn't been sure.

The snow had stopped, and the roads were clear, so we got back to the hotel by 8:40. I wasn't that surprised when I opened up the door, and saw Blackstone and Special Agents Levi and Francis.

"Well," Blackstone said, "if it isn't the prodigal fucking journalist."

"You're early," I said.

"Yeah, and I'm having some doubts," Blackstone said. "I see you found your daughter."

"Who the hell are you?" Sarah snapped at him. "What are you doing in our hotel room?"

"Mr. Blackstone here," I said to her, "is our local federal pain in the ass." I nodded at the two others. "His friends are Special Agents Levi and Francis. FBI."

"Assigned to your kidnapping, Miss Maxwell," said Agent Levi. From his expression, I think he took my little walk out of the hospital personally.

"Oh," Sarah said.

"Francis?" Blackstone said. "Will you and Levi take her in the other room and get a statement. And for God's sake, keep an eye on her."

"Dad?" Sarah looked at me.

"It's okay, they're cops. And I need to talk to Mr. Blackstone."

"Damn right you do," Blackstone said.

I watched Francis and Levi lead Sarah out of the room. When the door closed, Blackstone looked at me. "Okay, I'm not heartless. I know you scammed me so you could get your daughter. If it was me, I'd probably pay anything to get her back. But now she's back, and you better come clean with me. What did you pay, and to whom, to ransom her?"

I limped over to one of the chairs and eased myself down into it. I sighed.

"Christ, what happened to you?"

"Blackstone? I told you, you're early."

"Don't start playing games now, I could—"

There was a knock on the door. Blackstone stared at me.

"You gave me until nine AM."

The door knock sounded again.

I smiled at Blackstone, "Maybe you should get that. It's nine o'clock."

Blackstone looked at me, shaking his head. "I don't believe this," he muttered as he walked over to the door.

He opened it, and a line of solemn-looking dwarves walked into the room. "What?" Blackstone said.

The first dwarf stepped forward and nodded his head in a short bow. "I am Gwentarian of the clan Parthalán. I bring the board of directors of Magetech, Inc. We wish to offer the federal government a deal."

Blackstone turned toward me and said, "You bastard, how long have you been sitting on this?"

"You better get negotiating," I told him. "These guys are used to making deals with the Devil."